UNFINISHED PORTRAIT

Rona Parish is asked to write a biography of reclusive artist Ellie by her concerned sister. Ellie has seemingly disappeared, and the mystery surrounding her whereabouts has fuelled a new interest in her work. But when Rona discovers that Ellie's closest friend committed suicide, Rona wonders whether Ellie, wracked by guilt over her friend's death, could have been driven to do likewise...

UNFINISHED PORTRAIT

Anthea Fraser

Severn House Large Print
London & New York

This first large print edition published 2011
in Great Britain and the USA by
SEVERN HOUSE PUBLISHERS LTD of
9-15 High Street, Sutton, Surrey, SM1 1DF.
First world regular print edition published 2010 by
Severn House Publishers Ltd., London and New York.

British Library Cataloguing in Publication Data

Fraser, Anthea.
    Unfinished portrait.
    1. Parish, Rona (Fictitious character)--Fiction. 2. Women
    authors, English--Fiction. 3. Women artists--Fiction.
    4. Missing persons--Investigation--Fiction. 5. Detective
    and mystery stories. 6. Large type books.
    I. Title
    823.9'14-dc22

    ISBN-13: 978-0-7278-7941-7

Severn House Publishers support The Forest Stewardship Council
[FSC], the leading international forest certification organisation. All
our titles that are printed on Greenpeace-approved FSC-certified paper
carry the FSC logo.

MIX
Paper from
responsible sources
FSC
www.fsc.org   FSC® C018575

Printed and bound in Great Britain by the
MPG Books Group, Bodmin, Cornwall.

ONE

Rona could hear the phone ringing as she put her key in the door. In one complicated manoeuvre she nudged the dog inside, pushed the door shut, dropped her carrier bags on the floor, and caught up the instrument.

'Hello?' she said breathlessly.

'Rona? Good! I was just preparing to talk to a machine!'

For a moment the voice eluded her. Then, with a touch of apprehension, she identified it as that of her editor at Jonas Jennings.

'Prue? How are you? It's been a long time...' Her voice tailed off in embarrassment.

'It has indeed! Still pursuing your journalistic career?'

'Well, I—'

Prue Granger laughed. 'Relax! I'm not about to pressurize you. But I have a project I think might be of interest – one that would combine your talents, as it were.'

'Sounds intriguing,' Rona said cautiously.

'I hope so, but it could best be discussed over lunch. Today's Tuesday; how about Thursday this week? Are you free? One o'clock at Papa Gigio's in Covent Garden?'

5

'That would be fine, Prue. Thank you.'

'See you then,' said Prue Granger, and rang off.

Rona looked down at the dog nuzzling her legs and bent to unfasten his lead. Then, picking up her shopping, she followed him down the basement stairs to the kitchen.

It was indeed a long time since she'd spoken to Prue, she reflected, starting to unpack her bags. Her career as a biographer had been on hold for eighteen months or more, following the abortive ending of her last project due to murder and a legal minefield her publishers were unwilling to enter.

While she regained her balance, she'd reverted to her secondary – and, up to then, spasmodic – work as a freelance writer for the glossy monthly *Chiltern Life*. But, incredibly, innocuous pursuits such as writing-up eight-hundred-year anniversaries, tracing birth parents, and researching the history of local firms had also resulted in death and disaster. Even befriending her next-door neighbours had proved a perilous undertaking.

Murders seem to seek you out, her husband Max had once observed, and though she'd shied away from it, the phrase had lodged in her mind with an almost superstitious acceptance. If Prue wanted to speak to her, she reasoned now, it must surely mean she'd a biographical subject in mind. With luck, that might break the chain, though what 'combining her talents' meant, Rona had no idea.

On an impulse, she picked up the phone and rang her twin's office. It was twenty past five; she shouldn't have left yet.

'Lindsey Parish.'

'Hi, Linz, it's me. Are you seeing Dominic this evening?'

There was a pause. 'As it happens, no. Would you believe he's abroad again?'

'Then how about joining me at Dino's? There's something I'd like to talk over with you.'

'Sounds serious.'

'Not really. I'd just like a sounding board.'

'My primary function, of course. Actually, since I'll probably be here till about seven, it'll suit me quite well. Seven thirty OK?'

'Perfect,' Rona said, with a lifting of her spirits. 'See you then.'

Rona had given up explaining why, on the three evenings he held his art classes, Max spent the night at his cottage across town. Family and friends viewed the arrangement as at best bizarre, but since he wouldn't have got home much before bedtime, only to return to the studio first thing in the morning, it struck them both as a pointless exercise.

In fact the purchase of Farthings, with its airy upstairs studio, had in all probability saved their marriage; with both of them working from home, tempers had frayed when Max required loud music as he painted, and Rona total quiet in which to write. The outcome was that both now

7

had space to follow their careers, leaving them free to appreciate each other's company during his midweek return – following afternoon classes – and at weekends.

And it wasn't as though they weren't in regular contact. They spoke on the phone at least twice a day, the main call to exchange news of the day's happenings, the last, brief, one to say goodnight. That evening, Rona told him about Prue's summons.

'Will you be hauled over the coals for dereliction of duty?' he enquired humorously.

'She says not, but she's certainly got something lined up.'

'Well, you've nothing on hand at the moment, have you? It'll be good to have something to occupy you.'

Rona was silent, admitting to herself that the tragedy next door, though nearly two months in the past, still haunted her. It had taken all her willpower to complete the article she'd been working on, and knock it into shape for *Chiltern Life*.

'Sweetie?' Max prompted. 'You don't have to do it if you don't want to, you know.'

She shook off her musing. 'I know; the trouble is, the longer I put off doing another bio, the harder it gets. It's such a commitment, Max; so much easier just to toss off the odd thing for Barnie, than look around for something new.'

'But you're wasting your talents. You know that. At least keep an open mind till you hear her proposal.'

She sighed. 'Yes, of course. By the way, Lindsey and I are going to Dino's, so don't phone before eleven.'

'Right, I'll prop my eyelids open! Enjoy yourselves, and give Dino my regards. I'm only sorry I can't join you.'

Dino's was an Italian restaurant a brisk, six-minute walk from Rona's home, and she was a regular customer. Hating cooking as she did, when Max wasn't home to act as chef she invariably opted, according to mood, for ready-meals, takeaways or salads. And when she fancied none of them, she went to Dino's. Often, on arriving at the restaurant, she'd find friends already there, and the obliging Dino would lay an extra place at their table.

That evening, though, there was no one she knew, and she was led to her corner table with the effusive welcome always afforded her, and Gus the retriever settled resignedly beneath it.

Lindsey arrived minutes later, dropping into a chair and lifting her hair with both hands.

'This was good thinking, sis,' she remarked, reaching for the glass Rona had already filled. 'I've had the hell of a day; if we'd not arranged to meet, I might well have been there another hour.'

Lindsey was a partner at a firm of solicitors on Guild Street, Marsborough's main thoroughfare.

'Jonathan didn't help,' she added, picking up the menu. 'Ever since Dominic and I got together, he's lost no opportunity to be bloody-minded. I'd have got through hours earlier if he'd been more cooperative.'

Jonathan Hurst, a fellow partner at Chase Mortimer, had, despite being happily married, conducted a light-hearted affair with Lindsey over the past twelve months, while Dominic Frayne, a relative newcomer who interested her far more, had remained offhand and non-committal. It was only recently that he'd made a positive move, though after Lindsey's initial ecstasy, Rona guessed it hadn't progressed as far as she'd hoped.

Her sister's love-life had always been erratic, Rona reflected; her ex-husband, Hugh, was also still on the scene, willing to be strung along when she had no better offer.

Dino himself approached to take their order, and as he moved away, Rona enquired, 'Where's Dominic this time?'

'God knows,' Lindsey replied shortly. 'He doesn't ring me daily, like your dutiful Max, who's only down the road anyway. With Dominic, it's a question of out of sight, out of mind.'

'I'm sure that's not true,' Rona said soothingly, then, when Lindsey didn't respond, 'Linz, everything is – all right, isn't it?'

Lindsey made an impatient gesture. 'When we're together, it couldn't be better. It's just that we're *not* together nearly as much as I expected. Business always comes first, and that means being closeted with bloody Carla.'

Carla Deighton was Dominic's attractive assistant, whom, since her flat was two floors below his in the same building, Lindsey referred to bitingly as his live-in girlfriend.

'She goes abroad with him?' Rona asked incautiously.

'Too right she does. Anyway – ' Lindsey straightened – 'enough of me. This meeting is to discuss something specific, is it not?'

'A phone call from Prue Granger,' Rona said.

'Ah! A call to arms?'

'To lunch, actually, the day after tomorrow.'

'But with the intention of extracting a bio?'

'That must come into it, but she said something about combining my talents, whatever that means.'

Lindsey thought for a moment. 'Well, I suppose you've done a fair bit of research recently.'

'But that wouldn't require combination – it's a large part of bios anyway.'

'How do you feel about tackling another?'

'Depends who the subject is. I have to feel some kind of ... rapport.'

'And there's no one who fills the bill?'

'No one who's not been written about a dozen times already.'

'Dominic's read all yours, you know. He's most impressed. Didn't realize I had such illustrious relatives.'

'Talking of illustrious relatives, weren't you going to meet one of his, the last time we spoke?'

'Oh, Crispin, yes; though that's not how Dominic sees him. He keeps emphasizing they're only second cousins.'

11

Rona looked surprised. 'Why is that?'

'He reckons some of his activities don't bear scrutiny.'

'Really? I've never heard that.'

'Too nebulous to get into the press; they concentrate on his celebrity status – fast cars, loads of money, famous girlfriends. Oh, he's been fined for possession of drugs, drink driving and so on, but it didn't tarnish his image – just made him one of the boys.'

Lindsey smiled at the waiter as he laid a plate of steaming pasta in front of her.

'If Dominic has such a low opinion of him,' Rona said, 'why did he accept his invitation?'

'It wasn't from him, it was from his parents, and he's quite fond of them. Anyway, it was a jolly good do, at the Dorchester.'

'But you did actually meet Crispin?'

'Oh yes, and believe me, he's quite something. Charm personified, and extremely good-looking. Photos don't do him justice.'

'Did you tell Dominic that?' Rona asked blandly, winding spaghetti round her fork.

Lindsey gave a brief laugh. 'What do you think? Anyway, on the subject of relatives, illustrious or otherwise, have you spoken to the parents recently?'

'I dropped in on Pops yesterday. I was up that way, and he gave me a cup of tea. He seemed in good form.'

'More than Mum does, at the moment.'

'Oh?' Rona looked up.

'She seemed a bit subdued when I phoned,

though she insisted nothing was wrong.'

Their parents had separated at Christmas, and while their father was renting a flat near the woman he hoped to marry, their mother, still in the marital home, had taken in a lodger, a teacher at the nearby primary school.

'I'll have a word with Max,' Rona said, 'and perhaps we could invite her over at the weekend. Sunday lunch. Will you be free?'

'In all likelihood,' Lindsey said gloomily. Then, with a shamefaced smile, 'Sorry – nothing personal. Thanks; if Mum's up for it, I'd be glad to come.'

Avril Parish, unaware that her daughters were discussing her, looked up at the sound of the front door.

'That you, Sarah?' she called, realizing too late the fatuity of the question. After all, who else could it be?

'Yes,' came the reply, as Sarah moved purposefully towards the stairs.

'Had a good evening?'

Intercepted, she'd no option but to put her head round the door.

'We went to the cinema. It was OK. I've put the snip down.'

Avril nodded. 'Thanks. Good night, then.'

'Good night.' And the door closed behind her.

Avril stared at the television screen, where, since she'd muted it on hearing the door, figures waved their arms about silently. How long, she wondered miserably, could she keep this up?

13

Including the summer break, Sarah had been with her six months, yet Avril knew her no better than on the day she arrived. But in the interval, through a variety of circumstances, she had met her father, Guy Lacey, and an attraction had sprung up between them.

While Sarah and her boyfriend spent a large part of the summer in France – he was a sports master at the school, so shared the long holiday – she and Guy had grown closer, and Avril was happier than she'd been for years. Unsure how the relationship would progress, they'd not as yet mentioned it to their daughters, but Avril knew, with sinking heart, that Guy was planning to tell Sarah when she went home to Stokely for the weekend.

It would have been so much easier, she reflected, if she and Sarah got on well, but Sarah had made it plain from the start that their relationship was a strictly business one. How would she react on learning her father and her landlady had been seeing each other?

With a sigh, Avril switched off the television and went to bed.

By the time Max came home the following evening, Rona had changed her mind a dozen times about whether or not she wanted to embark on a new biography. Would Prue expect an immediate answer to whatever she was proposing? Should Rona phone her agent to tell him about the lunch? Or wait till she knew what Prue had in mind? It was as well, she reflected, that

Max would be home, or she'd doubtless have vacillated all evening.

Hearing his key in the door, she went into the hall to greet him, while Gus bounded joyfully about them. Max's face felt cool, and the scent of wood smoke clung to his coat. An illegal bonfire somewhere, no doubt.

He shrugged off his coat and lifted the mail from the hall table, leafing through it as he followed her into the sitting room.

'An airmail from the Furnesses, I see,' he commented. 'Why didn't you open it?'

'I ... thought I'd leave it for you,' Rona said, not meeting his eyes.

He flicked her a glance. The Furnesses were the owners of the house next door, renting it out to a series of tenants during their residency in Hong Kong. This was their first communication since the tragedy.

Max slit open the flimsy paper, ran his eye rapidly down its contents, then returned to the beginning to read it aloud.

'Dear Max and Rona: first, please accept my apologies for not having written before. Monica and I were appalled to hear what had happened at the house – even more so, since you were both so closely involved. Useless to rant at the letting agents – the tenants' references were impeccable and no one could have foreseen what would happen.

'As they point out, however, the notoriety is unlikely to tempt new enquiries – or at least, not

of the right kind – and we have decided to come home, look the place over, and decide what we want to do with it. In the present economic climate, putting it on the market is hardly an option, but nor is trying to let it again in its current state. Last time we were over, we realized it was badly in need of modernizing, and this seems the right time to go about it. At least it will then bear no resemblance to the house lived in by the Franks.

'An added incentive is that my contract out here is coming to an end, and we will shortly be needing a base in the UK. This will be an opportunity to decide if we want to return to number seventeen, or leave it on the agency books as an investment. We certainly intend to stay in the area, and as you know, Lightbourne Avenue has a great deal going for it.

'So this letter is to give you due warning of our arrival. We shall be flying to the UK on Monday 19th October and staying at the Clarendon. We'd be delighted if you would join us for dinner soon afterwards, and will be in touch to arrange this. In the meantime, renewed apologies for not having written earlier.

'Monica joins me in sending best wishes.

'Sincerely, Charles.'

Max looked up, meeting Rona's eyes. 'So there you have it. It'll be good to see them again; must be at least three years since they were over.'

'I'm glad they're going to do something to the

16

house,' Rona said. 'It's hopelessly old-fashioned, especially the kitchen.'

She stopped abruptly, not wanting to remember the kitchen next door.

Max moved to the drinks cabinet and poured
two glasses. 'Get this down you, my love. And
don't worry, the ghosts will be well and truly
laid.'

His words still reverberated in her head the next
morning, as she gazed out of the train window.
The ghosts in the house, such as they were, may
indeed be banished by refurbishment; it
remained to be seen how long they would stay in
her head.

With a sigh, she turned to the newspaper she'd
bought at the station, glanced at the gloomy
headlines, and opened it in search of lighter
reading. And at once her eyes fell on a photograph captioned *Crispin Ryder and friend arriving for the world première of the new Bond
film.*

His photos don't do him justice, Lindsey had
said, but Rona could see his attraction, even in
the poor quality of the newsprint. The photographer must have called out his name, catching
him just as he turned with an enquiring smile,
one arm loosely round the fur-coated girl at his
side. Though in his late forties, he looked lean
and boyish, his frilled shirt-front and the jacket
slung carelessly over his shoulder proclaiming a
confident insouciance that was immediately
appealing. So Dominic suspected him of nefari-

ous dealings; doubtless they would only add to his attraction.

London looked its best in the mellow October sunshine, and in Covent Garden buskers were busy, guitarists, jugglers and pavement artists attracting their own crowds. The restaurant Prue had nominated was on the first floor, the street level being given over to a delicatessen. Rona made her way upstairs, and, emerging at the top, immediately caught sight of her.

Prue stood as she approached, her short, curly hair and over-large spectacles making her look, as always, like a precocious child.

'Good to see you!' she exclaimed, leaning forward to touch cheeks and kiss the air before standing back to survey Rona with her head on one side. 'Well,' she pronounced, resuming her seat, 'you look none the worse for your adventures.'

'I'd say I'm relatively unscathed,' Rona confirmed, sitting opposite her.

'I can't imagine how you manage to get yourself into those situations.'

'Nor can I. Max says if he hadn't gone grey in his twenties, he certainly would have by now.'

'Ah yes, how is that clever husband of yours? Still teaching?'

'Very much so; evening classes Mondays, Tuesdays and Thursdays, afternoon classes Wednesdays, and the Art School ten till four on Thursdays.'

Prue shook her head wonderingly. 'And in his

spare time, he turns out masterpieces!'

Rona smiled. 'Not sure about that, but he keeps busy, certainly. He's been commissioned to do several canvases for the boardroom in a prestigious new building in Buckford.'

'Well, all power to his paintbrush! Now – ' she picked up the menu – 'what can I tempt you with?'

They spent several minutes discussing their choices, and Prue ordered a bottle of Frascati to go with them.

'Incidentally,' she said, 'before we go any further, I should tell you I invited Eddie to join us, but admittedly it was short notice and he had a prior engagement. He sends his best.' Eddie Gold, small, rotund and ebullient, was Rona's agent.

Prue sat back in her chair, her eyes owlish behind their horn-rimmed spectacles. 'Now – tell me – what do you know of Elspeth Wilding?'

The question was so unexpected that for a moment, Rona stared at her blankly. 'The artist, you mean?'

'The artist.'

Rona's brows drew together. 'Is this by any chance why you were quizzing me about Max?'

'Just answer the question, my dear.'

'Well, she's one of the big names, isn't she? Pictures in Tate Britain, the Hayward Gallery, Somerset House – you name it.'

'Anything else?'

Rona thought for a moment, and memory

19

stirred. 'Didn't she hit the headlines about a year ago? Went missing, or something?'

'She did indeed,' Prue confirmed portentously, 'and, despite extensive searches, hasn't been seen since.'

'Really? I'd no idea; I assumed she must have turned up again.'

'Unfortunately not. What's Max's opinion of her?'

'Oh, he thinks she's brilliant, among the greats.'

'Yet he never wondered if, as you put it, she'd "turned up" again?'

'Prue,' Rona said slowly, 'what *is* this?'

She didn't answer directly. 'Elspeth was a child prodigy – did you know that? Had her first pictures hung at the age of thirteen, and there's hardly a prize she hasn't been awarded. It's an amazing career.'

'But someone must know where she is, surely?'

'It seems not.'

Rona straightened suddenly. 'Oh now look, Prue, I hope you're not suggesting what I think you are.'

Prue leant forward earnestly. 'Rona, it's an assignment tailor-made for you. Damn it, you're a biographer with a reputation for solving mysteries. What could be better, when it's quite likely a clue might lie in her past? So, you research her life, and, in tracking down her friends, relatives, associates, etc., there's an excellent chance you'll come up with the answer. She could be living incognito somewhere, having lost her memory.'

Not that again! Rona thought involuntarily. She said quickly, 'So that's what you meant about combining my talents.'

'Exactly. The only drawback is the biography would have to be classed as unauthorized, even though the family have requested it.'

Rona looked up quickly. 'The family have?'

'I was coming to that; I had a phone call from Elspeth's sister. I don't know if you're aware of it, but the family live in Buckfordshire, so she's heard all about your exploits, and, I gather, read your previous work. She also knows your husband's an artist, and hoped that might help influence you. Rona, she literally *begged* me to persuade you; poor woman, she doesn't know if her sister's alive or dead, and it's driving her demented.'

Their food arrived, but, delicious though it was, Rona scarcely tasted it as her mind swung between considering the idea and rejecting it outright.

'Surely someone's already done her?' she asked suddenly, unwittingly breaking into Prue's conversation.

'Not, incredibly enough, for ten years. She's a very private person, hates publicity of any sort. Apparently it was a mammoth task to persuade her even to attend functions held in her honour.'

'Then perhaps she just wanted to escape from it, once and for all. As simple as that.'

Prue held her eye. 'Then prove it.'

'Prue, I—'

'Look, Rona, don't discount it out of hand. I'm not asking for an instant decision, but assuming you do eventually want to return to biographies, the longer you put it off, the harder it will be. If you don't use it, you'll lose it. The magazine stuff you're doing is all well and good, but it's pretty ... ephemeral, isn't it? This could ease you gently back – a kind of halfway house.'

Rona smiled reluctantly. 'You're a good advocate, I'll give you that. All right, tell me what you know about her sister and the family.'

'Virtually nothing; only that the sister's name is Naomi Harris, and she lives in Sunningdene.'

'She didn't say anything about Elspeth's disappearance?'

'No, it's of no interest to me.' Prue paused and smiled. 'Though it seems to be to you.'

'Does Eddie know about this?'

'That Mrs Harris approached me, yes.'

'What did he think?' Behind her agent's laid-back manner lay a razor-sharp brain, and Rona valued his opinion.

'That it was up to you – he's the soul of diplomacy, our Eddie. No doubt you'll phone him, and – also no doubt – you'll want to discuss it with Max. If, as you say, he thinks highly of Elspeth, I imagine he'll be in favour of your tackling it.'

'Don't gang up on me, Prue!' Rona protested, and Prue laughed. 'So, what happens now?'

'You know the form. If you decide to go

22

ahead, we'll draw up the contract. Until it's signed, you'll obviously have no contact with Mrs Harris.'

'And if I decide not to?'

'I'll offer it to someone else. Now, I think we've said enough on the subject. Would you like a dessert?'

Since Eddie had pleaded a prior engagement, Rona waited till she reached home before phoning him.

'Dear girl!' he greeted her. 'Been wined and dined by the Honourable Prudence?'

'I have; bearing out the adage that there's no such thing as a free lunch.'

'Twisted your arm, did she?'

'She had a pretty good go at it.'

'And seriously, what do you think of the proposal?'

'God, Eddie, I don't know. I've been turning it over in my mind ever since. One minute I think I'll do it, the next I'm backing away.'

'From what, exactly?'

'Mainly, I admit, the commitment; I've got out of the habit of setting aside a couple of years or so on one project. Also, Prue seems to think I enjoy being an amateur detective, while the truth is, it's been thrust upon me. I certainly never intended it. In fact, one reason I've been considering another bio was as a means of escape from mayhem and murder.'

'But that, if I remember correctly, was where it started. Have you spoken to Max?'

'Not yet. It's his day at the Art School.'

'So, what's the present state of play?'

'Up in the air. I'll have to sleep on it, probably several times, before I reach any decision.'

'Well, if you want my unbiased opinion, I think you should take it. You've been frittering along for a while now; it's time to get down to some serious work. However, I'm not going to lean on you, nor will I try to change your mind, whatever you decide. That's a promise.'

'Thanks, Eddie. I'll let you know.'

'God, Rona, that would be amazing!'

Rona sighed. Prue was right; Max was in favour.

'A big name like that, just falling into your lap!'

She said sharply, 'You do know she's disappeared?'

'*Disappeared*? That's putting it a bit strongly. I know she's been lying low for a while, but she's always hated publicity.'

'More than lying low, Max. According to Prue, she vanished off the face of the earth, and extensive searches have failed to find her.'

'Oh God,' Max said flatly. 'Here we go again.'

'Precisely my reaction.'

'Does that mean you're not going to do it?'

'It means,' Rona said with heavy emphasis, 'that I would welcome an informed discussion of all the pros and cons before reaching any decision.'

'Obviously I don't want you taking any risks,

24

but, as you know, I've been trying for ages to steer you back to bios, and this has been handed you on a plate. Think of it – no worry about choosing a subject, then persuading your publisher, then waiting for agreement from the estate. If you ask me, Fate is telling you to get back on the horse.'

'Fate can mind her own flaming business,' Rona said.

But as she put down the phone and prepared to take Gus for his walk, it seemed to her that the decision had already been reached.

TWO

Rona spent a large part of the next day on the Internet, looking up references to Elspeth Wilding. A lot of the information was repetitive, though minor facts varied from site to site. By mid-afternoon, she had copied and pasted from several different sources to open a file of her own, which, she assured herself, could be deleted if she decided to go no further.

She stretched, rubbing her back. So, what had she learned? That Elspeth Mary Wilding had been born in Buckford on 4th April 1968, the third child of Richard and Hazel Wilding. That she had shown a precocious gift for painting, and had had a picture displayed in the Royal

Academy's Summer Exhibition of '81. That she was considered one of the most important artists of the twenty-first century. That she'd been awarded the Royal College of Art gold medal for her year, among the first of her many prizes. Her unwillingness to appear in public was well documented, and borne out by the same, unsatisfactory, photograph on all sites, in which her face was partially screened by a sheet of pale hair. *It doesn't matter what I look like*, she was quoted as saying, *it's my art that's important*.

The widest divergence came in reports of her disappearance, varying from wildly imaginative scenarios to the more cautious statement that she had 'dropped out of circulation' in May 2008. What was abundantly clear, however, was that nothing had been heard or seen of her since.

'Well?' Max said eagerly, coming into the kitchen that evening. 'Made up your mind yet?'

Rona returned his kiss. 'No; I told you, I want a full-blown discussion.'

'Even though you've slept on it?'

'Not too well, as it happens. I was turning it over most of the night.'

'Then the sooner you make your mind up, the better. Can't have you losing your beauty sleep.' He glanced at the printed sheets she'd brought down. 'Been genning up on her, I see. I could have told you most of that.'

'Except for her disappearance,' Rona reminded him.

'Well, this lot don't seem any better informed.' He poured the drinks and handed her a glass. 'Was she officially reported missing, do you know?'

'Prue didn't say, but I suppose she must have been.'

'I doubt if there'd have been much response from the police. They'd only pursue it if the person who disappeared was a child, vulnerable in some way, or a criminal on the run. Otherwise, their line is that an adult has every right to go off without telling their family.'

'Prue mentioned searches, but perhaps it was the family who organized them; I'll ask Mrs Harris. If I ever meet her, that is,' she added, catching his amused glance.

Tom Parish stood at the window of his flat taking deep breaths, his fingers prodding experimentally at his chest. Though he'd previously had two heart scares, it was a year since the most recent, and he couldn't recall the exact symptoms. God, this was all he needed! He and Catherine were flying to Portugal next week.

The doorbell sounded. That would be her now. Rather than going down to meet her, as he usually did, he pressed the buzzer and listened to her ascending footsteps.

'Tom?' There was a note of anxiety in her voice.

He turned from the window, forcing a smile. 'Good morning, my love.'

She came quickly towards him, scanning his face. 'Are you all right? You look a bit pale.'

'I *feel* a bit pale. Indigestion, probably.'

Her voice sharpened. 'You've a chest pain?'

'Not a pain; just a little ... discomfort.'

She took his arm. 'Come on – you're coming with me.'

'What's the hurry?' he protested. 'Surely we've time for a coffee before—'

'Forget the shopping trip. We're off to A&E.'

'Oh now look, Catherine, there's no need for that! It's—'

'With your history, there's every need.'

'Then let me give Ben a ring.' Ben Pierce was their GP and a family friend.

'Better to go straight to the hospital; time could be all-important. Now don't argue, there's a love. This is non-negotiable.'

He sighed, allowing himself to be led down the stairs and out to her waiting car. Guild Street when they reached it was thronged with Saturday shoppers – they should have been among them, he thought in frustration – and their progress was slowed by congested traffic.

'I feel OK now,' he said hopefully.

'As in toothache vanishing when you see the dentist. Sorry, won't wash. I want someone to have a good look at you.'

At last they were turning into Alban Road and, within minutes, the entrance to the Royal County. Catherine pulled up at the door.

'You go and sign yourself in. I'll park the car and be with you in a minute.'

Reluctantly, since he'd no option, Tom did as she said.

'Hello, Gorgeous!'

'Dominic!' Lindsey took the phone over to the sofa and curled up with it. 'Where are you?'

'Still in Athens, unfortunately. I'd hoped to be on my way home by now, but there's a contract still to be finalized and the signatory's not available till Monday.'

'So you'll be back then?'

'All being well. What have you been up to?'

'Fairly busy at the office, otherwise not a lot. I'm lunching with Rona and Max tomorrow.'

'Give them my best. The four of us should get together sometime.'

Lindsey's heart lifted. Neither Max nor her parents had met Dominic as yet, and Rona only briefly. She'd been chary of suggesting he 'meet the family' till she was more sure of him.

'That would be great,' she said.

'In the meantime, I'll phone as soon as I land, and if I'm home in reasonable time, I'll send the car for you. All right?'

'Great,' she said again. It was still a novelty to be chauffeur-driven everywhere in Dominic's Daimler.

'See you soon, angel.' And he rang off. He never indulged in long telephone conversations, Lindsey thought regretfully; if he did, it might make his frequent absences more bearable.

She leant back against the cushions, letting her eyes move round the room with a now-familiar sense of dissatisfaction. Although she'd bought the flat nearly four years ago, it was still furnished with pieces she and Hugh had chosen together, and split between them when they parted. They were no longer to her taste, and what she'd really like to do was throw everything out and start again from scratch.

Damn it, she thought impatiently, she could still see Hugh sitting in the chairs, which had been disconcerting to say the least when she was with Jonathan. Dominic had not as yet set foot here, and she realized suddenly that she didn't want him to until it was refurbished. Time, then, to put an end to vague discontent and do something about it. Redecoration would be the first step; the walls throughout were the bland magnolia slapped on by the builders, but thankfully the carpet, a nubbly oatmeal throughout, was still in good condition and would go with any colour scheme. And, by a stroke of luck, two of her friends ran a decorating service; they'd be able to advise her.

Fired with sudden enthusiasm, Lindsey swung her feet to the floor, retrieved a pad and pencil from the bureau, and began a methodical survey of her home.

Tom's heart and chest had been listened to, his blood pressure taken, and after an ECG and blood test, he'd been sent on his way with a bottle of aspirin and a spray to use if his symptoms recurred. Angina, he was told, but nothing too serious.

'A waste of time,' he remarked, dropping into his usual chair in Catherine's sitting room. 'I told you it would be.'

'On the contrary; we now know what was wrong, and can take steps accordingly. We could not have gone away with that hanging over us.'

'Talking of which, we still have those last-minute things to buy.'

'And we've Monday and Tuesday in which to get them.' She smiled at him. 'Admit it: what's really bugging you is the time deducted from our weekend.' Although they habitually spent Saturdays together, on Sundays Catherine drove to Cricklehurst, to visit her son and daughter-in-law.

He grinned shamefacedly. 'Am I that transparent?'

'Yes, but you can relax on that score, too. You need a quiet weekend, and I intend to see you get it.' And, in answer to his questioning look, she added, 'I phoned Daniel from the hospital, to say I wouldn't be over tomorrow.'

'But that means you won't see them for three weeks,' Tom protested, trying to hide his pleasure. 'Think how many pounds Alice will have gained! You'll hardly recognize her!'

Catherine laughed. 'You can mock. Just wait till you have a grandchild.'

'A chance would be a fine thing. I despair of my daughters.'

'Then you can share Alice. She'll be your step-granddaughter, once we're married.'

He held out a hand to her. 'Seriously, are you sure about this? I'd be perfectly all right, you know.'

'I'm sure you would,' she replied, giving it a squeeze, ' but you gave me a fright and I want us to have a normal day together, with no hospital visits.'

'Me too,' he said, 'but promise me one thing.'

'Not to tell the girls?' She'd invited Rona and Lindsey to supper the following Tuesday, on the eve of their departure. Max, of course, would be at his evening class.

'Got it in one.'

'All right, I promise. Now, we've spent quite long enough discussing your health, Tom Parish; let's have another look at that hotel brochure.'

Sunday was warm and sunny, and the little walled garden the perfect place for pre-lunch drinks.

'This is the life!' Lindsey declared. 'What could be better than sitting in the sun, G and T in hand, with the gorgeous smell of roast beef wafting over us?'

'Almost like being back in Italy,' Avril remarked happily, 'especially with the paving and all the containers.' She and Lindsey had spent ten days there the previous month, an arrangement made, to Lindsey's chagrin, just before she and Dominic came together, and he'd proposed a holiday in South Africa – a proposal that, having necessarily been postponed, had so far not been rescheduled.

Max glanced at his watch; still fifteen minutes till the meal would require attention. 'So, what's everyone been doing since we last met?' he asked.

Lindsey drained her glass and put it on the table, shaking her head as he mimed a top-up. 'I've decided to revamp the flat,' she said. 'New colour-scheme, new furniture, new curtains. The lot.'

'You said you'd like to, when we looked round Willows',' Rona remarked. Willows' Fine Furniture, the emporium on Guild Street, was the last local firm whose history she'd researched. 'I didn't realize you were serious.'

'I probably wasn't, then, but the idea's been growing on me. I thought I'd ask Nina and Nicole for suggestions.'

'It'll cost you,' Max said shrewdly.

'Well, I've nothing else to spend my hard-earned cash on, and I'm sure they'd give me a discount.'

'What will you do with the things you have?' Rona asked.

'Send them for auction. Anything they fetch can go towards the new stuff.'

'I sometimes wish I could do that,' Avril remarked.

Rona and Lindsey exchanged a worried glance. Selfishly, they preferred 'home' to remain the same, even though they no longer lived there.

'But it's perfect for you, surely?' Rona said tentatively. 'Especially since the alterations you had done, before taking in lodgers. En suite and everything.'

At the thought of Sarah, Avril's face clouded; had Guy broached the difficult subject yet?

'Mum?' Lindsey's voice reached her. 'Is something wrong?'

Avril shook herself. 'No, no. At least, I hope not.'

'What do you mean, you hope not?'

She hesitated, then made up her mind. 'It's just that Sarah's father and I saw quite a lot of each other during the summer, and we're wondering how she'll react when she finds out. He's ... intending to tell her this weekend.'

'But Mum, that's wonderful!' Rona exclaimed. 'It's about time you had some fun!'

'Certainly is!' Lindsey confirmed. 'Isn't he the one we saw at the Clarendon?'

Avril nodded, her face colouring. 'It's ... not really serious, or anything. Just that we enjoy each other's company. I knew you two would understand,' she added in a burst of gratitude, 'but Sarah's reaction's not as easy to predict. She's had her father to herself all her life.'

'But she's not living at home now,' Rona objected. 'And didn't you say she has a boy-friend?'

'She has, yes.'

'I'm sure she'll be fine about it,' Max said firmly. 'It sounds an excellent arrangement.' He turned to Rona. 'We've heard your sister's and your mother's news, darling. Are you going to tell them yours?'

Avril and Lindsey looked at her expectantly.

'Nothing's settled yet,' she said defensively.

34

'But?' Lindsey prompted.

'I've been asked to do another bio.'

'So that *was* what Prue wanted!'

'I still haven't decided...' Rona's voice tailed off, and, catching Max's smiling glance, she knew it was no longer true. 'Well, perhaps I have,' she amended.

'So who is it?' demanded Avril.

'The artist, Elspeth Wilding.'

'Well, she's certainly a big name,' Lindsey remarked. 'Well done, sis.'

'You say you've been asked,' Avril said. 'Does that mean you didn't choose her yourself?'

'No, her sister approached my publishers.'

'Hang on,' Lindsey broke in. 'Wasn't there something funny about her? I seem to remember—'

'She disappeared,' Rona said bluntly. 'About eighteen months ago.'

Avril looked puzzled. 'She's still alive, then? I thought you usually—'

'We *hope* she is,' Max put in. 'But part of her sister's reason for approaching Rona is because she's also known for solving mysteries.'

Lindsey sat back. 'Uh-oh.'

'All I'm committing myself to,' Rona said firmly, 'is the bio. I am not – repeat not – going out of my way to solve any mystery. If something surfaces during normal research, fair enough, but I'm certainly not digging for it.'

'Well, just be careful, dear,' Avril said uneasily. 'You've given us enough frights over the last year or two.' She glanced involuntarily at the high wall between their garden and that next door.

Max, intercepting it, said, 'The Furnesses are coming back, did Rona tell you?'

Avril brightened. 'Permanently?'

'Not immediately, but they want to look over the house with a view to modernizing it, and in the process erasing any reminders of ... past occupants.' He glanced at Lindsey. 'More work for your friends at *Double N*, perhaps.' He got to his feet. 'Excuse me – time to make the gravy. Lunch in ten minutes, ladies.'

'Good morning, Eddie.'

'Dear girl! Have you reached a decision?'

'Yes, I'll go for it. It would be foolish not to; it's bound to attract a lot of interest.'

'My thinking exactly. Fine, I'll get on to Prue and come back to you with her offer. Then, once the contract's signed, you can approach the family.'

The die was cast, Rona thought fancifully as she put down the phone; she only hoped she wouldn't come to regret it. In the meantime, she should warn Barnie Trent, the features editor, that she'd be taking a sabbatical from *Chiltern Life*.

'So you're returning to your first love?' he observed, when she'd explained the position. 'Well, I'm glad for you, though obviously sorry we'll be losing you, at least for a while. As you know, your series have proved very popular.'

'I've enjoyed doing them, and part of me

wants to continue, but it was always an interim arrangement; I've carried on longer than I should – sheer laziness, really.'

'We're running the Willows one next month. I suppose, as it turns out, it'll be your last in that series?'

'Probably, but in any case I've covered most of the firms eligible.'

'Well, despite the hiatus on the business side, we still have the social. Dinah was saying the other day it was some time since she'd seen you. I'll get her to give you a call.'

'That would be great. Thanks, Barnie.'

'And good luck in the meantime,' he said.

'Avril.'

'Oh, Guy, you've been on my mind all weekend! How did it go?'

'Sarah's left the house?'

'Yes, five minutes ago. She's been pretty ... monosyllabic.'

'I thought she might be. Look, I have to come over this morning. Can we meet for lunch?'

'Yes, yes, of course, but I'm at the library till one. Will that be too late?'

'No, but it'll save time if I come out to you.' Belmont, the suburb where she lived, was a twenty-minute drive from Marsborough. 'Where do you suggest we meet?'

Avril thought for a moment. 'The Jolly Wagoner, in the High Street?'

'No chance of running into my daughter?' She heard the smile in his voice.

'I doubt if the school encourages lunchtime drinking.'

'Right, I'll be there at one, and bag us a table. See you then.'

It didn't sound as though their news had been well received, Avril thought anxiously, as she shrugged on her coat and let herself out of the house. The local library, where she worked part-time, was within walking distance, as, for that matter, was the primary school where Sarah taught – the reason she'd chosen to come to Avril. Oh dear, she did so hope it would be all right. But there was no point in worrying; Guy would put her in the picture soon enough.

Lindsey had taken a packed lunch to work, and ate it hastily at her desk, a weather eye on the door. It was not a practice approved of at Chase Mortimer, particularly among the partners, and one she seldom engaged in. Today, however, she'd an important errand to see to, and, having dusted the crumbs off her lap and disposed of the evidence, she left the office and set off in the direction of *Double N.*

She had known Nicole and Nina since school-days, and even then they'd been interested in art and design. After obtaining their degrees, they'd set up a small business together, which, in succeeding years, had continued to flourish, until they now owned handsome premises on Guild Street, offering a complete personal service with a wide range of options.

Lindsey pushed open the door and went inside, pausing to take stock of the Aladdin's cave around her. Materials and fabrics of every kind hung suspended in a riot of colour down the length of the shop – brocades, velvets, chintzes, soft furnishings, plain, patterned, rough and smooth. To her left stood a row of sloping stands bearing a dozen or so wallpaper books; two of the high stools in front of them were occupied.

A smiling salesgirl approached her. 'Can I help you, madam?'

'I'd like a word with the proprietors, please.'

'If I could have your name, I'll see if they're available?'

'Lindsey!'

She turned, to see Nicole Standing hurrying towards her. 'How are you? I haven't seen you for ages!' She nodded at the assistant. 'It's all right, Deirdre, I'll see to this.'

'Actually,' Lindsey said, 'I'm in search of professional advice.'

'Then come into the office and tell me about it.'

The room at the back of the premises looked, to Lindsey's mind, more like a sitting room than a workplace, furnished as it was with easy chairs and sofa as well as the obligatory desk.

'Look who's here!' Nicole carolled as they went in.

Nina Martin looked up from a sheaf of papers, her face breaking into a smile. 'Lindsey – hello! How are things?'

'In need of a make-over,' Lindsey replied. 'On the home front, at least. I've decided to scrap everything and start again.'

'Then you've come to the right place.' Nicole went to a coffee percolator and poured out three cups.

'So what's the first step?' Lindsey asked, seating herself on the sofa and accepting her coffee. 'Do you have a selection of brochures to look at, or do I just go through the fabulous materials out there and select something?'

'We do have brochures, yes, but we usually start by coming to your home to take measurements, while you give us a rough idea of what you have in mind.'

'That's just it – I haven't anything, beyond clearing everything out. The flat's quite modern, so I'd like a contemporary feel, but at the moment it's all so *bland*. I want to change that – make it a statement about *me*!'

Nina laughed. 'That could be tricky! You say you're ditching the lot – does that include furniture?'

'Except for the odd piece, yes. Thankfully the carpets are OK, but I'll be wanting new curtains, bedspreads, cushions, furniture. A total makeover.'

'Obviously, we'll be more than happy to oblige. How many rooms are we talking about?'

'Sitting room, two bedrooms, and the hall, stairs and landing. Not that it's really a hall, just a tiny entrance before the stairs begin. The kitchen and both bathrooms are fine.'

'You've saved yourself several thousand there!'

'So the first step is for you to come round and measure?'

'That's right. We can fix a time now, if you like.' Nina went to the desk and brought back an appointments diary.

'I'm afraid it'll have to be an evening or weekend,' Lindsey said apologetically. 'I can't take time off work at the moment.'

'No problem. How about this evening?'

Lindsey hesitated. Dominic was hoping to be back...

'Or tomorrow?' Nina suggested, glancing at the diary.

'Sorry, no, I'm out tomorrow. Better make it Wednesday, if that's all right? After six thirty?'

'Wednesday it is.'

Lindsey leant back and drew a deep breath. 'I can hardly wait!' she said.

Avril saw him as soon as she entered the pub, and he raised a hand in greeting, standing up as she reached him to give her a quick kiss.

'As you see, it's pretty busy; I suggest we order our food straight away, then we can settle down to talk. What do you fancy?'

They opted for salmon fishcakes, and Guy fought his way to the bar to order them, returning minutes later with a tankard of beer and a glass of white wine.

'So?' Avril enquired, almost as soon as he'd seated himself. 'What happened?'

He lifted his tankard in a toast, and drank deeply before setting it down again.

'She was totally unreasonable,' he said then, his face hard. 'Accused me of putting her in "an untenable position", if you please. Damn it, her mother died when she was a baby; she can't resent you on her behalf. All these years I've been there for her, and barely looked—'

'But that's just it,' Avril interrupted. 'As you say, all these years there've been just the two of you, totally self-sufficient. It's understandable that she should resent someone else coming on the scene.'

'No, Avril, it's *not* understandable! She's not a child, for God's sake. She's simply being unforgivably selfish.'

There was a pause, while they both reflected on what had been said.

'In a way,' Avril mused, 'it's a pity it started while she was abroad – behind her back, as it might seem. If she'd been around, seeing it unfold gradually, it wouldn't have come as a shock – a fait accompli.' She looked down at her glass, forcing herself to say what she'd prepared, but prayed would not be necessary.

'Guy, the last thing I want is to come between you and Sarah. Might it be best if we just...' She stumbled to a halt, aware of his sudden stillness.

'Just what?'

'Let it go?' she finished miserably.

There was a pulsating silence. Then he said harshly, 'Is that what you want?'

She reached impulsively for his hand. 'Of course not! It's been wonderful these last few months.'

He gripped her hand in both his. 'It's not what I want, either. Rightly or wrongly, I've started to hope that – well, when your divorce comes through...' He gave his head an impatient shake. 'Anyway, be that as it may, I've no intention of letting that selfish little minx come between us. I love her dearly, but perhaps I've been guilty of spoiling her, letting her think only her wishes count. Dammit, she has a boyfriend – it's quite likely they'll marry before long. Then what am I supposed to do?'

He sighed, adding more calmly, 'I want to keep the peace with her, Avril, of course I do, but she's not going to dictate how I lead my life.'

Avril's mind was spinning. This was the closest he'd come to hinting at a future together and she knew, beyond doubt, it was what she wanted above all. But at the cost of severance from his daughter? She moistened her lips, trying to be reasonable.

'Is it me she objects to, do you think, or would it be the same with anyone?'

'How could she object to you?' he demanded. 'You've been kindness itself, even giving her advice that time she fell out with Clive. No, what she can't take is the thought of not being the sole object of my affections. Well, I'm sorry, but she'll have to lump it.'

He looked up at her. 'Did you tell your two?'

She nodded.

'And?'

'Well, they were ... pleased for me. But there's

43

no reason why they shouldn't be,' she added quickly. 'After all, Tom has someone else. We've all ... moved on.'

'Exactly,' Guy said grimly. 'And that's just what I intend to do.'

THREE

When Avril returned from her lunch date, it was to find a message from Sarah advising her that she was going out straight from school, and wouldn't be back till later.

Avril had been bracing herself for their next meeting, endlessly debating how to tackle the subject on both their minds. Now, she'd have to wait several hours more, and when Sarah did come in, she'd go straight up to her room. But they couldn't go on circling each other like a couple of wary dogs; for all their sakes, the situation *had* to be brought into the open and discussed.

She'd waylay her in the hall, Avril decided; block her route to the stairs, and suggest they had a coffee together. Short of downright rudeness, Sarah would at least have to pause, giving Avril the opening she needed.

Consequently, when, just after ten thirty, she heard her key in the lock, she immediately hurried out of the sitting room. Sarah, startled at her sudden appearance, said involuntarily, 'Mrs Parish!' Then, before Avril could speak, went on quickly, 'Actually, I was wanting a word with you, to let you know I'll be leaving soon.'

Avril stared at her, completely taken aback. 'Oh, now, Sarah, surely—'

'Clive's buying a flat, and once it goes through, he wants me to move in with him.'

Avril brushed that aside. 'I've been wanting to talk to you, too, about your father—'

Sarah made a dismissive gesture. 'That's none of my business.'

'But I don't want you to feel you have to leave, just because—'

'I told you, I'm moving in with Clive. It was always on the cards, once he got a place of his own.'

'We still need to talk,' Avril said desperately.

'Obviously I'll let you know as soon as we have a firm date, but I wanted to give you time to find someone else.'

'Sarah, I really—'

'Now, if you'll excuse me...' And she brushed past and started up the stairs.

Defeated, Avril turned back into the sitting room. *Now* what should she do?

Dominic didn't phone till eleven fifteen, and then only to say goodnight. Lindsey, who had waited in all evening, had retired, disgruntled, to bed, and was on the point of switching off the light. The weariness in his voice, however, precluded an acid comment.

Instead, she asked, 'Did you get the contract signed?'

'Eventually, but not till gone six. They kept raising further points. I'm sorry, angel; I was hoping to see you tonight.'

'Me too,' Lindsey said.

'So it'll have to be tomorrow. Collect you at seven?'

'Dominic, I'm sorry; I can't make tomorrow.'

There was a pause. Then, simply, 'Oh?'

'I'm going to Catherine's for supper. She and Pops are off to Portugal this week.'

Another silence, and she remembered, with a mixture of annoyance and anxiety, that he disliked having his plans thwarted.

'You have to go?'

'Yes,' she said tightly, 'I have to go, and what's more, I *want* to. It's not my fault you were delayed this evening. I postponed an appointment to wait in for you.'

His voice was cool. 'If we're apportioning blame, Lindsey, it wasn't my fault, either; I couldn't leave Athens without that contract.'

'Fair enough; just don't expect me to cancel an engagement to suit you.'

There was a short silence and she held her breath, wondering if she'd gone too far. Then he said evenly, 'Perhaps we should postpone this conversation until we're both less tired.'

'Perhaps we should.'

'Goodnight, then.'

'Goodnight.' She jammed her finger on the off-button and, flinging the phone down onto

46

the bed, buried her face in the pillow and pounded it with her fist. Why, she demanded of herself, did she have to fall for such an infuriating man? Why couldn't he be like Hugh, always there at her beck and call? Or, she wondered in a moment of self-analysis, if he were, would she treat him in the same way?

She rolled on to her back, uncomfortable with the thought. He'd phone tomorrow, she assured herself, and she'd be all sweetness and light. He'd probably suggest Wednesday, and then they – oh hell! Nina and Nicole were coming! But that would take only an hour or so; she'd ask him to make it seven thirty. If he phoned.

But when she set out for Catherine's the next evening, there'd been no word from him and she was back on the emotional see-saw. She'd thought, a few weeks back, that they'd gone beyond that, but it seemed she was wrong.

She reached the bungalow in Willow Crescent just as Rona was drawing up, and they went down the path together. Catherine, elegant as always, opened the door and kissed them in turn.

'Lovely to see you! Do go on in. Tom's on bar duty.'

'It's very noble of you to entertain just before going away,' Lindsey remarked. 'I doubt if I could do it.'

'Well, we both wanted to see you, and we have to eat, after all. I'm afraid, though, it's family fare tonight, rather than cordon bleu.'

47

'A very well-fed family, mind you!' Tom commented, coming into the hall and kissing his daughters. 'How are you both? You look positively blooming!'

Rona's forehead creased slightly. 'Not sure that you do, Pops. Are you OK?'

'Absolutely fine. Just in need of a holiday.'

'Surely now you've retired, your whole life's a holiday!' Lindsey teased.

'Then perhaps it's sea air I need,' Tom amended. 'Now, what are you drinking? The usual?'

They preceded him into Catherine's pleasant sitting room, familiar to Rona, less so to Lindsey, who, siding with her mother in the break-up, had remained hostile to Catherine for some time. Even now, she wasn't quite at ease with her. She seated herself on the sofa and checked her mobile was switched on.

Tom, having served their drinks, sat down beside her. Across the room, Catherine had produced a brochure of their hotel, and she and Rona were discussing it.

'So, how are things, Lindy-Lou?'

It was a pet name he hadn't used for years, and in her rocky state it brought a lump to her throat.

'Fine,' she said.

'And the man in your life?'

'Fine too, last time I saw him.' Her voice sounded brittle; she hoped he wouldn't notice.

'And when was that?'

'Oh, God, Pops, I don't know! Two or three weeks ago.'

She felt his quick glance, and added defen-

48

sively, 'Everything's OK, you know.'

'Is it? I worry about you, sweetheart; I just wish you could find the right one and be happy, like Rona.'

'Well, you always said our similarity was only skin-deep.'

He laughed. 'That's true, and I wouldn't have it any other way.'

Lindsey took a quick sip of her drink, willing the tears not to come. When she and Rona had quarrelled as children, she'd always run to their mother, Rona to their father, and she'd grown up suspecting – no doubt quite wrongly – a corresponding bias on the part of her parents. It was oddly comforting to know her father worried about her.

His large, warm hand closed briefly over hers. 'Just remember I'm in your corner,' he said.

She nodded, incapable of speech, and, realizing this, he turned back to the others.

'Well, Rona, what have you been up to since we last met?'

She smiled across at him. 'You'll be glad to hear I've agreed to another bio.'

Tom and Catherine exclaimed together. 'Now, that *is* good news!' Tom went on. 'And who's it to be this time?'

'The artist, Elspeth Wilding.'

'Really?' Catherine's interest quickened. 'Did you know that as a child she attended St Stephen's? Well before my time, of course!' Catherine had been head of the Buckford primary for twelve years. 'She was one of our

49

most illustrious old girls!'

Rona leant forward eagerly. 'Did you ever meet her?'

'Unfortunately, no. We kept inviting her to present prizes at Speech Day, but she always declined.'

Disappointed, Rona sat back again. 'That's par for the course; she seems to have shunned any kind of publicity.'

'I did see her occasionally, about town. It was odd, though; you'd expect people to recognize her, since she's so famous, but no one ever seemed to.' Catherine smiled. 'I always thought she was a bit like Alec Guinness.'

Tom gave a bark of laugher. 'I think that requires an explanation, darling!'

'Well, you know how brilliant he was at looking completely different every time you saw him? Most actors, however good they are, *look* the same, even if the characters they play are entirely different. But he was like a ... a blank canvas, seeming to paint on a different face for each part.'

'You mean she looked different, every time you saw her?' Rona asked with a frown.

'Not exactly; it was as if she *was* that blank canvas. What I'm trying to say is there was nothing memorable about her, no distinguishing feature you could latch on to. Apart, that is, from her hair, which was silver-blonde and often bundled under a hat anyway.'

'Didn't she die a year or two ago?' Tom asked.

'No,' Rona corrected, 'she disappeared, and

hasn't been seen since.'

'I trust finding her isn't part of your remit?'

She smiled. 'I've a feeling that's what her family's hoping, but I'm not to be drawn. A bio is what they requested, and a bio is what they'll get. Full stop.'

'But you'll have to look into it, surely?' Catherine said. 'It's something that happened in her life, after all.'

'Thankfully, it'll be some time before I come to it,' Rona replied. 'When I do, I'll play it by ear.' She glanced at Catherine. 'You knew about her disappearance?'

'Yes; I'd left Buckford by then, but it was reported in the press. "Her family are anxious to contact her" sort of thing, and a rehash of her career to date, presumably to keep up the interest. There were several reported sightings, but nothing ever came of them. So, when do you start work?'

'Eddie phoned this morning with the publisher's offer, which I've accepted. So once the contract has been drawn up and signed, we're away.'

'Then let's toast the latest magnum opus!' Tom said, raising his glass. 'May it equal or even outshine the success of its predecessors!'

'Linz.'

'Hi, Rona. Going in for breakfast calls now?'

'Well, you don't like me phoning the office, but we didn't get a chance to talk, either on Sunday or last night, and I was wondering how things are?'

'Comme ci, comme ça.'

'Heard from his lordship yet?'

'Briefly.'

'I'm not trying to pry, Linz; I just thought you were a bit quiet at Catherine's.'

'Twin radar?'

'It happens. Are you free for lunch? Once I start work, I'll be pretty tied up.'

'OK, you're on. The Gallery or the Bacchus?'

'Let's make it the Gallery; it's less formal.'

'About one?'

'See you there.'

Rona replaced the phone thoughtfully. She needed to clear her mind as well as her desk before starting on the biography, but as always her family weighed heavily: Lindsey, because of the confounded Dominic, whom she'd hoped had come to heel but apparently hadn't; her mother, in case her lodger put a spoke in a promising romance; and her father, because there'd definitely been a strained look about him the previous evening. And the frustrating thing was that she could do nothing about any of it.

What she needed, she decided, was fresh air and exercise.

'Walk, Gus!' she said. The dog looked up expectantly as she took down his lead, then bounded ahead of her up the basement stairs and waited on the front mat, tail wagging, as she shrugged on a jacket.

It was still early, and the overnight mist was clearing slowly as the sun broke through. Dew still lay on the decorative railings and on the tops of cars whose owners had not yet left for work.

At the corner they turned right, then right again into Charlton Road, where an enterprising builder had erected a row of garages to serve the houses in the Avenue, which, being Georgian, lacked them. Rona and Max owned one, and she'd soon be collecting her car to drive to Buckford. Today, however, she was making for the slip-road that led from here to Furze Hill Park.

It was their favourite walk, hers and Gus's; hers because the park, with its bird's eye view of the town, gave her a feeling of space from the problems that beset her; his because, up at the top end, he could run freely, retrieving anything Rona might throw for him. Today, she'd slipped a ball in her pocket.

A group of schoolgirls, neat in their green uniforms, were emerging from the passage, using it, no doubt, as a short cut from the houses up in Park Rise. Where, Rona remembered, Dominic had his penthouse. In fact, the only time she'd met him had been at the top of the park, when he'd briefly mistaken her for Lindsey. To her surprise, she'd found she liked him, but that liking would be short-lived if he continued to upset her twin.

She and Gus emerged from the alley opposite the park gates and made their way up the steeply sloping path past neat beds of chrysanthemums and dahlias, the duck pond and the children's play area, to the uncultivated area at the top, a favourite haunt of dog-walkers. Rona released Gus from his lead and he ran joyously ahead, ears flapping in the breeze that was always present up here.

To her right, the town below her still lay shrouded in mist, through which chimneys and steeples were gradually emerging. Hidden beneath it, Lindsey would be arriving at her office, Max setting out his paints for the day's work. And her father and Catherine would be leaving for the airport. She did hope the break would take away that tightness she'd noticed round his eyes and mouth. For eighteen months now, she'd lived with the constant fear of another heart attack.

Gus had returned and was bounding up expectantly. Rona laughed.

'Quite right!' she told him. 'I came up here to forget my problems, not to dwell on them.'

And, taking the ball from her pocket, she flung it as far as she could up the slope.

It had been good to see Rona for lunch, Lindsey thought, as she threaded her way through the home-going traffic. They could speak more freely to each other than to anyone else, and it usually proved therapeutic.

It was Rona, always the more practical one, who'd raised the question as to what Lindsey would do during the refurbishing.

'Presumably all the furniture will have gone, and the place will smell of paint. You'd better

54

move in with us for a week or two.'

Incredibly, she hadn't thought that far ahead. 'Wouldn't you mind? Or Max?' she'd asked.

'Well, Max isn't there half the week, and come to that, I might be away the odd night myself, in Buckford. But provided you can face the camp bed, you're welcome to the studio.'

There was no guest room at number nineteen, but on the top floor, like those below it, dividing walls had been removed. The resulting large, light space had been intended as Max's studio, but since the purchase of Farthings it had degenerated into a junk room.

'Don't worry, we can soon clear a space,' Rona had assured her. And then she'd raised an interesting point: whether Lindsey's resolve to refurbish was a declaration of independence, a means of showing Dominic she wasn't expecting to move in with him.

'Would you, though, if he asked you?' Rona had asked, when she'd denied it. And, forced to consider the question, she'd been surprised to find she would not.

'Not as things stand, anyway,' she'd added. 'I'd feel vulnerable, with no bolt-hole to run back to. Also, he's away so much; I'm better off in my own little pad. Of course, if marriage was on the cards...'

Her voice had tailed off, and Rona squeezed her hand sympathetically. 'I shouldn't hold your breath,' she'd advised, and Lindsey knew she was right.

She sighed, and switched on the radio. She'd

left the town behind now and was on the northern stretch of Alban Road leading out to the small development where she lived. And minutes later, as she turned into the gateway of number six Fairhaven, she felt the usual lift of coming home, and knew she'd be loath to give it up.

She garaged the car and let herself into the flat, pausing just inside the door to survey the walls stretching up to the landing above. Bland magnolia, she thought; but what did she want in its place? She'd neither the time, nor, frankly, the inclination, to spend hours poring over pattern books and paint charts. If only she could wave a wand and have it all finished, without having to agonize over it!

Ten past six; she'd just time for a final tidy before her friends arrived. She was putting away the breakfast things, left draining on the sink, when the telephone shrilled through the flat.

Dominic! she thought, heart pounding, as she hurried to pick it up. But it was Hugh on the line, and she felt a spurt of irritation.

'Just phoning for a chat,' he said.

'This isn't a good time, Hugh; I'm expecting Nina and Nicole – they're coming to advise me on redecorating the flat.'

'*Double N*, eh? Wouldn't a can or two of paint be cheaper?'

'No doubt, but I'm throwing everything out and starting again.' She paused as a thought struck her. 'The furniture's going in to auction, together with some pictures and ornaments. Is there ... anything you'd like first claim on?'

He gave a brief laugh. 'It's so long since I've been in your flat, I can't remember what's there.'

'Oh, for heaven's sake! Three-piece suite, bedroom furniture, bookcase...'

'Finally ditching old memories?'

She bit her lip. 'If you put it like that.'

She heard him sigh.

'Hugh, they'll be here—'

'Yes; yes, you said. All right; I won't have room for much, but I would like a quick look, if that's OK. Shall I drop in later, when the girls have gone?'

Lindsey hesitated, but really, the sooner he came, the better; she'd need to clear the flat before any work could begin. And yet again, Dominic hadn't phoned. She was damned if she'd put everything on hold to suit him.

'Better make it eight o'clock, then.'

'You won't have had time to eat, will you?'

'Hugh—'

'Don't panic; I'm not suggesting a night of unbridled passion, merely a pie and pint at the Peacock.'

Lindsey laughed in spite of herself. 'All right,' she said.

Nina and Nicole stood in the middle of the sitting room, looking about them. Nicole had dropped a bulky envelope and some heavy sample books on the sofa, but so far their contents had not been examined.

'We were running through some ideas before we came,' Nina said. 'Duck-egg walls were a thought, with curtains and coverings in café au lait. But am I right that you face north here?'

Lindsey nodded.

Nina shook her head doubtfully. 'Might be a bit cold, then.'

'We could reverse it?' Nicole suggested. 'Pale coffee walls and light blue furnishings? That would be warmer.'

'Look,' Lindsey said, 'I've been thinking about this. I'm up to my eyes at work, and what with various other things' (*such as Dominic*), 'I honestly haven't the time to give this the consideration it deserves. Added to which, I've not an artistic bone in my body. What I'd really like is to give you completely free rein, so I can just come back in a few weeks' time, and admire the fait accompli. Is that OK with you?'

'Certainly, if you're really sure?'

'Oh, I am!' Lindsey breathed a sigh of relief: one less thing to worry about. 'Now, can I get you a coffee or anything, before you start?'

'No, thanks, we're fine.'

Lindsey watched them for a few minutes as they set about measuring walls, fireplace and windows. Then she sat down on the sofa, picked up one of the pattern books, and idly flicked through it. 'I'd be hopeless at making up my mind,' she commented. 'Any of these would be great.'

Further measuring was done on the landing and in both bedrooms.

'What about furniture?' Nicole asked, as she put away the tape.

'Again, I leave it to you. Something modern, in keeping with the flat.'

'This is going to be fun!' Nina said. 'So what kind of figure are we aiming at?'

Lindsey named one. 'Will that give you enough scope?'

'More than enough, since you qualify for mates' rates. So, we'll mull it over during the next few days, then send you a set of plans, with suggested wall covering, soft furnishings, etc. Your bedroom would benefit from built-in furniture, instead of those large, free-standing pieces. There are some very pretty designs around.'

'Sounds good,' Lindsey said. 'When can you start?'

'Fairly soon, once you've OK'd the suggestions and removed what's to be sold. Aren't you keeping any of the furniture?'

'Only that little bureau, which I love. Hugh's coming to look over the rest, before it goes under the hammer.'

'How is Hugh? It's a while since I've seen him, though David met him for a drink last week.'

'He's fine,' Lindsey said briefly.

Nicole flicked her a glance. 'And the enigmatic Dominic?'

'Also fine.'

She laughed. 'I get the message! Well, regards to both of them, as and when appropriate. And we'll be in touch within a day or two.'

'Coast clear?' Hugh asked, smiling at her from the doorstep.

'Coast clear,' she confirmed. 'Come on up.'

He followed her up the stairs, and, as always, she was intensely and infuriatingly aware of him. The attraction between them was as strong and vibrant as ever, even though love – at least on her part – had long since departed. It had, in fact, led to her spending a night with him back in the summer, a totally irresponsible act that had given him false hopes.

'So,' she said a little breathlessly, as she led the way into the sitting-room, 'take your pick.'

He looked about him. 'You're chucking the lot?'

'Apart from the bureau and the odd picture. Let's face it, Hugh, it doesn't owe me anything, and it was, after all, bought for an entirely different house.'

'Well, you've seen my place, so you'll appreciate space is limited. I've always liked that clock, though, if you're determined to get rid of it?'

'You're welcome. Feel free to wander round while I get us a drink, and see what interests you. Whisky and water?'

'Please.'

Hands in pockets he began a slow perambulation of the room, pausing occasionally to study a picture or lift an ornament. Lindsey, pouring the drinks, watched him out of the corner of her eye, trying to analyse what it was about him that still lit fires inside her. He wasn't conventionally good-looking, with his lean, pale face and red hair, but there was an indefinable magnetism about him that still pulled at her, however hard she might resist.

'I could make use of the coffee table,' he remarked, taking the glass she handed him. 'And the bookcase, come to that. It'll be a squeeze, but I could just about fit them in, if you're sure. And perhaps the Venetian picture, for auld lang syne.'

Lindsey flushed, avoiding his eye. It was a painting they'd bought on their honeymoon.

'Oh, and the clock, of course. That's about it. How much do you want for them?'

She looked startled. 'Oh, I didn't—'

'Nonsense; they were part of your settlement when we split, so you should be recompensed. And,' he added, as she started to protest, 'I'll only take them on that condition.'

'But I've not the faintest idea what they're worth,' she objected, hating the thought that a spontaneous offer had turned commercial.

'Then I'll check what they'd be likely to fetch at auction.'

'Hugh—'

'Consider the matter closed. How soon do you want rid of them?'

'As soon as possible, I suppose. I'll be getting on to the auctioneers tomorrow.'

'Then I'll hire a van and collect them at the weekend, if that's OK?'

'Fine,' she said numbly.

'You'll need somewhere to put the books in the meantime,' he added. 'Have you any boxes?'

'I'll get some. Rona's kindly offered to put me up while it all goes ahead.'

'Is anything going into store?'

'I'll decide that when I know how much I'm keeping. I've not made a definitive list yet.'

Hugh drained his glass. 'Right. If you're ready, let's go and eat.'

'I've invited Lindsey to stay while her flat's being decorated,' Rona said, watching as Max stirred a béchamel sauce for the evening meal. 'You don't mind, do you?'

'Oh, God!' He turned to look at her, the wooden spoon dripping back into the pan. 'How long for?'

'No need to sound so thrilled!' Rona snapped.

'Sorry, love, but as you well know, the less your sister and I see of each other, the better we get on.'

'Well, you won't *be* seeing much of her, will you? You're only home two evenings a week and she might well be out anyway.'

'And the weekends?'

'Same thing applies; she has a busy social life, you know. *Other* people enjoy her company.'

There was a brief silence, then Max returned his attention to the pan. 'Sorry,' he said, his back to her. 'Of course she must come.'

Slightly mollified, Rona set about laying the table, but Max, stirring rather more vigorously than was called for, remained ill at ease. His relationship with Lindsey was a state of armed neutrality, and he continually marvelled that his wife's twin, so unnervingly like her in appearance, could be so totally different in character. Nor could he forget – though God knew he'd tried hard enough – that, in the throes of her divorce four years ago, she had driven round to Farthings one night, and begged him to make love to her. But that was something he'd never told Rona, and never would.

Though Hugh and Lindsey did, indeed, go to the Peacock, an upmarket pub on the outskirts of Marsborough, they dined not on the proposed pie and pint, but beef Stroganov and full-bodied red wine. He was good company, and despite the usual underlying tensions, Lindsey enjoyed herself.

It was eleven o'clock when he dropped her back at the flat, and the light was flashing on the answer phone. She pressed the button as she took off her jacket, pausing as Dominic's voiced filled the room.

'I shall call for you at seven tomorrow evening,' it announced baldly. 'And if you tell me you can't make it, I shall personally wring your neck!'

Lindsey smiled to herself. So, having got over his sulk, he'd found she wasn't sitting at home awaiting his call. Which was just as it should be.

Humming to herself, she prepared for bed.

FOUR

The contract for the biography arrived on Friday, its unusual promptness indicative of Prue's desire to get the project under way – lest Rona change her mind, perhaps. Having duly signed it, she wrote a brief note to Naomi Harris, whose address Prue had supplied, suggesting a preliminary meeting.

As she dropped both envelopes into the pillar box, her hand lingered momentarily in the slot, as though wishing she could snatch them back. Then, with a sigh, she withdrew it and turned away.

That evening, to celebrate, Max took her to Dino's, where they arrived at the same time as their friends Magda and Gavin Ridgeway.

'Telepathy!' Magda exclaimed, bending to pat Gus, who was nudging her legs. 'We only decided to come half an hour ago. Thought about phoning you, but it seemed too short notice.'

Dino himself guided them to a table and fussed around taking orders for drinks and producing menus, and it was only when he moved away that Max volunteered the reason for their own visit.

'Rona's taken the plunge and opted for another biography,' he announced.

'Well!' Gavin exclaimed. 'Cause for celebration indeed! Who is it this time?'

And Rona explained again about Elspeth, her ultra-private life and her disappearance.

'Which aspect will you be concentrating on?' Magda asked shrewdly.

'Definitely her life; I've had my fingers burned too often to look into any more mysteries.'

'Oh, come on!' Gavin mocked. 'You know you love it!'

Rona shook her head with a smile. 'Enough about me; what have you two been up to?'

He grimaced. 'Her ladyship here's been on the fashion bandwagon.' Magda, a childhood friend of Rona's, was the owner of a string of highly regarded boutiques. 'Living it up, while yours truly was left to exist on baked beans!'

'Don't believe a word of it!' Magda advised them. 'From what I hear, he made full use of the golf club restaurant, spurning the gourmet selection I'd left in the freezer.'

'And it was a worthwhile exercise, the fashion week?'

'Most definitely. It always is, but this year was extra special, because the British Fashion Council's celebrating twenty-five years. Lots of socializing, and so on.'

'Shaking hands with the great and the good?' Max enquired. 'Rather you than me!'

'Oh, it had its moments!'

'Come on, then,' Rona encouraged her. 'Name

some names!'

'Crispin Ryder, for one.'

'The Playboy of the Western World?' Max scoffed. 'What, pray tell me, is his interest in women's fashion?'

'I'd say it's more the women than the fashions,' Gavin replied. 'He was all over Magda.'

His wife flushed. 'Oh, Gavin, really! He was just being helpful.'

'Funny you should mention him,' Rona said; 'Lindsey was talking about him the other day. Seems he's vaguely related to Dominic, and she met him at a do they went to.'

'And what was her impression?'

'I think the phrase was "charm personified".'

'Sounds about right.'

Remembering Dominic's distrust of his second cousin, Rona thought it wise to change the subject. 'So, what are we in for this autumn, fashion-wise?'

And talk turned to less controversial subjects. It was only as they were leaving that Ryder's name came up again.

'You'll be getting the usual invite to my show,' Magda told Rona, while the men settled the bill. 'Choice of either Thursday the twenty-ninth or Friday the thirtieth, eight o'clock at the Clarendon. And if you fancy meeting Crispin, he's promised to bring a crowd on the Thursday. A foot in that door would be quite a coup!'

'It'd have to be the Thursday anyway; the thirtieth's Max's birthday.'

Magda laughed. 'Lucky it's that way round!

Admit it – you're dying to meet him!'

'I'm certainly curious.'

'You won't be disappointed!' Magda promised her.

They had just finished breakfast the next morning when the phone rang, and Rona reached to retrieve it.

'Miss Parish? This is Naomi Harris.'

Rona widened her eyes at Max. 'Good morning, Mrs Harris.'

'I do apologize for interrupting your weekend – I hope this isn't inconvenient?'

'No, not at all.'

'As you'll have gathered, I've just received your letter, and needless to say, I'm delighted you've agreed to take this on.'

'I'm sure it'll be very interesting,' Rona murmured.

'You suggest meeting, and I presume you'd like it to be as soon as possible? I'm free on Monday, if that's any use?'

'Well, yes, thank you; I could certainly manage that.'

'I was thinking if we met in Buckford, rather than at my home, we could have a preliminary talk over coffee, then I could take you to Elspeth's studio?'

'That sounds an excellent idea.'

'How long will it take you to get there?'

'About two and a half hours, depending on the traffic.'

'Then suppose we say between eleven and

eleven thirty, at St Stephen's Coffee Shop? It's in Market Square, near the main library.'

'I know it,' Rona said. She'd frequented it while researching Buckford's eight hundred years of history.

'Splendid! Till Monday, then.' And Naomi Harris rang off.

'She's not letting the grass grow, is she?' Max commented from behind his newspaper.

'Suits me. The sooner I get down to it, the better. She's going to show me Elspeth's studio, which should be interesting.'

Max lowered his paper. 'I wonder if her canvases and sketches are still there.'

'Wouldn't they be too valuable to leave in an empty house?'

'Depends, I suppose. If they're still expecting her to reappear one day, they'd be likely to leave as much as possible in situ.'

Rona leaned back in her chair, and looked at him consideringly. 'What do *you* think happened to her, Max?'

'God knows. She could have had a complete breakdown, and be in a psychiatric home somewhere.'

'But then her family would know, surely?'

'Perhaps they do,' Max said enigmatically.

Rona stared at him, and he went on, 'She'd peaked, you know, some years ago. Her stuff wasn't going for the sums it used to. Perhaps it was an elaborate publicity stunt, to bring her back into the limelight.'

'You old cynic! And has it worked?'

He shrugged. 'There was a surge in prices when she disappeared, but it's settled down again now.' He flashed her a grin. 'Your bio should revive it nicely.'

Rona threw her napkin at him.

'Seriously, I'd say the likelihood is that she's dead, though how, where, or when is anyone's guess. Again, perhaps that's where you come in.'

'I told you, Max, I've no intention—'

'And I'm glad you haven't. But the family don't know that, do they? They're probably hoping you'll produce her – abracadabra! – out of a hat.'

'Then they're in for a disappointment.'

'Perhaps you should make that clear on Monday.'

'Perhaps I will.'

Rona finished her coffee in a thoughtful mood.

Slowly, reluctantly, Lindsey awoke. From the strength of light behind the curtains, she judged it to be about nine. Hugh would be here with his van in a couple of hours. Which, of course, was a pain. Dominic had suggested, on Thursday evening, that they go away for the weekend, and once again she'd had to disappoint him.

'You're turning me down for your ex?' he'd demanded incredulously.

'He's hired the van, and arranged for a friend to help him with the furniture. I can't let him down, Dominic. Anyway, I want the flat cleared as soon as possible.'

'Why the hurry, all of a sudden?'

'Because I've put it off quite long enough, and the decorators are almost ready to start.'

He'd given her a searching glance, and she remembered Rona's point about it being a show of independence. Had that thought also occurred to him?

Lindsey sat up and swung her feet to the floor. Odd to think that she wouldn't be spending many more nights in this bed. It, like the rest of the furniture, had been bought for the home she and Hugh had set up together, eight years ago. Remembering all its associations, good and bad, she decided not to attend the auction. It would be too painful, seeing part of her life put up for sale and handed to the highest bidder.

Feeling vaguely sad, she went for her shower.

Because Rona was unsure what her movements would be, Max had taken Gus to Farthings on Monday morning, promising to give him a walk at lunch time.

The drive to Buckford brought back memories of fifteen months ago, when, during her researches, she'd lodged two nights a week with Nuala Banks and her family in Parsonage Place. This time, there wouldn't be the need to spend so long there; having seen over Elspeth's house, she was hoping Mrs Harris would allow her to remove any papers she needed, and work from home.

It was just after eleven when Rona reached Buckford and parked her car in the multi-storey.

Memories assailed her as she made her way past the church and turned into ancient Clement's Lane, where the houses leaned towards each other, and old Miss Rosebury had seen the ghost of a little boy. Now she herself was one of Buckford's ghosts, part of its many-layered history.

It was with a sense of relief that Rona emerged from its narrow confines into the openness of Market Square and its weathered stone cross. On her left, a flight of steps led up to the library, and across the square was St Stephen's Primary School, where Catherine had once taught and where, years earlier, Elspeth Wilding had been a pupil. It was obviously breaktime, and children's voices, laughing and shouting, drifted towards her.

Rona turned right, towards the bow window that fronted St Stephen's Coffee Shop. The familiar scent of roasting beans and fresh pastries greeted her as she pushed open the door. Most of the tables were occupied, and she hesitated, glancing from one to another, until a woman at the far side rose to her feet with lifted hand. Naomi Harris, no doubt.

As Rona approached her, she was forming her first, lightning impressions: shorter than herself, neat figure, flyaway fair-to-grey hair, hesitant smile. Altogether not so confident a figure as her voice on the phone had indicated.

'Miss Parish – I'm so pleased to meet you. I've admired your work for some time.'

'That's kind of you.'

They sat down, and Naomi Harris beckoned a waitress, who took their order. Her eyes dropped momentarily to her clasped hands, then met Rona's with a smile.

'I'm not sure where to start!' she said apologetically, and Rona warmed to her.

'I believe there was a biography of your sister some ten years ago?' she prompted.

'Yes, but it wasn't at all satisfactory. Elspeth was extremely uncooperative, refusing access to any letters, diaries or papers, and the poor man ended up rehashing what was already public knowledge. A waste of everyone's time.'

'Am I likely to fare any better, since I won't even be able to meet her?'

'Definitely,' Naomi Harris said firmly, 'because without her breathing down my neck, I can tell you all you want to know from a close personal angle – about her childhood, her likes and dislikes, the start of her career and so on. And, of course, we're very much hoping you might discover why she left so suddenly – if she'd been planning it for some time, or it was a spur-of-the-moment thing. I've looked through her diaries and letters, but your trained eye might pick up something I missed.'

Warning bells rang in Rona's head. 'Mrs Harris, I'm sorry, but there's absolutely no way I could go through them.'

Naomi Harris stared at her. 'But surely, if I give you permission—?'

Rona was shaking her head. 'Unless and until there's proof of her death – which we all hope won't happen – her right to privacy stands, and any personal papers remain her "intellectual property".'

Seeing Naomi's bewildered disappointment, she added, 'I shall, of course, be anxious to look through files and papers that *aren't* private, and I'll be grateful for any personal memories you and your family can supply. But I must emphasize that my interest lies in her life and work, her place in British art, and so on; I'm neither qualified nor, frankly, willing, to look into her disappearance.'

Naomi Harris was looking crestfallen. 'I appreciate that. But on the other hand, you've solved quite a few puzzles over the last few years, and we were hoping you might ... add one more to your list. Though, of course, if you can't go through her papers...'

Coffee and butter-soaked crumpets arrived, and a brief silence ensued while cups were filled and crumpets distributed. Rona was grateful for it; but now the disappearance had been mentioned, she might as well get the facts. As Catherine had said, she'd need to cover it eventually.

So, as the waitress moved away, she asked, 'When did you first realize she'd gone?'

'The eleventh of May last year – my daughter's seventeenth birthday. She'd had a party for her friends on the Saturday, and the family celebration was the next day. Naturally, Elspeth was invited; she's Gillian's godmother as well as her aunt.'

She paused, toying with the crumpet on her plate. 'But ... she never came. We waited for a while, and phoned both her home and her mobile, without success. Then we started worrying she might have had an accident driving out to us.'

'When had you last seen her?' Rona interrupted.

'Earlier that week. My last words to her were, "See you on Sunday."'

'And she seemed all right then?'

Naomi hesitated. 'It's difficult to say. She'd been ... unpredictable for quite a while.'

Rona leaned forward, interested, despite her resolution. 'Unpredictable how?'

'Well, she'd been through a period of intense depression, worried that she'd lost her way, and couldn't paint any more.' Naomi Harris looked down, biting her lip. 'But it wasn't only that, it was the body-clock thing. She was over forty, and she'd never even had a love affair – been too wrapped up in her work. She felt life was passing her by.'

'Did she actually say so?'

Naomi smiled wryly. 'She was as private with me as with everyone else, but I do remember her saying once, "I live a very narrow life, Naomi. To be a *great* artist, I need to experience it far more fully."'

Rona stirred uneasily. Max had said Elspeth's work had fallen off; he also suspected she was dead. Severe depression, loneliness, loss of her talent – might they have led to an undiscovered

74

suicide?

'But then,' Naomi was continuing, 'about three months before she left, she suddenly seemed to throw off her depression, became much brighter. I half-wondered if she'd met someone, but there was no hint of that and she refused to give any explanation, except to say she'd pulled herself together.'

'I interrupted you,' Rona apologized. 'You were telling me about the dinner party?'

'Yes. Well, as time went on and there was no sign of her, my parents in particular became more and more anxious, so Leonard, my husband, got the car out and went to look for her. He drove all the way to Buckford along the route she'd have taken, even knocked at her front door But the house was in darkness, so he came back again. We phoned the hospitals, but there was no record of her having been injured or anything. Then, later, when we went to the house, we found Gillian's birthday present, ready wrapped, in her sitting room. Surely that meant she'd intended to come?'

'She hadn't told friends she was going away?'

'Miss Parish, she had no friends. Not really. The only person she was close to, Chloë, had – died a year or so earlier.'

Rona frowned. 'Died how?'

Naomi gave a little shudder. 'Threw herself under a train, actually. It was all very distressing, and Elspeth was knocked sideways.'

'That was when her depression started?'

'No, actually; it had begun some months

earlier.'

'So who was this Chloë?'

'Chloë Pyne. She was an artist, too, though not as successful as Elspeth. They met at secondary school, went on to university together, then the Royal College of Art. They were inseparable, really. Until a month or two before Chloë died.'

'What happened then?'

Naomi Harris sighed. 'The old story: a man entered the equation. He fell for Chloë, kept phoning her, sending flowers. It wasn't mutual, but Elspeth was ... I suppose jealous is the only word for it. Anyway, there were heated exchanges, and when Chloë died, they'd not spoken for several weeks. Elspeth blamed herself for her unreasonable behaviour, and for not being there for Chloë.'

'Who was this man?' Rona asked after a moment.

'Yet another artist. Nathan Tait.'

'Nathan Tait?' Rona repeated in surprise.

'You know him?'

'Not personally, but I've heard my husband speak of him.'

'Of course – Max Allerdyce. I was forgetting. Did he ever meet Elspeth?'

Rona shook her head. 'Unfortunately not.' She paused. 'Who else was at that family dinner?'

'My parents, as I said; my brother and his wife; Gillian, of course, and Toby, our son. The whole family, in fact.'

'And there's been no contact since?'

Naomi's eyes dropped. 'Actually, there's

76

something I need to tell you.' She hesitated, her hands twisting in her lap. 'Everything I've said so far is right: she was expected at the dinner, she didn't come, and we were all very worried. The next day, we reported it to the police, but to our amazement they weren't interested, maintaining she'd every right to disappear if she wanted to. And without their authorization, her bank refused to tell us whether or not she was still withdrawing money, using her credit card, and so on.'

Naomi paused to refill their coffee cups. 'So it was left to us, and we set about organizing searches, persuading the press to run the story, and so on.' She sighed. 'But it was a nine days' wonder; when there were no developments, everyone lost interest. Artists,' she added bitterly, 'don't have the widespread appeal of pop stars.'

'So then what happened?' Rona pressed.

Naomi looked up, steeling herself. 'Toby, our son, came to us one evening, very red in the face and close to tears, saying he had a confession to make. The long and the short of it was that during the party the night before the birthday dinner, he'd deleted a message from the answer phone. I don't know about you, but in our house messages build up and are never cleared, and you have to wade through a whole lot of what you've already dealt with before coming to anything new. So we'd recently introduced a policy of deleting a message as soon as it had been played.

'Well, as I said, the phone went in the middle of the party, he answered it – as it happened, a wrong number – and saw the red light flashing. And when he heard Elspeth begin to speak, he thought it was the message she'd left earlier in the week, so he deleted it, went back to the party, and never gave it a second thought, even when she failed to show up the next day. Fifteen-year-old boys, I'm afraid, aren't the most reliable of mortals. And by the time he *did* remember, we were all running round in circles, the story had appeared in the press, and basically he'd been too scared to come forward till his conscience got the better of him.

'But he remembered that as he pressed the delete button, he heard her say, "I want you to tell everyone, while you're all together, that I'm going—" And that was it. Well, we were frantic, as you can imagine. Elspeth obviously thought we all knew what she was planning, but we'd no idea where she was or how long she'd be away, and to add to our worries, her mobile account had been closed the day after she left. There was absolutely no way to contact her.

'After a lot of discussion, to spare Toby's blushes, and also, admittedly, because we'd look foolish, we decided not to make it public, but just let the story die down. No one seemed very interested, anyway.'

'But surely you've heard from her since?'

'That's just it! We expected her back in a week or two, or at least some kind of contact – a postcard or phone call. But all we've received is a Christmas card – seven months, mind you, after she left –wishing us well and saying she was fine. It was posted in London, but there was no address and no hint of when she was coming home. And this is where I owe you an apology, because I thought that if you agreed to write her biography, she might hear of it and be annoyed, which would bring her out of the woodwork.'

'Well, thanks!' Rona said.

'Oh God, that came out quite wrong! I'm sorry! I *do* want you to do it, and so do my parents, though I have to tell you Richard and Marcia are totally against it.'

'Are they prepared to speak to me?'

'I don't know, to be honest. But it would be worth seeing them if you can, because Elspeth was always closer to Richard than to the rest of us.'

'I'll need their address, then, and also those of anyone else who knew her. Did she have help in the house, for instance?'

'Yes, Mary Strong. She still goes in once a week to dust around, open windows, and so on, and her husband keeps the garden tidy. I'll look up their address for you.'

'Thank you.' Rona hesitated. 'What about Chloë's family? Do you think they would see me?'

Naomi looked surprised. 'I really don't know. You could try.'

'You're not in touch with them?'

Naomi shook her head. 'I only met them briefly at her funeral. Elspeth had begged me to go with her, and it was all pretty harrowing, as you'd imagine. Her father's disabled in some way – he was in a wheelchair.'

'Was Nathan Tait there?'

'Yes, but keeping a low profile, and he didn't go back to the house.' She glanced at Rona's empty cup. 'If you're ready, shall we go?'

Naomi's car was on a meter in a road just off the square, and they drove to an area on the outskirts of town, where the houses were widely spaced, hidden behind high walls or hedges. Having parked, Naomi pushed open a gate to reveal, to Rona's surprise, not a substantial house but an attractive-looking cottage dating, she judged, from the eighteenth century.

'It's a listed building,' Naomi said over her shoulder, as she opened the front door, 'but thankfully the plumbing's twenty-first century. Hang on a minute, while I switch off the alarm.'

The door opened on to a small square hall, with the staircase straight ahead, and it was clear any necessary modernizing had not destroyed the character of the place; the doorways were low – Max would need to stoop to go through them – the windows mullioned, and the rooms small by today's standards, but the overall effect was enchanting.

'It's a little gem, isn't it?' Naomi said. 'I came with Elspeth to view it, years ago, and we both fell for it at once. But it will be the studio that interests you, I imagine, and that's in the back garden.'

Rona turned in surprise, and Naomi laughed.

'She couldn't put extra windows in the house, but an additional selling point was a stone building outside, not visible from the road, which she could modernize to her heart's content. Come and see.'

At the back of the hall was a small but fully equipped kitchen, and through its window Rona had her first sight of the studio.

'It's larger than I was expecting,' she said. 'Are there two storeys?'

'Yes, you go up a ladder-cum-staircase to the studio itself.'

The garden, mainly laid to lawn but bordered by beds of peonies and dahlias, was neat and tidy, testament, Rona presumed, to Mary Strong's husband, and only a few recently fallen beech leaves lay scattered on the grass.

Naomi unlocked the sturdy wooden door, and the air that met them was unexpectedly warm.

'Central heating,' she said briefly. 'It comes on twice a day at a low temperature, to keep the place aired. We can't risk damp canvases.'

'Max wondered if you'd removed her work, in case someone stole it.'

'We thought of it, but there's an alarm system, as you see, and anyway, Elspeth's work is so distinctive they'd have difficulty selling it. Also, her later paintings are very large – six feet across in some cases – and removing them would involve taking out a window and lowering them to the ground. A laborious and expensive business, and, I should think, enough to deter all but the most determined thief.'

The ground floor of the building comprised a minute hall with two rooms opening off it, one a washroom, the other a kitchenette with sink, hob and fridge, and a drop-down table with stool alongside.

'When she was in full spate,' Naomi explained, 'she'd have lunch and even dinner out here, rather than break off to go back to the house.' She gestured to the open staircase. 'After you.'

It was a similar approach to Farthings, Rona thought, emerging from the stair head into a large space overflowing with light, though in addition to accoutrements similar to Max's – easels, trolleys with tubes of paint, brushes in jars, turps and linseed – there was also a small desk bearing a computer and printer.

Naomi, emerging from the staircase behind her, saw her glance at it. 'Her assistant sometimes works up here,' she explained.

Rona nodded, looking about her with interest. There was a row of canvases against a wall, but unlike Max's, they were covered and facing inwards, and a couple of large, wall-mounted paintings were similarly draped. In fact, only one was open to view, a cloudscape measuring some three feet by six, but she'd barely glanced at it when Naomi gave a sudden exclamation.

'God, is that the time?'

Rona, glancing at her watch, saw it was approaching one o'clock.

'I must go – I'd no idea it was so late. I was

intending to buy you lunch, but I'm playing bridge at two thirty. God, I'm so sorry! What must you think of me, driving you all the way out here, then immediately dragging you away again?'

'Don't worry,' Rona said quickly. 'I want to get home myself in time to walk the dog before dark.'

'Tell you what, I'll arrange for Gwen Saunders to meet you here. She's Elspeth's part-time assistant, and much more competent than I am to discuss her work. It was her job to organize exhibitions and see to the correspondence, though Elspeth called on her less and less during that last year. She still looks in once a month to see if anything needs doing, and asked me to tell you she'll be pleased to help in any way she can.'

Naomi scrabbled in her handbag for notebook and pen. 'Let me just list the phone numbers you'll need, while I remember. There's Gwen, my parents, my brother, the Strongs, the Pynes – can you think of anyone else?'

Rona smiled. 'That'll be fine to be going on with.'

Locking up as they went, they hurried across the garden and through the house to Naomi's car, and she drove swiftly back to the town centre.

'Where can I drop you?' she enquired.

'Anywhere will do. My car's in the multi-storey, but I'll have a sandwich before I leave.'

'I feel dreadful dumping you like this—'

'Really,' Rona assured her, getting out of the car, 'it's fine. Thanks for everything.'

'I'll phone this evening, with the numbers you need.' And then she was gone, the car accelerating away in the direction of Sunningdene.

'It was frustrating in the extreme,' Rona said, 'to be in the same room as her paintings, only to be dragged away without so much as a glance at them.'

They were in the kitchen at Farthings, Max having broken off work to join her for a cup of tea before she took Gus home.

'However,' she went on, 'the big news is that Elspeth *did* tell them she was leaving, but they never got the message.' She explained what Naomi had told her.

'Bang goes my theory about her being dead,' Max said resignedly.

'Not necessarily; they haven't heard from her since Christmas.'

'Less likely, though, which is all to the good. So, you're telling me that after all that, you never even saw her work?'

'As I said, we ran out of time. There was a canvas on the wall, though, showing clouds racing across the sky.'

Max nodded. 'A cloudscape – that figures. She's well known for them; must have painted a couple of dozen at least.'

'Heavens! You'd think she'd get tired of them.'

'Ah, but then you're not an artist! Seriously,

though, clouds are her trademark. There's Monet and water lilies, and Hockney and swimming pools, and Wilding and clouds.'

'Perhaps, when I go to see them, you should come along.'

'God, I'd give my eye teeth to! Do you think anyone would mind?'

'I can't see why, but I'll check with the PA.'

Rona finished her tea and looked down at the dog lying at her feet. 'I must go, if Gus is to get any walk at all. It's too late for the park.' The afternoon had clouded over, which would hasten the onset of darkness. 'Back home, then once round the block will have to do.'

'He'll be fine; he had a decent outing at lunchtime, as instructed.' Max walked with them to the door. 'I'll ring you at bedtime,' he said.

FIVE

During the next couple of days, Rona felt she was marking time. Naomi had called as promised on Monday evening, but having passed on Gwen Saunders' number, warned of a delay.

'I rang her when I got back from bridge, but she's away for a few days, so I left a message saying you'd contact her. As for the other numbers, if you give me your address, I'll ask her to email them – easier than dictating over the phone. And when you're ready to interview me, or if there's anything else you need, just phone.'

She hadn't known, when Rona enquired, when Ms Saunders was due back, and Rona's attempt to reach her the next day was again met by the answer phone. There being no point in repeating Naomi's message, she had rung off.

Wednesday morning brought a postcard from her father in Lisbon, crammed with news of all the sights they were visiting. Rona hoped he wasn't overdoing it, though Catherine was sure to be monitoring him.

Lindsey phoned at lunchtime. 'The auction people are clearing the house on Saturday,' she announced, 'after which, I shall be a displaced person. I trust you haven't rethought your invitation?'

'Of course not. When are the decorators starting?'

'Monday. They reckon the painting and papering will only take a week, but the soft furnishings have to be ordered, and some of the furniture has a delivery time of two to three weeks. Will that be OK?'

'Of course it will. Are you getting rid of all the furniture?'

'Except for a few pieces, which can be covered in sheets. It's not worth putting anything in store, but I'll have to bring some boxes of books and ornaments with me, not to mention my entire wardrobe.'

'Just as well there's plenty of room up there.'

'I'm not sure how long it will be for, but the carpets will be down, so as soon as I have the basics – i.e. a bed and somewhere to sit – I can move back in.'

'There's no hurry, Linz, honestly. It'll be great to have you. We might even meet Dominic while you're here.'

Lindsey brightened. 'Yes, he said he'd like that.'

'So, you'll be arriving on Saturday?'

'Late afternoon, if that's OK. Tell Max I'll cook the evening meal, to help earn my keep!'

'He'll be delighted!'

Rona passed on the message when Max returned that evening. He grunted in reply, and she slid an arm round his neck.

'You won't be grumpy with her, will you, darling?'

He smiled reluctantly. 'I'll welcome her with open arms!' he said, turning to pick up the ringing phone.

'The eagles have landed!' proclaimed a voice. 'It's Charles, Max. We're at the Clarendon.'

'Charles, hi! Did you have a good flight?'

'Long and tedious, actually, but we're just about over the jet-lag. We were wondering if you and Rona would be free to have dinner with us on Friday?'

'That sounds great, but hang on while I check with my social secretary.' He put a hand over the mouthpiece. 'Dinner at the Clarendon on Friday?'

'Wonderful!' Rona confirmed.

'We'll be delighted, Charles. Seven thirty in the bar? Excellent. We'll look forward to it, and to hearing all your news.'

As he switched off the phone, Rona said a touch anxiously, 'We won't have to go through the murders again, will we?'

Max gave her a reassuring squeeze. 'I'm sure not; they're already feeling guilty about our involvement. I hope they do decide to come back,' he added. 'They seem a nice couple; it would be good to know them properly, instead of a brief meeting every couple of years. Odd to think that house has been let ever since we've lived here.'

'To get back to Linz,' Rona said, 'we'd better go up and see what state the studio's in.'

Max groaned, but followed her protestingly up three flights of stairs to the top of the house. The large space was cluttered with suitcases, empty computer boxes, rolls of surplus carpet and several of Max's discarded canvases.

'God, I'd forgotten all about these,' he remarked, lifting one up and examining it critically. 'Not at all bad, considering.' He moved on to the next one, and stopped with a frown. 'Hang on – this isn't mine! What the hell...?'

He peered down at an almost indecipherable signature in the bottom corner. 'Good God, it's one of Nathan's. They must have got mixed up, when we went on that painting weekend.'

Rona straightened. 'Nathan? Nathan Tait?'

'Yes. I'd better return it, I suppose. Wonder if

he missed it?'

Rona looked over his shoulder at the canvas he was studying. It was an abstract, slashes of vibrant reds, greens and blues zoning in from all angles, crossing and recrossing in a riot of colour that made the eyes ache, and creating a powerful effect of confusion.

'Strong stuff,' she said. 'Did you ever meet a friend of his, Chloë Pyne?'

Max turned from the painting to stare at her. 'However did you come up with that name?'

'Did you, Max? Meet her?'

'No, but I certainly heard a lot about her that weekend. Nate was well and truly smitten.' His brows drew together. 'How did you come across her?'

'She was Elspeth Wilding's best friend, and she threw herself under a train.'

'My God!' He stared at her. 'Poor old Nate – he'd have been devastated.'

'He didn't tell you?'

'I've not seen him since that weekend. What a thing to have happened.' He frowned. 'Was that before or after Elspeth left?'

'A year before.'

'No connection, then.'

Rona said slowly, 'I'm not so sure.'

Max gave a short laugh. 'Well, if there is, I'd put my money on your finding it. Now, enough speculation: what do you want to do with all this stuff?'

Rona forced her mind back. 'If we stack everything in one corner, that'll leave plenty of room. She's bringing the contents of her wardrobe – and here's just the thing – that old clothes rail you had before we were married. That'll be ideal.'

'For roughly a third of it, perhaps,' Max commented. 'But more importantly, where's the camp bed?'

They found it buried beneath a box of Christmas decorations, Max put it together, and an hour later, the open space looked more like a rudimentary guest room. Rona had balanced a mirror on top of a tea chest to serve as a dressing table, and brought up a chair and spare lamp from her study.

'That should do,' she said, surveying the result of their endeavours. 'I'll put a hot water bottle in the bed to air it, and she should be fine.'

'Right,' Max said, 'then let's go down and get dinner under way.'

Thursday's call to Gwen Saunders struck gold.

'Oh, Miss Parish! I'm so glad you rang; Mrs Harris asked me to look up some addresses and phone numbers for you, and I'm just about to email them.'

'Thank you, they'll be very useful. She said you'd kindly volunteered to help, and I'd very much like to see Miss Wilding's paintings.' If the assistant was being formal, Rona reckoned so should she.

'Of course. And I can provide catalogues, lists of paintings and exhibitions, trips abroad and so on.'

'That would be wonderful. When would be convenient?' Rona asked, mentally crossing her fingers. She was eager, now, to start work.

'I could manage tomorrow, or is that too soon?'

'No, it would be ideal.' Rona paused, remembering Max's interest. Friday was the one day in the week when he'd no outside commitments. 'I wonder – would it be all right if my husband came with me? He'd love to see—'

'Mr Allerdyce?' Sudden animation warmed her voice. 'It would be an honour to meet him! I've been to all his exhibitions, and attended a lecture he gave some years ago, here in Buckford.'

'That's kind of you,' Rona murmured, taken aback. 'Tomorrow morning, then? About eleven?'

'That will be perfect.'

When she had rung off, Rona texted Max at the Art School. *Have arranged for you to come to Buckford with me tomorrow, to see Elspeth's studio etc. OK?*

A minute later the reply came back. *Great! Well done!*

So things were moving at last, Rona thought with satisfaction.

'Avril?'

'Hello, Guy. You must be psychic – I've just walked through the door.'

'From a library stint? Actually, that's why I'm ringing: is this coming Saturday a working or a free one?'

'Free, why?'

'I was wondering if you'd like to come here for the weekend.'

Avril's hand tightened on the phone. 'Well, I...' She swallowed. 'What about Sarah?'

'She'll be with Clive – and all next week too, in fact, as it's half-term. Surely she told you?'

'She hasn't yet.' Avril drew a deep breath. 'In that case, I'd love to come.'

'Excellent! I'll collect you tomorrow evening about seven.'

'Oh, no need for that! I can easily drive over.'

'As I said, you'll be collected, and safely returned on Sunday evening.' He paused. 'Talking of Sarah, how's she been this week?'

'I've hardly seen her, but when I did she was perfectly civil. Distant, but civil.'

Guy snorted. 'She'll come round in time.'

'I hope so,' Avril said.

Sarah did, in fact, belatedly advise Avril of her plans that evening, and Avril, hiding her prior knowledge, said brightly, 'Well, enjoy yourselves! The weather forecast's good, at least for the weekend.'

Though when, she asked herself as Sarah went on up the stairs, did two people in love ever care about the weather? Which brought her, with a rush of nervousness, to her own weekend. Despite their growing closeness, Guy always treated her with what was now, sadly, regarded as old-fashioned respect, and had never suggested they spend the night together. So how was she supposed to regard this invitation? By accepting, had she tacitly agreed to go one step further, or would she decorously be shown to the guest room? And which alternative would she prefer?

It's not serious, she had told her daughters. But over lunch last week, he'd hinted that it might be, and ever since her mind had been in a turmoil. She would just, she told herself with false calm, have to take things as they came.

A blue Renault was already parked at Elspeth's gate, and as they drew up behind it, Gwen Saunders emerged and came to greet them. She was a plain woman in her fifties, with prominent teeth and round glasses, and, though it was Rona's hand she shook first, Max obviously commanded most of her attention.

'It's such an honour to meet you, Mr Allerdyce,' she gushed. 'I've always thought Buckfordshire has been blessed indeed, to be home to two such eminent artists!'

Rona could see Max was embarrassed. 'That's kind of you, Ms Saunders, but I'm hardly in the same class as your employer!'

She gave a brief smile and reverted to her role as guide. 'I have the key to the side gate,' she said briskly, 'so we don't need to go through the house.'

They waited while she released first the padlock and then the Yale, and followed her down a narrow path alongside the house to the back garden. A few more leaves had fallen since

Rona's last visit; it seemed Bill Strong had not returned in the interval.

Once in the studio, Max moved round it like an acolyte in a temple, examining with interest the tubes of paint and selection of brushes, before being called into service to help Rona and Ms Saunders lift the canvases ranged along the wall and turn them to face the room. Only when all had been turned did the PA, with a flourish worthy of a conjuror, whip off the dust sheets, one after another, to reveal the paintings beneath.

For a full minute, the three of them stood in silence, studying the first canvas, before beginning to move, infinitely slowly, along the row. Rona would have liked Max to talk her through them as he did with his own paintings, but the presence of Gwen Saunders inhibited her from asking. She was, however, able to regard each one with a modicum of knowledge, noting its composition and the means used to draw the eye deeper into the picture. Several were the cloudscapes for which Elspeth was known – great washes of sky painted at varying times of the day, from dawn, through the heat of midday, to the flame and gold of sunset. But still life was also represented – polished tables bearing vibrantly coloured jugs of flowers – and a few portraits, one of an old woman who gazed out of the canvas with such a wealth of despair that Rona caught her breath.

Eventually, as they at last reached the end of the row, Gwen Saunders broke the silence. 'As you can see, they're in various stages of completion. She'd get bored with one and start on another, going back and forth between them as the mood took her.'

Rona, who'd not realized they were un-finished, could only nod, but Max was saying, 'I've done that myself.'

For a moment longer he stood gazing at the final canvas – a view of the house from the end of the garden, executed with the misty luminosity of Impressionism, before turning to Ms Saunders almost angrily.

'Why in God's name didn't she finish them?' he demanded. 'Most of these only require a few more touches, and they'd be great – far more accomplished than what she'd been doing latterly. It looks as though she'd turned the corner and was back on form.'

'Oh, I wish she could hear you say that!' Gwen Saunders exclaimed. 'She was so dispirited! You might like to study the ones on the wall – feel free to remove the covers – while I look out the brochures and so on for your wife.'

She went to a filing cabinet, unlocked it, and removed several files and folders.

'We have here an almost complete record of Miss Wilding's career to date,' she said proudly. 'A cuttings book with critical reviews, her awards and certificates, brochures of all her exhibitions, solo and group, and details of her foreign travel. And, as they're all in the public domain, there's no reason why you shouldn't make use of them.'

Naomi must have passed on her reservations about 'intellectual property', Rona thought. 'That's wonderful,' she said. 'They'll be invaluable. Thank you.'

'I shall, though, have to make an inventory of everything I pass to you, for my own records.'

'Of course.'

She waited, glancing through the cuttings album, while Gwen went to the desk and began to type out her list. Max, having finished his scrutiny of the wall paintings, was working his way along the bookshelf, removing an occasional magazine or volume to leaf through.

Gwen finished her inventory and printed off two copies of it, which she and Rona both signed. Then she packed the folders and files into a cardboard box, and, the purpose of the visit completed, they made their way back to the car, where Gus, tail waving, greeted them with enthusiasm.

'What a gorgeous dog!' exclaimed Gwen predictably, as Max released him from his pen and clipped on his lead. Playing as always to the gallery, Gus nuzzled and licked her hand.

'Thank you so much for your help, Ms Saunders,' Rona said, slipping her copy of the inventory into her bag.

'A pleasure. And please don't hesitate to call me if there's anything else I can help with.'

They waited while she climbed into the little Renault, and, with a wave of her hand, drove off.

'You have a lifelong fan!' Rona remarked.

Max ignored the comment. 'Right, once round the block with Gus, then a pub lunch before we start back. OK?'

'OK. I could have done with your comments back there,' she added, 'to get the full value out of the paintings. For instance, you realized straight away that they were unfinished, but they looked perfectly OK to me. When I come to writing up her paintings, I might well need your help.'

'My charges are quite reasonable,' he said.

Richard Wildling looked up as his wife came into the room. 'Naomi phoned while you were out. The biographer woman has made contact.'

'Oh God!' Marcia Wilding took off her rain-hat, tossed it on the sofa, and ran her hands through her straight, shining hair. 'Well, I suppose it was only a matter of time.'

'At least she's refused point-blank to touch the letters and diaries. I told Naomi that would happen, but she couldn't believe anyone'd turn down the chance to get her hands on them.'

Marcia shrugged out of her raincoat. 'At least she has scruples.'

'More likely guarding her own back. I'm surprised she's prepared to go ahead, though, without Ellie's personal input. She's unlikely to do much better than the last poor bugger.'

'Does Ellie know about it, do you think?'

Richard shrugged. 'Presumably not, unless there's been an announcement of some sort in the press. "Biographer hopes to solve mystery of

97

missing artist" or some such.'

'But shouldn't she be ... warned?'

'And how do you suggest we do that, when she won't entrust us with either her address or phone number? We'll just have to wait, as always, until she contacts us, and that could be weeks.'

'All this cloak and dagger stuff!' Marcia exclaimed irritably. 'Who the hell *cares* where she is?'

'I do, for one.'

'And that's what's bugging you, isn't it? That she's not even confided in her beloved elder brother.'

Richard flushed as the barb struck home, unfurling his long frame from the chair. 'Be warned, though,' he added, as Marcia, bending to retrieve her discarded rain-hat, moved towards the door, 'this woman will want to interview us, and she has our contact number.'

'You can tell her how you used to pull Ellie's pigtails,' Marcia returned flippantly, leaving the room.

The Furnesses were in the bar, and Charles came forward with hand outstretched.

'So glad you could make it! Good to see you again.' He kissed Rona's cheek, and, as he greeted Max, she turned to his wife.

Monica Furness, tall and fair, was an ex-model whose radiant smile had, in its time, graced many a magazine cover. She was not smiling now, and her brown eyes were full of concern.

'Rona – how are you?' she asked after a quick kiss, and it was no formality.

'I'm fine,' Rona answered brightly, hoping to ward off reference to recent trauma, and Charles, taking orders for drinks, provided a welcome distraction. She feared, though, that it would be short-lived.

'What have you done with your offspring?' Max asked, as they seated themselves. 'Are we to have the pleasure of seeing them?'

'Not this evening, no,' Charles replied. 'At thirteen and fifteen, they can safely be despatched to the cinema and a burger bar.'

'I doubt if I'd recognize them. We were reckoning it must be three years since we saw you.'

Monica nodded. 'Though we've been over to stay with relatives in the interval.'

'So how long are you here for this time?'

Charles sat back and crossed his legs. He was a thin, wiry man, an inch or two shorter than his wife, and his crinkly brown hair had receded in the years they'd known him, but his eyes, bright and alert, still gave the impression that they missed nothing.

'Well, as you know, our main objective is to settle the business of the house. We went round it yesterday with a builder in tow, and are now awaiting his estimate. Frankly, we were appalled by the state it's in – no blame to the tenants, merely wear and tear over the years. The trick, of course, will be to modernize without destroying its original character, but I'm pretty sure we can achieve it.'

'Does that mean you'll move in yourselves?'

'I think so. It'd be foolish to spend all that money improving it for someone else's benefit, when we'll be wanting somewhere ourselves. Still, no hard and fast decisions at this stage. The only thing that's certain is that it can't be left in its present state.'

The barman brought their drinks over, and again Rona was glad of the interruption, but as soon as he'd gone, Charles, with a swift glance at her, began, 'We would just like to apologize again for everything you went through. I appreciate you don't want to rake it up, and I shan't mention it again, but you knew them fairly well, I believe?'

Rona took a quick sip of her drink. 'I'm not sure I'd agree with that. There was a great deal I *didn't* know, as I found to my cost.'

'But you went to the house several times? From what I gather—'

'Charles,' Monica leant forward and put a hand on his arm. 'I really don't think Rona wants to talk about it.'

He looked momentarily nonplussed. 'Oh – I'm sorry.'

Max said steadily, 'Let's just say it's great from our viewpoint that it's being done over, and it'll be even better if you come and live there. Now, tell me what you'll do when your contract expires; will you be assigned another job in the UK?'

And as the two men settled back to discuss

100

business, Monica said softly, 'I'm sorry about that. He didn't mean to upset you.'

'I know. I'm sorry too, it's just—'

'You don't have to explain. The subject is now closed and won't be raised again. Ever.'

'Thank you,' Rona said.

The rest of the evening passed pleasantly, and over the excellent meal a variety of topics were discussed, including changes in the town over the last few years, the need to find schools for the Furness children, and Rona's career. To her relief, the name Elspeth Wilding seemed to mean little to the Furnesses, so there was no need to go into increasingly repetitive explanations.

'Let us know what you decide,' Max said, as they made their farewells in the foyer.

'Of course, and apologies in advance for the succession of workmen who'll be clogging the road for the foreseeable future.'

'OK, sweetheart?' Max asked, slipping an arm round Rona as they walked to the car.

'It was a bit dicey at first, but I suppose it's only natural for them to be curious.'

'Well, the house will be totally different by the time they've finished,' he said with satisfaction. 'Nothing remaining to remind us of anything.'

'Amen to that,' she said.

The Rubicon had been crossed, Avril thought sleepily, and in the most easy, natural way imaginable.

Guy had called for her as arranged, and during the drive to Stokely she'd still felt apprehensive about what might lie ahead. However, his relaxed manner soon put her at ease, and by the time they reached his home, she was looking forward to the visit.

The house they drew up outside was not unlike her own, built between the wars of solid red brick with painted gables. But this was a busier road than Maple Drive, and almost directly opposite was a bus stop and a parade of six or seven shops.

Noting her glance at them, Guy said with a smile, 'Handy if I run out of bread! What's more, there's a fish and chip shop, for when I'm feeling lazy.'

'You do your own cooking?' she asked, surprised the thought hadn't occurred to her.

'Needs must, since Sarah left. Don't be apprehensive, though; I long since graduated from the tin-opener!'

He took her case out of the boot and accompanied her up the drive, put his key in the lock, and as the door swung open on to a palely panelled hall, any resemblance to her own home vanished. The outlay of the rooms, the position of the staircase, the décor and furnishings, were all totally different, which, oddly, Avril found a relief.

'I'll show you your room,' Guy said, leading the way upstairs, 'and while you settle in, I'll check on the meal. It's been slow-cooking all day, so should be just about ready.'

'It certainly smells good.'

Her room. Avril surprised in herself a feeling of disappointment, and the wish that he wasn't quite so much of a gentleman. The door he opened revealed a fairly small room with a double bed covered in old-fashioned white candlewick, and she was touched to see he'd placed a vase of late roses on the dressing table.

'I thought, since you live in a quiet road, the traffic might disturb you,' he said. 'Being at the back, you won't hear it in here.'

'Thank you.'

He nodded. 'Come down when you're ready.'

Avril went to the window, which overlooked the small back garden. Though too dark to see much, light from a window below revealed a modest terrace and flowerbeds. For the rest, it seemed mostly laid to lawn, though at the far end she could just make out the shape of an arched trellis with a wooden bench beneath it and, to one side, the dark ripple of a pond. This, she thought, was where Sarah had grown up, a motherless girl in the care firstly of nannies, then housekeepers. How had that shaped the prickly, independent young woman she had become?

Guy had a drink waiting for her when she went down, and gave her a quick tour of the downstairs. 'We're eating in the dining room in your honour,' he said. 'I usually sit at the kitchen table, watching TV.'

The meal was coq au vin, followed by apple pie. Avril was impressed, and said so.

'Packet pastry, I'm afraid,' Guy admitted. 'I enjoy cooking, though I confess I don't eat like this every day!'

She helped him load the dishwasher, and dried the glasses he washed by hand. Then he made coffee, which they took through to the sitting room. Avril studied the wedding photograph on a side table, of a much younger Guy with considerably more hair, and a laughing girl who bore a distinct resemblance to Sarah.

'Sarah's like your wife, isn't she?' she said softly.

He came to stand beside her. 'Yes, and I admit I found that difficult to cope with, especially as she grew older. But Sarah's very much her own person – far more forthright than Sally ever was, and now the resemblance is more of a comfort than a pain.'

'You must still miss her. Your wife.'

'And you your husband.'

Neither statement was either confirmed or denied, and they moved tacitly away from both the photograph and the topic, sitting by the fire he'd lit and listening to a CD. And eventually the time came, as Avril had known it must, to go upstairs.

They went up together, and on the landing Guy took her gently in his arms and kissed her. Instinctively, she pulled him closer, wondering if he could hear the clattering of her heart.

His lips moved to her throat, and after a minute he said softly, 'Avril, I want very much to make love to you. But I don't want you to think that was why I invited you here, because it wasn't, and if you're not ready, or would rather not, I'll quite understand.'

'I'm ready,' she said.

SIX

Though Rona was anxious to start work on the papers she'd brought back, she had to curb her impatience. It was the weekend, and furthermore Lindsey would be moving in that evening.

'Our last meal à deux,' Max commented over lunch.

'Only for a couple of weeks,' Rona reminded him. 'You're not going to be difficult, are you?'

He raised his eyebrows. 'Moi?'

'Anyway, Linz said she'd cook the meal tonight, remember, so relax and enjoy it. I hope she'll be all right in the studio,' she added worriedly. 'It *is* a bit barn-like.'

'Just as well, since she'll bring everything but the kitchen sink.'

'I thought we might invite Dominic over while she's here.'

'You don't want me to ask his intentions, do you?'

Rona ignored that. 'I think you'd like him.'

'As you know, I don't usually admire your

sister's taste in men.'

Or anything else about her, Rona thought sadly. The veiled animosity between her husband and her twin was an ongoing regret.

Lindsey seemed unusually downcast when she arrived that afternoon, barely speaking as the three of them unloaded her car – parked in the nearest space, some way down the road – and transported boxes and cases up two flights of stairs to the studio. And when Rona came up with the last box, she surprised her sister with tears in her eyes.

'Linz!' she exclaimed. 'Whatever is it?'

Lindsey dabbed angrily at her eyes. 'I'm being stupid,' she said savagely. 'Stupid and sentimental. But seeing what amounts to the last eight years of my life being carted away and the flat completely stripped, as though I'd died or something...' Her voice caught. 'I just wanted to snatch everything back, say I'd changed my mind.'

Rona put an arm round her. 'Think how lovely it will be, when you're back there with everything new.'

Lindsey sniffed inelegantly. 'I know. The computer images are stunning.'

'There you are, then. And in the meantime, it'll be great having you to chat to, especially on the evenings Max is teaching.'

Lindsey gave her a squeeze. 'Thanks, sis.'

'Advance warning, though: I have two dates next week, Magda's fashion show on Thursday

– though I'm sure you'd be welcome if you'd like to come – and it's Max's birthday on Friday, so I'm taking him to *An Inspector Calls* at the Darcy Hall.'

'I hadn't forgotten! And actually, that fits in perfectly. Dominic's whisking me off somewhere unspecified for the weekend, and, much as I'd enjoy the fashion show, Thursday is book group.'

'First I've heard of any book group!'

Lindsey smiled. 'I've only just joined, but they're an interesting crowd, and it gets me reading books I mightn't otherwise come across.'

'Fair enough, then, but I have to tell you you'll miss seeing the delectable Crispin.'

'How so?'

'He's bringing a crowd to the Clarendon. Magda would give her right arm to get that set on her database.'

'Good luck to her. And I'll be interested in your opinion of Mr Ryder.'

To Rona's relief, that first evening passed off well. True to her promise, Lindsey cooked a delicious meal, which they ate by candlelight overlooking the shadowed patio.

'I could get used to this!' Max commented. 'An excellent meal, Lindsey. Thank you.'

'High praise indeed, from the master chef!'

Rona began to clear the table. 'I meant to ask you, Linz, is Mum away? I've been trying to get hold of her, to invite her to lunch tomorrow.'

Lindsey shook her head. 'Not that I know of, but I've not spoken to her this week. When did you ring?'

'Last night, and several times today, but it's always the answer phone. I hope she's OK.'

'You'd have heard if she wasn't,' Max said.

'Try again now,' Lindsey suggested.

Rona did so, but, as before, only the recorded voice replied. 'Perhaps she's at a bridge tournament, or something.'

'She should be back by now.'

'A bridge weekend, then. She's been on them before.'

'No point in worrying,' Max said firmly. 'Avril's well able to take care of herself. Now, would anyone like a brandy with their coffee?'

Sunday was the usual lazy day. After a late breakfast, Rona spent some time in the paved garden, removing dying plants from the containers and generally tidying up, and in the afternoon all three of them took Gus for a prolonged walk in the park.

'It makes me realize how little exercise I take,' Lindsey commented, brushing her hair back as the wind played havoc with it.

'You should get a dog,' Rona advised.

'I couldn't leave it in the flat all day – it wouldn't be fair.'

'Then join a gym!'

'I'm far too lazy, as you well know.'

'OK, another idea: instead of a leisurely lunch, come over sometimes and take Gus for a walk.

We'll lend him to you!'

'I just might, at that! I'd forgotten how great it is up here.'

That evening, as they relaxed over the Sunday papers, Lindsey said suddenly, 'I'm going to try Mum again.' She reached for her mobile, and Rona, watching as she tapped in Avril's number, relaxed when her twin's face brightened.

'Mum! It's me. How are things? ... Great. I'm phoning to let you know I'm at Rona and Max's ... Yes, everything was cleared out yesterday, so I'm a displaced person! ... I'm not sure exactly; about two weeks, depending on the arrival dates for the furniture ... Of course, you'll be one of the first to see it! Actually – ' she glanced at Rona – 'Ro tried to phone, to invite you to join us for lunch. Have you been away?'

Lindsey's eyes grew round as she listened to her mother's reply, and she gave Rona a totally inexplicable thumbs-up.

'And everything ... went well? ... Well, that's great, Mum! Good for you! ... Oh – yes, of course ... We'll speak later in the week, then. Yes, I will. Bye, Mum.'

Lindsey rang off.

'That was an abrupt ending,' Rona remarked. 'And why the thumbs-up?'

'She said there was someone at the door, though I suspect it was just an excuse. She sends her love, by the way, and says she'll phone you during the week.'

'And?' Rona demanded impatiently.

'AND – she *was* away for the weekend – with Guy Lacey! How about that?'

'Away where?'

'At his house in Stokely.'

'Well, well, well,' Rona said slowly. 'That's certainly a step forward.'

'And why not?' Lindsey flashed. 'She's a free agent, isn't she, and Pops has Catherine.'

'Linz, I'm not criticizing, just saying it's a step forward. I think it's great she's found someone, and he seemed very nice when we saw him.'

Lindsey subsided. 'Sorry,' she mumbled. 'I didn't mean to bite your head off.'

'Wasn't he supposed to be telling Sarah the position, the weekend Mum came for lunch? I wonder how that went.'

'Perhaps we'll learn more next time we speak to her,' Lindsey said hopefully.

By eight thirty the next morning, Max had left for the studio and Lindsey for the office. Rona cleared away the breakfast dishes with mounting anticipation. Now at last she was free to retreat to her study and examine her treasure trove.

The cardboard box was on the study floor, where Max had dumped it on their return from Buckford, and she lifted it carefully on to the table by the window and began to remove its contents.

The cuttings book looked of particular interest; it had been compiled – by Gwen, Rona guessed – as a scrapbook, and hotel bills and airline tickets were interspersed with notices announcing exhibitions in cities as diverse as New York, Madrid and Tokyo, as well as the prestigious British Painters of the Nineties held in London in '95. Then followed appraisals of those exhibitions by a variety of art critics from around the world. It would all have to be gone through carefully, but what she was after at the moment was an overall view – and, if possible, something that would bring the elusive subject of the biography to life.

Admittedly, there were a few manuscript notes in, presumably, Elspeth's handwriting, but nothing that gave any insight to her character, and Rona was forced to acknowledge the likelihood that anything personal would be confined to her diaries and letters, which must remain out of reach.

By the end of the morning, she was disappointed and more than a little dispirited. Though she'd a wealth of information on the mechanics of Elspeth's career, the artist herself had refused to come alive for her, remaining locked in the confines of her paintings. What she needed were personal recollections to put flesh on the bones.

She opened a desk drawer and retrieved the page of contacts she'd printed from Miss Saunders' email. Where to start? Perhaps, she thought, with Naomi Harris, whom she already knew. It was lunchtime; with luck, she'd be at home.

She was. 'Mrs Harris? It's Rona Parish.'

'Oh, Rona, hello!' There was a pause, then an

embarrassed little laugh. 'I hope I may call you that, since we'll be seeing a fair bit of each other? And I, as you know, am Naomi.'

'Rona's fine, thanks. I've been going through some papers, but so far I've not been able to get any handle on Elspeth herself. I wondered if I could come up and speak to you about her?'

'Yes, of course. Her childhood, do you mean?'

'To start with, yes; but if things occur to you out of context, fine. I can sort everything out later. When would be convenient?'

'I suppose you'd like it to be as soon as possible?'

'Ideally, yes.'

Naomi hesitated. 'Is it likely to be a long interview?'

How long is a piece of string? Rona thought. 'It depends really; I'll have a list of questions to start you off, and with luck, you'll be able to enlarge on the answers. I'll bring my recorder, if that's OK, to save having to write notes all the time.'

'Of course. How about tomorrow, then?'

'That would be great. Thanks.'

'Sunningdene's marginally nearer than Buckford, but you'll still have quite a drive. Suppose you come about eleven, and we can break for lunch?'

'Oh, please don't go to any trouble,' Rona protested.

'No trouble – it'll be something light. Now, do you know where we are?'

'I'll find you. I have your address, and Sunningdene's not very large, is it?'

'That's true. Very well, eleven o'clock tomorrow, then.'

Rona put down the phone and drew a breath of relief. That should start the ball rolling.

She set off the next morning just after nine, Gus curled up on the back seat. She'd be out most of the day – too long to leave him – and she could stop to exercise him on both the outward and return journeys.

It was a glorious day, mellow sunshine burnishing the remaining leaves to flame, and Rona was tempted to take the scenic route, meandering past Nettleton and Woodbourne and getting the full benefit of the autumn foliage. However, the Buckford road would be quicker; perhaps, time permitting, they could come home the other way.

After a gap of over a year, this was the third time in eight days she'd driven this way. Future interviews, though, should entail shorter journeys; according to the emailed information, Elspeth's parents had moved to Chilswood, and her brother and his wife lived in London.

Sunningdene was a small market town cradled in a valley, and it was in the countryside surrounding it that Rona stopped to let Gus have a run. Over to her right, rooks cawed and flapped over a small wood, while fields stretched away on either side, farm buildings clustered on the horizon, and ahead of her, in a gentle dip, lay the roofs of Sunningdene.

A distant clock chiming the three-quarters recalled her to the present, and, bundling Gus back into the car, she drove down the hill into town. As she entered the High Street, she saw to her surprise that the shops were confined to the left-hand side, the right being given over to parkland, whose trees and grass gave the impression it was still part of the countryside. Ahead, the road forked on either side of an area set out as a market place, where a cluster of stalls appeared to be doing a brisk trade.

Memorizing the map, Rona took the left fork, and almost immediately turned left again, following the road for a mile or so till the shops ended and it widened into an estate of executive-type houses and bungalows. She then threaded her way through maze-like streets for another five minutes, before finding that matching the Harrises' address.

Gus briefly raised his head as she left the car, then settled back resignedly, closing his eyes.

Rona was a little disconcerted when a tall, grey-haired man opened the door to her, but his smile reassured her that she had the right house.

'Rona Parish? How do you do? I'm Leonard Harris. My wife's expecting you.'

And Naomi appeared behind him, smiling a welcome.

'You found us all right, then?'

'No problem till I reached the estate.'

'I know, it is a bit samey. Come through, there's some coffee waiting. Leonard's working from home today,' she added, leading the way

114

through a pleasant-looking sitting room to the conservatory beyond. 'He'll be joining us for lunch, though I doubt if he can add much to your research on Elspeth.'

The conservatory, warm after the cool autumn air, looked over a back garden that, to Rona's mind, had the manicured air of professional landscaping. Mentally, and a little disparagingly, she ticked off its components: decking, water feature, gazebo, barbecue stand – while admitting that the overall effect was pleasing to the eye. Then, ashamed of herself, she turned to her hostess with a smile.

'Have you always lived in a bungalow?'

Naomi, engaged in pouring the coffee, shook her head. 'We moved here five years ago. At the time, it looked as though Leonard might be made redundant, and it seemed wise to move to a smaller house. Also, he has a wonky knee, so doing away with stairs was a bonus.'

'It must seem odd, not going up to bed!' Rona said.

Naomi laughed, handing her a coffee cup. 'It took a while to get used to.'

She waved Rona to a chintz-covered sofa, and sat down opposite her. 'You said on the phone that you couldn't "get a handle" on Elspeth. What exactly did you mean?'

Rona took out her recorder and set it up on the glass-topped table. 'I know I've barely started, but ... nothing is coming through, no hint of her personality.'

'I can't say I'm surprised,' Naomi rejoined,

and the contentious subject of the diaries hung in the air between them.

Rona waited for her to go on, and when she didn't, prompted, 'Could you tell me, then, what you remember of her as a child.'

Naomi sat back, staring into her coffee cup. 'I was five when she was born, and I can remember very clearly my first sight of her, scarlet face screwed up in fury, and tiny fists clenched. Though we didn't know it at the time, she was starting as she meant to go on. I've never *known* such a child for tantrums. If she didn't get her own way, she'd scream and scratch, tug at my hair, kick out at Richard. And she was a nightmare when Mother took her shopping. If she wasn't allowed a lollipop or whatever, she'd lie down in the middle of the street or supermarket, drumming her heels and screaming blue murder.'

Naomi broke off with a laugh. 'I assumed all children behaved like that, and was quite apprehensive when Gillian was born. But she turned out as docile as a lamb, bless her!'

'How long did these tantrums last?' Rona asked.

'Way past the terrible twos – almost until she started school. Then she went from one extreme to another, and for the first few weeks refused to speak at all. My parents panicked and took her to a child psychologist, who assured them it was quite normal. They were advised to keep chatting to her and ignore her silence, and gradually she started talking again. But after that, we'd never much idea what she was thinking.'

'I know you said she'd no friends when she was older, but had she at school?'

Naomi thought back. 'I don't remember her going to parties, but she had one or two, and was very possessive of them. Anyway, she continued to be difficult until she was about five, when she was given a paintbox for Christmas.' She shook her head wonderingly. 'It was though someone had waved a wand – she was a different child. She spent all her time painting – nothing out of the ordinary, mind you, just like any five-year-old, but it became a passion, and she was certainly much more amenable.

'The psychologist said the tantrums had been a sign of frustration, because she'd difficulty expressing herself in words. Once she found a medium she was more comfortable with, she was happier. It sounded like gobbledegook to me, and frankly still does.'

'It says on the Internet that she was a child prodigy, and had a painting exhibited at the age of thirteen.'

'That's true. Once she started at secondary school, the art teacher saw she'd real talent and gave her extra coaching. I know it sounds silly, but it was as if someone had opened her cage. The results were instant and ... spectacular.'

'How did she react in herself? Was she more approachable?'

Naomi shrugged. 'She'd met Chloë Pyne by then, so if she confided in anyone, it would have been her. It seems ridiculous when she's my sister, but I've never really felt I know her.'

'Has anyone else in the family shown artistic leanings?'

'Not really, unless you count my grandfather. He taught art at secondary school level and dabbled a bit himself, but in a strictly amateur way. My parents have a couple of his water-colours.'

'Was he still alive when Elspeth started painting?'

'Sadly, no, he died before she was born. I suppose she *might* have inherited his talent, but if so, she far surpassed it.'

She'd look into that later, Rona thought. 'You said Chloë was also an artist?'

'Yes; as children, they'd shut themselves away and paint for hours on end. They weren't interested in anything else. Later, as I told you, they went on to uni and then the RCA together. Elspeth was much the better artist, but Chloë never showed signs of jealousy. It would have been different, I can tell you, if it had been the other way round.'

'Elspeth was competitive?'

'Extremely. And there were no half-measures with her: she either loved you or hated you, often swinging from one to the other and back again in the course of a day. It was very wear-ing.'

'Surely this didn't continue after she grew up?'

'She still has mood swings, though not so intense.' Naomi reached down beside her chair

118

and produced a photograph album. 'You might be interested in this, though obviously there's nothing recent. Elspeth always hated having her photo taken, and from the age of fifteen, downright refused to. Her publicity people had a terrible time with her.'

Rona moved across, watching as Naomi turned the album pages to reveal yellowing snaps of long-ago summers. In virtually all of them, while the youthful Naomi and Richard smiled obligingly for the camera, Elspeth either pulled a face, covered it with her hands, or turned her back. Only when she'd been caught unawares could Rona catch a glimpse of the attractive-looking child she had been.

As Naomi came to the end, a loose sheet of paper slid out, a page torn from a glossy magazine. She picked it up with an exclamation.

'I'd forgotten about this. It's the last photo we have of her, taken only a month or two before she went. As you see, she's still managing to avoid the camera.'

She passed the sheet to Rona. It was headed *Famous faces at the opening of the Newbolt Gallery,* and showed groups of men and women in evening dress, glasses in hand, standing about chatting. They might be famous in the art world, Rona thought, but she didn't recognize any of them, apart from the slight figure with her head down and her hair falling across her face.

'She didn't want to go,' Naomi said. 'Her dealer had practically to force her.'

Rona, about to read the list of those present,

looked up. 'Her dealer?'

'Someone else whose name and address you'll need, though not, presumably, for a while yet.'

'Sorry to interrupt,' a voice said, 'but lunch is ready.'

They looked up to see Leonard Harris smiling at them from the doorway to the sitting room.

'Goodness, is it that time already?' Naomi exclaimed. 'I'm sorry, Rona, I'd meant to offer you a sherry before we went through.'

'Thanks, but I'd rather not, with the drive ahead of me.'

'You'll have wine with the meal, though?'

'Just a glass would be lovely.'

The small dining room also gave on to the back garden, and Rona assumed the bedrooms must be at the front of the house. Naomi and Leonard between them brought through a golden-topped quiche and a bowl of salad.

'I can't claim any credit,' Leonard said, in response to Rona's appreciative comment. 'My wife made the quiche last night. All I had to do was put it in the oven at the right time, and dress the ready-prepared salad.'

'Team work!' said Naomi with a smile. 'Rona's trying to gauge Elspeth's character, darling,' she continued. 'Any contribution to make?'

'That's a tough one,' Leonard replied, pouring the wine. 'Off the top of my head, I'd say she's intense, passionate about what interests her, dismissive of what doesn't. And she can be both thoughtless and very generous, depending on mood. How's that for a summary?'

'Pretty accurate, I'd say.'

He glanced at Rona. 'I wish to God you could find her,' he said in a low voice.

Rona felt her colour rise. 'That's not my remit, Mr Harris.'

'I'm sorry – of course I know that. It's just that this prolonged absence is putting such a strain on everyone.'

'That's what you meant about her thoughtlessness?'

'I suppose so, yes. Perhaps self-centred would have been a better description. She doesn't stop to consider how her actions might affect others.'

The rest of the meal passed without further reference to Elspeth, but when Rona and Naomi were back in the conservatory, Naomi said hesitantly, 'You know you said it didn't matter if I remembered something out of context?'

'Yes?' Rona leaned forward and switched the recorder back on.

'Well, I told you she'd never had a love affair, and to the best of my knowledge that's true. But she did have a passionate crush on someone when she was about sixteen. I wonder sometimes if we underestimated that.'

'Who was he?'

'A master at the school – Mr Palmer, we knew him as. She was totally besotted with him, though I can't remember how we knew that – certainly not from her. What *did* hit the headlines was that he was dismissed for having an affair with one of his pupils. Elspeth was distraught – there's no other word for it. I suppose she'd built up a fantasy that he loved *her*, and learning in the most brutal way that he didn't almost destroyed her. My mother wrote it off as puppy love, insisting she'd soon get over it, but I'm not sure she ever did. Certainly she never risked being hurt again.'

Rona pondered over that during the drive home. Naomi might have a point: in as complex and intense a nature as Elspeth's, what must have appeared as rejection could indeed have had a lasting effect. She wished passionately that Chloë, who surely would have known all about it, was still alive and could fill in the gaps. Though even without her, Rona felt she'd come some way towards understanding the woman behind the averted face and screen of pale hair.

Max's mobile rang as he was cleaning his brushes after the day's work.

'Charles here, Max.'

'Hi there. Thanks again for the meal the other night.'

'A pleasure, and please thank Rona for her note – there was no need to write. This is just a courtesy call to put you in the picture, and I'm phoning your mobile to spare Rona hearing about the house.'

'That's good of you. So, what's the news?'

'We've taken the plunge and decided to come and live there ourselves.'

'That's excellent, Charles. It will be good to

have you as neighbours.'

'Thanks, but as you'd imagine, there's the hell of a lot to do in the meantime. I've arranged for a clearance firm to remove the entire contents. There's nothing there of value, and frankly Monica doesn't fancy any of it, after what happened. The carpets particularly are in a parlous state, some with pieces actually cut out of them. For forensic purposes, I suppose, though I'd rather not know. And, of course, we've a lot of our own furniture in Hong Kong, some of which we took out in the first place, so we'll be shipping all that home.

'We've ordered the fittings for a total refit of the kitchen and bathroom, and we're putting in a shower room and loo on the top floor for the kids. So there'll be the hell of a lot of drilling and hammering going on. I should invest in earplugs if I were you!'

'You seem to have organized a great deal in a short time!'

'It's been a rush to fit it all in before we leave, but we're just about there. We fly back at the end of the week.'

'So when do you hope to move in?'

'Spring next year, when the contract ends. With luck, we'll be settled in by Easter.'

'Well, anything Rona or I can do in the meantime, just let us know.'

'Thanks; we've booked a pretty reliable firm to supervise everything, but if I may, I'll give them your number, in case of emergencies. So, it just remains to say it was great to see you both, apologies again for the ordeal, and we'll be back next year.'

'We'll look forward to it,' Max said, 'and in the meantime, bon voyage!'

SEVEN

Rona's mood was decidedly more positive the next morning, and she worked steadily, transcribing her conversations with Naomi Harris and transferring them to the file she'd previously set up. And listening to Naomi's voice without the distraction of her presence, it struck Rona, with a sense of surprise, that she was not overly fond of her sister. True, it could be argued she'd been specifically asked about Elspeth's childhood, but the descriptions of her tantrums, her sulkiness, the attacks on her siblings, were surely more detailed and judgemental than was strictly necessary, perhaps indicating resentment of a talented younger sister.

Yet according to Prue, Naomi had begged her to commission the biography. Why? In the hope, as she'd half-admitted, that it might spur Elspeth into returning home? Or, as Max had cynically suggested, to increase the worth of her paintings?

That evening, as they were enjoying their pre-dinner drinks in the kitchen, Max announced that he'd arranged to meet Nathan on Friday, to hand over his painting.

'But Friday's your birthday!' Rona objected.

'I'm aware of that, darling, and that we're going out in the evening. This is at lunchtime.'

'Where are you meeting?'

He gave a short laugh. 'Nowhere exotic – Toddington service station. He's driving up to Yorkshire for an exhibition, and as he now lives in London, it's the most convenient place.'

'Who's Nathan?' Lindsey asked. 'Do I know him?'

'I doubt it,' Max replied, reaching down a pan. 'He's an artist friend of mine. We went on a painting trip about three years ago, and I must have scooped up one of his canvases. I found it when we were clearing the studio.'

'I'd like to meet him myself,' Rona said. 'Perhaps he could throw more light on the Chloë connection.'

'And who's Chloë?' Lindsey again.

'Elspeth's best friend; Nathan was in love with her.'

'Was being past tense?'

'As past as it gets. She's dead.'

Lindsey groaned. 'I might have known. Murdered, no doubt?'

'No, actually she killed herself. Under a train.'

'Ye gods!' Lindsey shuddered.

'I'm not sure it would be wise to broach the subject,' Max said mildly, above the hiss of melting butter. 'He's unlikely to relish being

125

quizzed about his dear departed.'

'It was two and a half years ago,' Rona protested. 'You can't wrap him in cotton wool for ever. Anyway, it's not so much Chloë I want to discuss, as Elspeth. He must have known her.'

'All roads lead to Elspeth,' Lindsey said resignedly.

'The trouble is, most of them are cul-de-sacs.'

'Why's that?'

'She's an intensely private person. Even her own family don't seem to know her.'

Lindsey finished her drink. 'Then it sounds to me as though you're on a hiding to nothing,' she rejoined.

'Hi,' Lindsey said.

It was four hours later, and she was leaning on the studio windowsill, mobile in hand, gazing down at the street below.

'How did the move go?' Dominic asked. He'd been in Frankfurt for the past week.

'As well as can be expected. I cried when the van drove away.'

'*Off went the van, with my home in it*? Poor baby. When's the auction?'

'Next week, but I shan't go. If I did, I'd probably buy everything back.'

'So much for your desire for a clean sweep.'

'I know, I know. Ignore me – I'm feeling a bit rootless at the moment, though Ro and Max have been great.'

'Well, you've the weekend to look forward to.'

'I know.' She brightened. 'You haven't said where we're going?'

'Sailing,' he replied.

'*Sailing*? At this time of year?'

'The forecast's good; it'll be perfect.'

'I trust you're not expecting me to hoist up sails or anything?'

Dominic laughed. 'Hardly. No, it's what's known as a luxury yacht, property of a friend of mine, and comes complete with crew and cordon bleu chef.'

'Ah, that sounds better!'

'I thought it might. There's an extra surprise, but that'll keep for the moment.'

'Dominic, you know I hate secrets! Tell me now!'

'Sorry, you'll have to wait till Friday. Sleep well.' And he rang off.

Lindsey clicked her mobile shut and went on staring down into the road. From this height, she could see the streetlights in Fullers Walk leading up towards Guild Street. Immediately below her, a man was walking his dog, allowing it to stop and sniff at every tree. In no hurry to go home, evidently.

She turned and, still leaning her elbows on the sill, surveyed her studio bedroom, lit softly by the lamp Rona had found for her. There were no curtains up here, just vertical blinds to pull across if the sun was too hot. In daytime, the room was flooded with light. At night, it held mysterious shadows. Her eyes moved across the spaces to the heaped shapes against the walls.

127

God only knew what they were; some must be Max's paintings, since among them he'd found one by his friend, whose girlfriend jumped under a train.

The radiator clicked suddenly, startling her. Oh God, she wished she was in her own cosy little flat!

She pushed herself away from the window and started to undress, thinking over the conversation with Dominic. She wasn't sure that she'd enjoy sailing, even with a crew. She'd been seasick as a child, and had tended to avoid boats ever since. She hoped grimly she could do justice to the chef's gourmet offerings.

And that surprise Dominic had up his sleeve: why did he mention it, if he'd no intention of telling her what it was? Just to be annoying, probably. Sometimes, she thought as she climbed cautiously into the camp bed, she wished she didn't love him so much.

The next morning, Rona continued sorting through files and folders, jotting down odd points as they occurred to her. It struck her suddenly that Catherine might know who'd been the head at St Stephen's in Elspeth's time. With luck, whoever it was would still be alive and living locally. And as the thought came, the front door bell rang, and Rona answered it to find Catherine herself on the step.

'I do hope I'm not interrupting anything,' she said. 'I've been shopping, and thought I might as well hand-deliver a little something we brought back from Portugal.'

'I was just thinking about you!' Rona told her. 'Come in! Did you have a good holiday?'

'Perfect. We paced our sightseeing, so had plenty of time to relax. And, of course, we ate extremely well.'

'And Pops?' Rona asked diffidently, leading the way into the sitting room.

'Is looking a lot better than when we went away.' Catherine handed Rona a little package wrapped in green tissue paper, which contained three brightly painted cockerels in diminishing sizes.

'They're lovely! Thank you.'

'You see them all over Portugal,' Catherine said. 'There's a legend dating from the fourteenth century about a pilgrim who was wrongly accused of theft, for which the penalty was death. He prayed to St James for justice, and went to see the judge who was due to sentence him. The judge was sitting down to dinner, which happened to be roast chicken, and the pilgrim said, "If I'm innocent, that cockerel will get up and crow!" And of course it did, and he was released.'

Rona smiled. 'I hadn't heard that. Have you time for some coffee?'

'If you're sure I'm not interrupting.'

'Actually, I wanted to ask you something. Come down to the kitchen.'

While the coffee brewed, Rona arranged the little cockerels along the shelf above the Aga. 'I'll have to remove them when we cook chicken!' she said.

'So what did you want to ask me?'

'I wondered if by any chance you knew who was head of St Stephen's while Elspeth was there.'

'When would that have been, exactly?'

'1969 to '75.'

'It would probably have been Miss Burbage, but I can check for you.'

'Did you know her?'

'Not personally, no.'

'Do you know if she's still around?'

'She was when I left, three years ago. I'll ring an ex-colleague, and ask her.'

'Thanks – and, for that matter, any other staff who were there at the time. It'd be fascinating to hear their impressions of her.'

'They might be tinged by hindsight,' Catherine warned. 'Where did Elspeth go on to?'

'Buckford High. I'll have to contact them, too.'

'So how's it going?' Catherine asked curiously. 'Have you met any of the family yet?'

'Just her sister and brother-in-law. It was Naomi who pressed for the bio.'

'And was she helpful?'

'Ye-es.' Rona pressed down the plunger and poured the coffee.

'But?'

'I'm not sure there is a "but". She arranged for me to see Elspeth's studio and bring home some files. And when I rang again, she invited me to lunch and answered all my questions. It's just that I got the impression there wasn't much love lost between them, so it might have been a somewhat biased account. I'll have a better idea when I've seen the rest of the family.

'And by the way,' she added, passing Catherine a mug, 'Elspeth's disappearance wasn't quite as mysterious as we thought; she *had* left a message for the family, but only a bit of it was recoverable, so they don't know where she is.'

Talk reverted to the Portuguese holiday, and shortly afterwards Catherine rose to go.

'I won't take up any more of your time.' She opened her bag and took out a package in blue tissue. 'You're likely to see Lindsey before I do; would you give her this, with our love?'

'Of course. Actually, she's staying with us at the moment.'

Catherine looked up in surprise. 'She's moved out already? I must tell Tom; he was intending to ring you both this evening, but now he can catch you together.'

'Not tonight, I'm afraid. Lindsey's meeting her book group, and I'm going to Magda's fashion show at the Clarendon. And tomorrow Linz is off for the weekend, and I'm taking Max to the theatre.'

Catherine nodded. 'For his birthday. We have something for him, but it looks as though it'll be Saturday before we can deliver it.'

'Come for lunch,' Rona suggested, opening the front door.

'Oh, there's no need—'

'Need doesn't come into it. Linz won't be

here, but Max and I would love to see you both.'

'Well, if you're sure...'

'It's a date,' Rona said firmly.

Lindsey was working at her desk when, after the briefest of taps, the door opened and Jonathan Hurst came into the room.

She looked up, eyeing him uneasily. 'Yes?' she said.

'Not the warmest of greetings, my love. Or should that be ex-love?'

'What do you want, Jonathan? I haven't time to play games.'

'Hoity-toity!' To her annoyance, he perched on the edge of her desk. 'Not a game, lovely lady, business with a capital B. Remember, in our more harmonious days, working together with old man Steinbeck?'

'That extremely complicated will? What of it?'

'He's fallen out with son number two, and wants to strike him off without the proverbial. And he's asked particularly to see us both, since we drew up the original will.'

'I can't see that's necessary,' Lindsey objected.

'It's necessary,' Jonathan said with quiet emphasis, 'if we're to keep an extremely wealthy client happy.'

Though not relishing the thought of working with him, she accepted there was little she could do.

'When does he want to see us? My diary's

pretty full next week.'

'Then it shouldn't be a problem; we're to meet tomorrow evening at six, after which he'll take us to dinner at the Clarendon. Now *that's* the kind of client we should cultivate!'

Lindsey flushed with annoyance. 'You should have checked with me before arranging anything; as it happens, I can't make tomorrow. I'm going away for the weekend.'

He looked at her blankly. 'Then cancel it,' he said.

'I'm sorry, I can't do that. I've been working late every night for I don't know how long, but tomorrow I have to leave on time.'

He leaned forward till his face was only inches from hers. 'I'm not sure you understand, Lindsey. If we don't play ball, he might move all his business elsewhere. You can imagine how popular that would make us.'

'Then you go, and present my apologies. Say I've been stricken down with yellow fever – anything you like. I can catch up later in the proceedings.'

'Look,' his tone became more placatory, 'you need only postpone it for a few hours. Dinner's sure to be over by nine, and—'

'I can't, Jonathan. We're going sailing, and we have to catch the tide.'

He sat back again, his face flushed with anger. 'Well, well, you *are* hitting the high spots! Lover-boy picking you up by helicopter?'

'I'll ring and apologize if you like,' she offered, refusing to rise to the bait, 'and as I say, I can soon pick up the threads. Tomorrow, though, is out of the question.'

He slid off the desk. 'I won't forget this, Lindsey,' he said. And the door closed behind him.

The fashion show was being held in the Clarendon's Albany Suite, which, decorated in white and gold, provided a pleasant but understated background designed not to detract from any colour scheme favoured by its patrons. In constant demand for dances, wedding receptions, whist drives, and any other function requiring space, it had its own ante-room, where, this evening, wine and canapés were being served.

The buzz of conversation reached Rona as she made her way towards it, and she paused in the doorway, hoping to see a face she recognized. A waiter materialized beside her with a tray of glasses.

'Red or white wine, madam?'

'Oh – red, thank you.'

'Rona!'

With a sense of relief, she caught sight of Magda, flushed and excited, making her way towards her. They embraced, taking care not to spill their drinks.

'Quite a turnout,' Rona commented.

'Yes, isn't it encouraging, when everyone's supposed to be tightening their belts?'

'Gucci, of course! But remember, it doesn't cost anything to look!'

'Oh I'm not listening to you! I always get a

raft of orders after these shows, and tonight will be no exception.'

'I'm sure you're right.' Rona's eyes were raking the chattering crowd. 'Has your pal Crispin arrived?'

'Yes indeed, accompanied by the promised jet set. Come and meet him.'

She took Rona's arm and they wove their way between groups, several times being waylaid by people touching Magda's arm with questions or comments.

'There they are, over by that pillar,' she said, and Rona, glancing in the direction indicated, stopped suddenly, frowning.

Magda glanced at her. 'What's the matter?'

'Nothing, really. I ... just had the feeling I've seen him before. Quite recently.'

'Well, that's no surprise! He's always in the news.'

'Yes, of course.' Rona allowed herself to be led over to the group, and Magda tapped the only man among them on the shoulder.

He turned with a smile.

'Crispin, may I introduce—'

'Oh, but we've already met!' he said, taking Rona's hand.

Magda, disconcerted, looked from one to another. 'Really? Rona was just saying—'

'That would have been my sister,' Rona interrupted smoothly. 'At the Dorchester? My *twin* sister,' she added, as he continued to look bewildered.

'Well, as I was saying,' Magda continued, 'this

is Rona Parish, a very good friend of mine. Crispin Ryder.'

'My sincere apologies,' he said with a mock bow. 'I'm delighted to meet you, Rona Parish. But you and your sister should come with a health warning! Now, may I in turn introduce my friends?'

All six were glamorous women, beautifully dressed, in their thirties or forties, and, interestingly, they all wore wedding rings. No wonder Magda was keen to get them on her books.

Someone claimed Magda's attention and she turned away, but Crispin drew Rona into their conversation, dispelling any awkwardness, and she was grateful. Lindsey had been right about the charm; he had it in spades. Over six feet – a fact not apparent from photographs – he was broad-shouldered and narrow-waisted, an athletic build. His face was faintly tanned, and there were lines round his eyes as though they were perpetually narrowed against some foreign sun. She sensed a certain recklessness in his manner, as though he were careless of what others thought, but perhaps that was a product of her imagination, in the light of what she already knew about him.

A bell sounded and a loud male voice requested that everyone make their way to the other room; the fashion show would start in five minutes. Rona, not wishing to intrude any longer on their party, excused herself with a smile and went ahead of them into the main room, where, to her relief, she was immediately hailed by two friends.

'Rona! We saw you across the room, but couldn't get to you! Come and join us!'

She followed them between the lacquered chairs and into the third row from the front, where they took their seats.

'A husband-free zone!' Rona remarked with a smile. 'Max is working, but what have you done with yours?'

'It's hardly their scene,' Hilary Grant replied, 'so we're having a girls' night out. We've booked a table at the Bacchus afterwards – might as well make the most of it!'

'Come and join us,' Georgia Kingston added. 'You've no one to hurry home for, have you?'

'Well, Lindsey's staying with us while her flat's being renovated, but she's out this evening, and said she wouldn't be back till eleven. So yes, I'd love to.'

Minutes later, the lights over the catwalk came on, the buzz of conversation ceased, and Magda appeared, to enthusiastic applause.

From then on there was an anticipatory silence, broken only by murmurs of appreciation and the odd burst of applause, as one model after another appeared, dressed in a succession of attractive outfits, progressing from leisure wear to smart casual, evening dresses to nightwear, and ending, as always, with a selection of stunning wedding gowns.

'Does she really stock all these?' Georgia whispered to Rona.

'She has eight boutiques, don't forget,' Rona

replied. 'If she doesn't actually stock them, she can certainly get hold of them, and there's a very quick turnover.'

'I bet. I really covet that tweed trouser-suit.'

Rona didn't see Crispin again – nor Magda, who was surrounded by a crowd as they made their way out. She'd phone her in the morning. They emerged on to Guild Street, shivering in the change of temperature, and crossed Alban Road into Market Street, the location of both the Bacchus Wine Bar and the local theatre.

'I'll be back here tomorrow,' Rona said. 'It's Max's birthday, and I'm taking him to *An Inspector Calls.*'

'Oh dear – does that mean the Bacchus two nights running?' The wine bar was popular with theatregoers, both before and after shows.

'No, actually, I've booked a theatre supper at Serendipity.'

'Oh, very posh!'

An extra chair was brought to their table, and they studied the menu, still discussing the fashion show.

'Anything you were tempted by, Hills?'

'That gorgeous cocktail dress – the one in bronze velvet. I'll certainly be speaking to Magda about that. It'd be great for Christmas.'

Georgia groaned. 'Don't talk about Christmas, for heaven's sake! We still have to survive Hallow E'en and Bonfire Night! What about you, Rona?'

'I loved them all, though I spent most of my time wondering what Crispin's crowd would go for.'

'Crispin's...?'

'Crispin Ryder. He brought half a dozen lovelies with him.'

Both her friends were staring at her. 'Crispin *Ryder* was there? At the show?'

'Yes; Magda introduced me to him.'

'Why didn't we see him?'

'Well, it's hardly surprising, among that crowd.'

'And you spoke to him? What was he like?'

'Suave, good-looking, licensed to thrill!' Rona laughed at their round eyes. 'No, actually, he was charming.'

'Do you believe all those stories about him?'

'Depends which stories. There's probably a germ of truth. He's related to Dominic Frayne.'

'Lindsey's Dominic? I never knew that.'

'I don't think he broadcasts it,' Rona said dryly.

Their attention was diverted by the arrival of the waiter, but later that night, as she prepared for bed, Rona remembered Hilary's question. *Did* she believe the stories about Crispin, having met him? And, despite his charm, she realized, with almost a premonitory tremor, that she probably did.

At breakfast, she reported on the evening to Lindsey.

'He mistook me for you,' she said.

'I must have made an impression, then,' Lindsey said complacently. 'Was he with the

Grayson girl?'

'No, six glamorous married ladies, designed to boost Magda's sales.'

'Wonder how many of them he's sleeping with!' Lindsey mused. 'Probably all six! What did you think of him?'

'Actually, he was very nice to me.'

'I bet!'

'Look, just because Dominic doesn't like him—'

'Seriously, Ro, he's bad news. Take my word for it. Attractive, certainly, but lethal.'

'That's a bit strong, isn't it? Plenty of other people break speed limits, take drugs and the rest.'

'Don't say you haven't been warned.'

Rona shrugged. 'What time are you leaving this evening?'

'Six fifteen. The car's collecting me first, as Dominic's meeting won't finish till half past.' She gave a twisted smile. 'I had a spat about it yesterday with Jonathan; just as well I'd the book group to go to; I was seething, and you weren't here to calm me down.'

'What was his problem?'

'A wealthy client wanted to see us this evening and take us to dinner afterwards. I said I couldn't make it, and he launched into a tirade, asking if Dominic was picking me up by helicopter!'

Rona laughed. 'A chauffeur-driven Daimler comes pretty close!'

'Don't you start!' Lindsey glanced at her

watch and pushed her chair back. 'Look, I must go, or I'll be in everyone else's bad books, too. See you.'

And she was gone, her high heels clattering up the stairs. Rona, with a bemused shake of her head, poured herself another coffee.

EIGHT

Lindsey leaned back against the luxurious leather and breathed a sigh of relief. She'd managed to avoid Jonathan all day – possibly because he was avoiding her – but she couldn't help wondering how the meeting with Mr Steinbeck was going. She wouldn't put it past Jonathan to make some snide remark about her. Still, she had two whole days away from the office, and determined to put all thought of it out of her mind.

She turned to Dominic beside her. 'Well, it's Friday now, so what's this surprise you wouldn't tell me about?'

'You'll know soon enough,' he said, then, forestalling her indignant movement, he laughed. 'All right, all right! Just that we'll have company on board.'

'You already mentioned the crew,' she said after a minute.

'Apart from the crew. I've invited my daughter and her fiancé to join us.'

Lindsey froze. 'Your *daughter*?'

'I thought,' Dominic continued imperturbably, 'it was a good opportunity for you and Olivia to meet, and for me to get to know Tristan. I've only seen him a couple of times.'

'But you might have warned me! I—'

'Why? Would you have brought anything different?'

'No, but—'

'Then what's the problem?'

Lindsey bit her lip. She'd not seen Dominic for over two weeks, and the prospect of having to share him appalled her.

'Did you keep her in the dark too?' she demanded.

He said evenly, 'She's aware you're coming.'

Lindsey looked at him quickly. 'So she does ... know about me?'

'As much as she needs to.'

'And what exactly does that mean?'

'What it says.' He paused. 'I hope you're not going to be this confrontational all weekend.'

There was a brief, pulsating silence. Then he put his hand over hers.

'All right, I'm sorry,' he said quietly. 'Perhaps it was unfair, but I thought you'd refuse to come if you knew Olivia would be there, and I ... wanted to see you. I've missed you. Am I forgiven?'

She turned her head to look at him, and her heart, fool that it was, turned over. 'I suppose so,' she said.

The play was good, the supper equally so. It was always a treat to come to Serendipity, Marsborough's newest and most exclusive restaurant. Part of its novelty was its layout, based on an Elizabethan knot garden, with a continuous waist-high partition snaking in and out around the tables, giving the illusion of privacy. Another was that counters displaying raw meat and fish stood either side of the room, and clients were invited to select their own, to be cooked on the grill behind the counter.

'I meant to ask how your lunch went,' Rona said, as they embarked on their dessert. 'Was Nathan pleased to get his canvas back?'

'Hadn't even missed it. I can't say I'm surprised; he hardly knew what he was doing that weekend. He's far more interested in this painting everyone's talking about – an unknown Castillo, by all accounts. It's being auctioned at Meredith's next month.'

Rona cracked the sugar on her crème brûlée. 'How do you mean, unknown?'

'No previous record of it. It's of a lady at the Spanish court, Doña Inez de los something or other, who was apparently the artist's mistress. He was court painter to the King of Spain in the early seventeenth century. It's the old story – it had been in someone's attic for years and no one had a clue what it was.'

'No provenance, then?'

'The term is "uncertain". In other words, it was probably looted by the Nazis during the war, and since no one's been able to establish a claim, the seller will get the lolly.'

'We should have looked more closely when we were clearing the studio!' Rona said. 'How was Nathan in himself, though? Did he mention Chloë?'

'No, but I felt I had to, so as soon as we sat down, I said I was sorry to hear about her, he nodded, and that was that. But later he asked after you, and when I said you were doing a bio of Elspeth Wilding, he was obviously interested. So I added that you'd like a word with him sometime, since Chloë was her friend.'

'And was he agreeable?'

'God knows. He started talking about something else, as though I'd never mentioned her.'

'Blast! I hope that doesn't mean he won't see me.'

'He'll probably be OK. You're not ready for him yet anyway, are you?'

'Not really, but I'm finding it increasingly hard to stick to my resolution to work chronologically. There are so many question marks about Elspeth's relationships with Chloë and with her family, not to mention, of course, where she's hiding.'

'So Prue Granger was right; the detective in you is coming to the fore.'

Rona grimaced. 'I was determined not to let it, but it's a losing battle. A compromise might be to see the family and let them talk freely about her, without trying to concentrate on her childhood. That way, I might get a more balanced

144

picture of her as she is now.'

Max said musingly, 'You know, I never thought of it before, but that phrase "a more balanced picture" brings it home. Writing a biography is much the same as painting a portrait, isn't it? We both work to build up layer after layer, until we have the complete person.'

'I suppose we do, but you're more likely to achieve it than I am.'

Their coffee arrived, and Rona leant back in her chair. 'So, have you enjoyed your birthday?'

'Very much. Lunch with an old friend, great presents from the family, and to crown it all, an evening at the theatre, followed by a cordon bleu meal!'

'There's more to come,' she reminded him, 'from Pops and Catherine.'

'I was rather hoping for more tonight!' Max said with a grin.

The rhythmic rocking of the boat, now at anchor, and the gentle slap of water should have been conducive to sleep, but Lindsey's brain was too busy analysing the events of the day. Dominic had told her, on the drive down, that he and his ex had finally managed to persuade Olivia, engagement notwithstanding, to stay on to take her degree. Though he'd not specifically said so, Lindsey gathered this weekend was by way of a reward.

What, she wondered now, was his verdict on the meeting between daughter and mistress? It had been awkward, there was no denying, not helped by Lindsey overhearing Olivia's reply to a sotto voce query from her fiancé: 'One of Dad's girlfriends.'

God, was that all she was? Was that how he'd described her to his daughter? When she'd first met him, Lindsey recalled, she'd been warned on all sides that he was a womanizer; several names had been bandied about, including Miranda Barrington-Selby, daughter of the Earl of Roxford. Was she herself just the latest in an ongoing line?

Beside her, Dominic slept, soundly and silently. She turned restlessly on to her side, staring into the luminous dark. And what of Olivia herself? She was pretty, certainly, her long hair carelessly caught up with a comb, her eyes clear grey and challenging. Did she resent 'Dad's girlfriends' on behalf of her mother? Or was she, as she somehow coolly implied, simply not interested?

The young man seemed pleasant enough, albeit, taking his cue from Olivia, slightly guarded towards herself. His main aim seemed to be to ingratiate himself with Dominic. It was clear the couple were very much in love, which, for all her reservations, Lindsey found touching.

Well, they had two days ahead of them in which to come to terms with one another. She could only hope harmony would prevail until they could all – surely thankfully – return to their respective homes.

Tom and Catherine's birthday gift was two

bottles of vintage port. 'We were just too late for the harvest,' Catherine said, 'but we had a wonderful day visiting the Douro vineyards, with lunch up there, and, of course, a tasting.'

'I'll make sure you're both present when I open a bottle,' Max promised.

They looked bronzed and well after their holiday, and Rona's anxiety about her father eased.

Later, when the men were talking, Catherine said to Rona, 'I phoned my friend in Buckford about Miss Burbage, and she is still alive, though she's moved to a retirement home. I have the number, if you'd like to contact her.'

'That's great, Catherine. Thanks.'

'Obviously, she could tell you about Elspeth's early schooldays, but your best bet, surely, would be the High School, where they first spotted her talent.'

'You're right, of course; I was trying to work chronologically, but as I told Max, it's getting increasingly difficult.'

'You want to skip to her departure?'

Rona smiled. 'How did you guess? After all, as long as the finished book's in sequence, it doesn't matter in what order I do my research.'

'Of course not!'

'You're laughing at me!' Rona accused her.

'Not really, but your father and I had a little bet as to how long you'd be able to resist.'

'How mortifying, to be so transparent!'

'So how do you propose to go about it?'

'By interviewing every single person she came into contact with, personally and professionally, right down to her cleaner and the person who cut her hair.'

'In the hope of what?'

'Uncovering something she might have said, some throwaway remark they'd not thought significant at the time. That she'd always wanted to live in Paris – that she'd like to visit Timbuktu – anything that might point me in the right direction and get this thing off the ground.' She gave a brief laugh. 'The trouble is, I'm out of practice on bios, and the time they take. My articles for *Chiltern Life,* even those needing considerable research, could be finished in a matter of weeks, and the more straightforward in days. I'll have to relearn patience.'

'It'll be worth it in the long run,' Catherine said comfortingly.

Citing the aftermath of seasickness, Lindsey left for work on Monday having skipped breakfast, and Rona, who'd not had a private talk with her since her return, feared the weekend afloat hadn't been an unqualified success.

'What are your plans for today?' Max asked, breaking into her thoughts.

'I really ought to track down Elspeth's paintings, which means a trip to London. I'll need to see as many as possible before I can write authoritatively, though I might need you to talk me through them.'

'Why not just go along to the Beaufort?' he asked, spreading marmalade on his toast. 'They-'ve got two or three there.'

Rona stared at him. 'Why on earth didn't you tell me?'

'I thought you knew. Didn't you see them when I had my exhibition?'

'I might have, but they wouldn't have meant anything then.' She sat back. 'That's good; I didn't really want to trail into London, though I'll have to eventually. You wouldn't like to come with me to the Beaufort, would you?'

'I would, but sadly I can't. I'm expecting a delivery from Amazon this morning. Another time.'

He pushed back his chair and bent to kiss her. 'Have fun. Speak to you later.' And he, too, was gone.

The Beaufort Gallery adjoined the Memorial Gardens, and as she passed them, Rona glanced at the stone column listing the dead of two World Wars. Within a few days, new wreaths of poppies would be laid on its steps.

At the entrance to the Gallery, she tied Gus's lead to a convenient post. 'I shan't be long,' she promised him.

The ground floor had been given over to a temporary exhibition, and she went up the open staircase to the rooms housing the permanent display. It was quiet this early on a Monday morning and she took her time, pausing in front of each painting and trying to see it through an artist's eyes.

The first Wilding she came to was on her right as she moved into the second room. It was titled

Cloudscape 4, painted in 1990, and measured eighteen inches by twenty-four. Photography was prohibited, but Rona took out a notebook and tried to put into words the overall impression it gave, a feeling almost of doom as heavy storm clouds banked over a darkening sea. It was not a comfortable picture, and she wasn't sorry to move on.

But if she'd hoped for work in a lighter vein, she was disappointed. Elspeth's second painting, farther down the room, was a still life, but not in any sense a straightforward one. While at first glance the subject appeared, conventionally enough, to be a selection of fruit heaped in a bowl, a second, closer look revealed that the bowl was cracked, most of the fruit rotten, and maggots were crawling over it.

Rona shuddered, turning with relief to a sunny landscape by an artist whose name she didn't know. The last of Elspeth's canvases was a portrait of a young girl in a party dress, and, bending to read the plaque, Rona saw it was titled *Gillian, 1999*. So the sitter was Elspeth's niece and god-daughter, Gillian Harris, on whose seventeenth birthday she had left home. As with the portrait in the Buckford studio, it radiated personality and, in this instance, the child's excitement, so that although Rona had never met the sitter, she immediately felt she knew her.

A couple had come into the room behind her and were studying the cloudscape, discussing it in low voices. As Rona passed them on her way out, she heard the woman say, 'Didn't she disappear or something?'

Indeed she did! Rona thought emphatically as she went back down the stairs; she only wished she knew why. At a desk in the foyer, postcards of assorted paintings were on sale, and she bought one of each of Elspeth's. She'd ask Max what he thought of them on Wednesday.

Gus greeted her with relieved tail-wagging. She untied his lead and they started back along Guild Street. Elspeth's paintings had depressed her, and she wasn't ready yet to return to the empty house. She'd stop for a coffee, she decided; with luck, she might see someone she knew.

But although the coffee was warming on a cool morning, and the general atmosphere relaxed and cheerful, none of Rona's friends were there, and she sat alone, Gus's head resting on her feet under the table.

Mentally, she gave herself a shake. It was pointless to let the paintings get to her; she must use them as a means of entering her subject's head and discerning her hopes and fears.

Having regained her sense of balance, she went home to the papers awaiting her.

She was still in her study that evening when Lindsey returned, calling up the stairs, 'I'm on supper duty tonight!'

'Be right down!' Rona called back.

'This is very noble of you,' she commented, entering the kitchen to find Lindsey unpacking a carrier bag.

'More self-preservation. I've no wish to survive on convenience food or takeaways, so when Max isn't here, I'm taking over as chef. Even when he is, if he'd like a break.'

'You're over your seasickness then?'

Lindsey flashed her a glance. 'Uh-huh.'

'Is that all you're going to say? How was the weekend?'

'A novel experience, in more ways than one – the prime being that we shared the yacht with Dominic's daughter and her fiancé.'

'Wow!'

'Wow indeed; especially as Dominic didn't tell me till we were actually driving down.'

'What's she like?'

'She regards me as "one of Dad's girlfriends", which pretty much sums it up.'

'Oh Linz, I'm sorry. Was she really sniffy?'

'Within the limits of politeness. She's a well-brought-up young lady.'

'And the fiancé?'

'Took his cue from her, though he thawed towards the end.'

'Well,' Rona said after a moment, 'perhaps it's a good sign, that Dominic took you to meet his family.'

Lindsey's only reply was an expressive sniff, and Rona thought it best to drop the subject.

They were finishing supper – rosemary-sprinkled lamb chops and sauté potatoes – when the phone rang, and Lindsey, being the nearer, picked it up.

'Rona Parish?' asked a voice.

'No; who shall I say is calling?'

Rona saw her twin's eyebrows go up, then she passed the phone across. 'Nathan Tait for you,' she said.

'Hello?' Rona hoped her surprise wasn't apparent in her voice.

'Oh, hello, Nathan Tait here. We haven't met, but I'm a friend of Max's.'

'I know; you had lunch together on Friday.'

'That's right; he told me you're writing Elspeth Wilding's biography, and want to ask me about Chloë. I'm afraid I cut him short – God knows what he thought. The truth is, it was a bit of a body blow, coming out of the blue like that. I just wasn't prepared for it.'

'I understand,' Rona said, though she wasn't sure she did.

'But I've had time to think about it, and though I didn't know Elspeth well, if my recollections could help at all, you're welcome to them.'

'That's good of you,' Rona replied, her spirits lifting. 'Perhaps we could meet somewhere?'

'Certainly. When are you next in London? I don't go to Buckfordshire these days.'

'I could come any day to suit you. I'm intending to go round the galleries, anyway.'

'Shall we say Thursday then? And to fit in with your plans, how about coffee at Tate Britain?'

'That would be great. Thank you.'

'Eleven o'clock?'

'Fine. How ... shall I know you?'

She heard him laugh. 'A carnation in my buttonhole, or a furled copy of *The Times* under my arm? Seriously, if you look for a stick insect with longish dark hair, you won't go far wrong.'

'I'll wear a red jacket,' Rona said. 'Till Thursday, then.'

Nathan's description of himself wasn't far out, Rona thought with amusement as she made her way towards him. His extreme thinness accentuated his height and, as if aware of it, he stooped a little. His hair was indeed overlong, curling over the collar of his open-neck shirt, and his eyes, deep in their hollows, were very dark. The hand he held out was large, bony and strong, and as it gripped hers, she had to stop herself flinching.

'I've heard so much about you over the years,' he said, pulling out a chair for her. 'I'm delighted to meet you at last.'

'And I you, especially after seeing your painting that we'd been harbouring all this time. I found it very ... challenging.'

He brushed that aside. 'First things first: how do you like your coffee, and would you like something with it?'

She requested espresso and an almond croissant, and watched while he threaded his way to the counter, returning minutes later with her order and a black coffee and Danish for himself.

'It might surprise you to know that I eat like a horse,' he said, unloading the tray. 'Though it never puts any meat on my bones.'

'A lot of my friends would envy you.'

He nodded and, niceties completed, moved straight from the banal to the business in hand. 'So, you're writing a biography of Elspeth Wilding.'

'Yes.' Tread carefully, Rona warned herself.

'I should make it clear there was no love lost between us. I imagine we resented each other in equal measure.'

'Because of Chloë?'

He nodded. 'She was the love of my life,' he said quietly. 'And it was reciprocated, till Elspeth put her spoke in.'

'In what way?'

'She was insanely jealous and did everything she could to split us up. Between you and me – and for God's sake don't quote me –' he lowered his voice still further – 'I was convinced she was in love with Chloë herself. She'd never had any men friends, Chloë seemed her only female one, and she was frankly terrified of losing her.'

He paused, staring down at the table. 'Well, she *did* lose her,' he finished bitterly. 'We both did.'

He looked up, and Rona saw the pain in his eyes. 'To be fair, Chloë was fond of her, too, and intensely loyal. She was torn in half between us, but I didn't realize the strain it caused until too late.'

His hands were clenched on the table, the knuckles white and shining. It seemed wise to steer the conversation back to Elspeth. 'You say you didn't know Elspeth well; how often did you actually meet?'

He gave his head a little shake, as though to clear it. 'Two or three times at most, and always at Chloë's instigation.' His mouth twisted. 'She tried her hardest to make us like each other, and failed miserably. But to start at the beginning, the first time I saw them was way back, at the RCA, though we were in different classes and never came into contact. Have you seen photos of Chloë? She was absolutely stunning. It was love at first sight, but I was too unsure of myself to make a move and, even then, Elspeth was ever-present.'

He bit reflectively into his Danish. 'After that, our paths separated. I had relationships over the years – of course I did – but I never forgot her, and it seemed nothing short of a miracle when, years later, we were exhibiting in the same gallery and met again. Even more miraculously, there was no sign of Elspeth. She'd far out-stripped us by that time, in both talent and fame. I took Chloë out for a meal, we went on to a club, had too much to drink, and she missed her last train home. So I took her back to my hotel and we spent the night together.'

He was silent for so long that Rona wondered if she should make some comment, though it was hard to know what. Then he started talking again, softly, as though to himself.

'It was perfect, beyond my wildest dreams, if you'll excuse the cliché. I was ... euphoric, scarcely able to believe it had happened. But it wasn't the same for Chloë; she was embarrassed by what had happened and blamed the champagne.

'I soon talked her round, though. I was still living in Chilswood then, so for a time – a very short time – we saw quite a lot of each other, even made love again. But then Elspeth realized what was happening and moved swiftly to nip it in the bud. God knows what she said to Chloë, but she changed, became cooler and began to make excuses. I knew it was down to Elspeth, and that there was a mental tug of war between us. And, damn her, she won.

'As you can imagine, I was distraught. After all those years, I had what I'd always wanted, only to have it snatched away again. I phoned, wrote, called at her house, all without avail. Then one evening when I drew up at her gate, her father came out to meet me. He said Chloë was very upset and asked me to give her a little space to sort herself out. He was very reasonable about it, so, against my will, I agreed. Six weeks later, she killed herself.'

The buzz of the café seemed a million miles away. Nathan's half-eaten Danish lay on his plate, the coffee in his cup grew cold. Finally, Rona said gently, 'I'm so sorry – I didn't mean to make you go through all that again. I just—'

'I know.' He looked up, and there were tears in his eyes 'But you see, it's impossible to speak about Elspeth without Chloë. They were inextricably entwined. It ... wasn't healthy, but there you are.'

'Have you seen Elspeth since?'

'Only across the grave at the funeral. She looked much the way I felt. I hoped she realized what she'd done.'

'So you never saw her without Chloë being there?'

He shook his head. 'Do you think she's still alive?' he asked after a moment.

The question took Rona by surprise; she'd forgotten the aborted message had not been made public. 'Yes, I do,' she replied. 'It turned out she left a message when she went, but it was erased before anyone heard it properly.'

'Did she now? Well, that's a new slant, admittedly. So where is she?'

'Ah, that's the million dollar question.'

'Well, she can burn in hell for all I care.'

And that was it, really. They'd both said all they could say, and soon afterwards they left the café, solemnly shook hands, and went their separate ways, Rona to find a corner in which to write down as much as she could remember of the conversation just ended.

Then, no longer in the mood to look at paintings, she went home.

NINE

That afternoon, Rona transferred to her computer the scribbled notes of her talk with Nathan, pausing over his opinion that Elspeth had lesbian leanings. He could, of course, know nothing of the adored schoolmaster, but was it possible, after that heartbreak, that she'd switched her affections from men to women? And, if so, was this of any significance?

Her best move, surely, would be to speak to Chloë's parents, and hear their side of the story. And while she was in Buckford, it would be useful to pay another visit to Elspeth's home; houses could reveal a lot about their owners, and she'd seen nothing of it except the garden studio.

As it was likely the Pynes didn't know of the biography, a letter of introduction seemed more appropriate than a phone call out of the blue. Accordingly she wrote one, regretting as she did so that her research would, of necessity, reopen old wounds. They could, of course, decline to see her, but she sincerely hoped they wouldn't; their opinion of Elspeth, whom they'd known far longer and far better than had Nathan, should be very interesting.

'I had a phone call from *Double N*,' Lindsey said that evening. 'The decoration's finished and everything's in place except the bed, which is due to be delivered tomorrow. So all being well, I can move back at the weekend.'

'As soon as that? I'd meant to ask Dominic for a meal while you were here, but the time's gone so quickly.'

'I've a better idea: you all come to me – an official opening, as it were. I've never cooked a meal for him, so it will be a chance to show off my prowess as well as the flat.'

'I'll miss my weekday chef!' Rona said ruefully.

'You could always cook for yourself,' Lindsey retorted. She leafed through the *Evening Standard* Rona had bought at the station, but been too preoccupied to read. 'I see our friend Crispin's in the news again.'

'What's he done this time?'

'Attended some function or other.'

Rona looked over her shoulder at the blurred photograph, and, as at the fashion show, felt a tweak of recognition, déjE0 vu. But now, staring at the static print rather than the living man, the memory slid into place. His stance, the angle of his head, the way he held his glass – all exactly as she had noted on approaching him at the Clarendon – *and had previously observed on the loose page in Naomi's album.*

'Hell's teeth!' she said suddenly, startling her sister. 'He was at the same do as Elspeth!'

Lindsey's eyebrows went up. 'When?'

'Shortly before she left. Naomi had a photo of her at the opening of a new gallery, and he was in the background.'

'So?'

'Well, they must know each other.'

'How do you make that out? They were at a public function, not a private party. How many people do you know at such do's?'

'But he was just behind her!'

'As, no doubt, were a lot of other people?'

'Well, yes, he was in a group, but—'

'Then it was probably pure chance the camera caught him when he just happened to be near her.' Lindsey paused. 'Anyway, would it be such a big deal if they did know each other? They're both public figures, after all. Though if Elspeth's as shy and retiring as you say, the same can hardly be said of Crispin, so it seems unlikely.'

'I still think it's an odd coincidence,' Rona said stubbornly, 'and I'm not sure I believe in them.'

Avril looked again at the clock. It was past eleven, and Sarah was still not back from the Parents' Evening she'd been attending at school. She might have gone for a drink with Clive, though that would be unlike her; she was scrupulous about avoiding late nights on week-days. Well, Avril reminded herself, it wasn't up to her to clock-watch – Sarah wasn't her daughter, after all.

Which brought to mind her own daughters,

and the fact that she'd not, as promised, phoned them back last week. But nor had they phoned her. Perhaps they'd seen through her fictitious 'someone at the door', and were giving her space. The implications of her weekend with Guy were, heaven knew, clear enough, but when Lindsey rang, they'd been too new and too precious to share.

She'd phone them tomorrow, she resolved; Lindsey should still be at Rona's. In the meantime, since there was really no need to wait up for Sarah, she'd go to bed.

Decision reached, she switched off the television and stood up. But as she turned to leave the room, a noise from outside startled her, an odd, shuffling sound. She froze, listening. There it was again, as if someone was stumbling about outside the window. Oh God, don't let it be a drunk!

Then, strident and shocking in the still house, came the clatter of the knocker, followed by a loud, continuous ringing of the bell. Avril gripped the back of her chair. What should she do? *God, what should she do?* Phone the police? But it'd take them ages to get here. Arm herself with a poker? And still the bell clarioned. Then, abruptly, it stopped, and it was silence that rang in her ears. She stood listening intently, praying for the sound of retreating footsteps. There was nothing.

Slowly, fearfully, she went into the hall and stood motionless, staring at the front door.

'Who's there?' Her voice came out as a croak.

She cleared her throat and tried again. 'The police are on their way!' How unconvincing that sounded! There was no response, not even the sound of someone leaving.

She could, of course, close her mind to it, go upstairs and lock herself in her room. But, she remembered suddenly, Sarah was due any time – overdue. She couldn't leave her to stumble unknowingly into whoever it was.

Avril tiptoed to the peephole and peered fearfully through. No one was in sight, and she drew a long, tremulous breath. Whoever it was had gone after all, but she needed to check, or she wouldn't sleep.

Slowly, silently, she slid back the snip of the Yale lock, at the same time turning the handle, and pulled the door open. Then, with a stifled scream, jumped back, as a dark shape that had been huddled against it fell forward across the threshold. It took her several paralysed seconds to realize it was Sarah.

'Move her as little as possible,' she'd been instructed over the phone. 'The ambulance will be with you shortly.'

So Avril sat on the hall floor, holding Sarah's hand, murmuring reassurances and praying for the sound of the siren. Her second phone call had been to Guy.

'I don't know,' she'd answered helplessly, as he questioned her urgently about the seriousness of the injuries. Better, perhaps, not to mention the blood. 'She has a bruise on her forehead, and

163

is drifting in and out of consciousness, but as far as I can see, nothing's broken. I should think—'

But he'd had no time for her theories. 'I'll see you at the hospital,' he'd said, and rung off.

And at last came the sound of an ambulance drawing up outside, and hurrying footsteps, and the calm efficiency of the paramedics. Under their ministrations, Sarah's eyes flickered fully open and she stared rather wildly up at them.

'You're all right, love,' the woman soothed her. 'You've some nasty cuts and bruises, so we're taking you to the hospital. Don't worry, your mum's here, and she's coming too.'

Avril, who'd been slipping on her coat, paused and caught Sarah's eye, but neither of them contradicted her.

'The police have been notified,' said the male paramedic. 'They're sending someone to watch the house till the locks can be changed.'

Catching Avril's blank look, he added, 'You say her bag's missing? With the door key in it?'

Avril moistened her lips. 'Yes. Yes, I hadn't thought.'

They lifted Sarah on her stretcher and carried her down the path to the waiting ambulance, and as Avril climbed in behind her, she was relieved to see a police car come spinning round the corner. Then they were on their way, and she lowered herself precariously on to the second bunk. Sarah, who'd been fitted with an oxygen mask, reached out a hand, and Avril took it between both hers.

'Your father's on his way,' she said.

Though it was a fifty-minute drive from Stokely to Marsborough, it was a good twenty minutes from Avril's home in Belmont, and she'd not been waiting long before Guy came striding down the corridor towards her. She jumped up and hurried to meet him. His face was drawn and he gripped her arms, demanding without preamble, 'What's happened? Where is she?'

'They're examining her now,' Avril said. 'Really, Guy, I don't think it's as bad as it seemed.'

His eyes had gone beyond her, searching the corridor. 'Who can I speak to?'

She was saved from answering by the appearance of a doctor in a white coat.

'Mr and Mrs Lacey? You can see Sarah now. We'll keep her in overnight for observation, but she should be able to go home tomorrow.'

'What are her injuries, doctor?' Guy demanded.

'Pretty minor, I'm glad to say. A few cuts on her face, one needing some stitches, and a nasty bruise that was responsible for the concussion. The police are waiting to interview her, but she's still in shock and I've asked them to leave it till morning.'

He glanced at his watch and, starting back the way he had come, gestured to them to follow. 'She needs to rest,' he said, over his shoulder, 'so please don't stay more than a few minutes.

You can phone in the morning to find out when to collect her.'

They halted at the entrance to a ward. 'In there,' the doctor told them. 'Ask at the nurses' station – they'll direct you to her bed.'

Nodding in response to their thanks, he hurried away. Avril stood to one side.

'You go in,' she told Guy. 'I'll wait here.'

He started to protest, but she nodded confirmation, and after a moment he went ahead. Avril seated herself on a bench against the wall, but almost immediately Guy reappeared.

'She wants to see you,' he said.

Avril looked at him in surprise. 'Are you sure?'

'Of course I'm sure! She asked where you were.'

He took her arm and they went in together. Sarah was in a bed halfway down on the right, and turned her head as they approached. There was a bandage round it, and her face, adorned with pads and plasters, was scarcely less white, though she managed a smile. She held out both hands, and, after a slight hesitation on Avril's part, they each took one.

'Sorry to have given you such a fright,' she said, her voice slightly croaky.

'Do you remember what happened?' Guy asked her.

'Only vaguely. I was walking home from school, past the parade of shops, and he must have been waiting in one of the doorways. He grabbed at my briefcase, and when I held on to it, hit me with something and knocked me down. I ... can't remember how I got home.'

Guy swore under his breath.

'Of course!' Avril exclaimed. 'For Parents' Evening, you'd have needed your briefcase. I was thinking it was your bag he took.'

'My purse and wallet were in it, though, so credit cards and about twenty pounds in cash, as well as my keys, mobile and laptop.' Her eyes filled with tears.

'Oh, love,' Guy said sympathetically. 'Did you get a look at him?'

'He was wearing a hood, and his breath smelt of beer. That's all I can remember.'

Feeling her hand tremble, Avril said quickly, 'Don't worry about it for the moment. The police will speak to you in the morning.'

Sarah nodded, tears of weakness coming to her eyes.

Guy said quietly, 'I think we should go, and let you rest – it's after one o'clock. Just relax, darling; you're safe now, and we'll be back in the morning to bring you home.'

Sarah gave him a shaky smile and turned to Avril. 'Thank you for being there,' she said. 'I could hear your voice, and it ... helped.'

'I'm glad,' Avril said, and, on impulse, bent down to kiss her cheek. Guy followed suit, and as they left the ward, Avril's own eyes were full of tears.

Rona spent some time the next morning listing as many of Elspeth's paintings as she could trace, and noting where they were displayed. The prospect of having to view a good proportion of them was daunting but would have to be done, and she was in the process of ticking them off when she was interrupted by a phone call from Naomi.

'Just wondering how you're getting on,' she began brightly, causing Rona to hope this wouldn't become a regular practice.

'Slowly, but I hope surely,' she replied cautiously.

'The reason I'm phoning is to ask when you're planning to see my parents? Ever since you were here last week, they've been gearing themselves up to be interviewed.'

Rona felt a spurt of irritation. 'I'm sorry, but where possible, I try to see people when I'm ready for their particular input.'

'So I can't give them a definite date?'

'Not at the moment, I'm afraid. I promise to give them plenty of notice, and arrange a time that's convenient for them.'

There was a brief silence, and Rona wondered if she'd taken offence. But then Naomi said quietly, 'I'm sorry; I did tell them we shouldn't hassle you, but they're rather uptight, as you can imagine, and made me promise to call you. Please don't worry that I'll be on the phone every five minutes – I assure you I won't.'

Rona released her breath. 'Thanks for being so understanding. I'm sorry, too, that I can't be more definite. Actually, there is something I wanted to ask you: I always try to visit the homes of my subjects – it's amazing how help-ful it can be – and if you remember, when you took me to Elspeth's studio, all I saw of the house was the kitchen. I was wondering if you'd have any objection to a return visit? Obviously I wouldn't invade her privacy in any way.'

'Just to look at the rooms, you mean?'

'Yes, that's all; so I can picture her living there.'

'Well, of course, if you think it would help. When are you thinking of?'

'Whenever's convenient for you. I'm hoping to be in Buckford one day next week; perhaps I could phone you when I know which? If it fits in with you, perfect, but if not, we can fix another time.'

'Right. I'll wait to hear from you.'

'Thank you.' A sudden thought struck her. 'Before you go, do you happen to know if Elspeth knew Crispin Ryder?'

'*Who*?'

'Crispin Ryder. You know, the millionaire playboy.'

'Good heavens, why ever should she?'

'He was standing behind her in that magazine photo.'

'*Was* he? You never said.'

'I didn't recognize him till later.'

'Well, I very much doubt she'd know him; he's just the type she'd run a mile from.'

It had been worth a try, Rona thought philo-sophically, and, as they ended the conversation, hoped the Wildings wouldn't learn of her decision to see Chloë's parents before them. But, particularly after meeting Nathan, she felt the Pynes' would be the more pertinent interview. It was doubtful whether Elspeth's parents could add much to what Naomi had told her, and, rightly or wrongly, Rona suspected that a broader view would be obtained by speaking to her brother, whom she intended to make her next priority.

Impatiently, she pushed back her chair and went to switch on the kettle, spoon coffee into a cafetière mug, and take milk from the fridge she'd had installed to save the two-flight trek to the kitchen. She felt in need of a stimulus before returning to her list of paintings.

A bark from Gus in the hall below indicated the arrival of the post, and Rona went down to investigate. A stiffened manila envelope lay on the mat, addressed to her in a hand she didn't recognize. She slit it open, and found herself gazing at a photograph of a young woman in cap and gown, holding a diploma.

She was absolutely stunning, Nathan had said of Chloë, and he was right. The most striking thing about her was her smile, which lit up her whole face. Her hair, curling under the cap, was a rich chestnut, her eyes a vivid blue, and there was an air of such infectious happiness about her that Rona found herself returning the smile.

She felt inside the envelope and extracted a scrawled note: *After our meeting, I thought you'd be interested to see the enclosed. No need to return it – I have another copy. Good luck*

170

with the book. Nathan.

He must have posted it within hours of leaving her, Rona thought, and hoped the memories she'd revived hadn't been too painful. Slowly, photograph in hand, she returned to the study.

They'd gone back to Belmont for what remained of the night, it not being worth Guy's driving back to Stokely. The policeman was still on duty, and had checked their identity before letting them into the house. The cloth Avril had used to stem Sarah's bleeding still lay on the floor, and she'd kicked it under the stand, hoping Guy hadn't noticed.

After an initial awkwardness, they'd spent the night together, both of them needing the comfort of each other's presence. Avril had felt a little guilty, not only that they were taking advantage of Sarah's assault, but making love in the bed she'd shared with Tom. Sensing this, Guy had offered to sleep in another room, but neither of them seriously considered it.

It had been agreed he would stay for the weekend, to be with Sarah while she recovered. 'And I'll make up the bed in Rona's room,' Avril said, 'so we can observe the proprieties, at least in public!'

They'd phoned the hospital straight after breakfast, and learned that Sarah had spent a comfortable night and would be discharged after the doctors' rounds at about eleven.

'Another cup of coffee, then,' Avril said.

'I should ring the locksmith straight away,' Guy advised. 'If he can come this morning, fine; we don't both need to collect her. In any case, the police have knocked off, now the house is occupied, and it shouldn't be left empty till the locks have been changed.'

'Though actually,' Avril mused, refilling his cup, 'since the attack happened by the shops and he certainly wouldn't have followed her home, he won't know where she lives.'

'There could have been something identifying her in the bag,' Guy pointed out. 'A letter addressed to her, or something. It's not worth taking the risk.'

Avril nodded reluctantly, and, taking out the *Yellow Pages*, made the call. They promised to send someone later that morning.

'Anyway, it's better you should go alone,' she said. 'It will give you some private time together.'

'She seems to have dropped her hostility towards you, though, wouldn't you say?'

Avril smiled ruefully. 'Only in the heat of the moment, because I'd helped her. It will probably come back!'

'Have faith!' he said.

The locksmith arrived soon after Guy had left for the hospital. It had been agreed that, since Sarah had only the front door key in her possession, only that one needed changing.

While he worked, Avril made up the spare room bed, picked some flowers from the garden for Sarah's dressing table, and planned the weekend meals. She had catered only for herself, as Sarah usually spent the weekends with Clive – who, Avril thought belatedly, ought to be told of the assault – why hadn't he walked her home? – though he'd no doubt have heard of it at school, which they'd phoned first thing to explain her absence. The receptionist had asked if she'd be back on Monday, but Guy couldn't tell her; it would depend on what he learned at the hospital.

The locksmith had finished, and, having supplied her with a set of three new keys, gone on his way. The dining room table was laid for lunch and a fish pie was cooking in the oven. Now the house could be safely locked, she could have dashed to the shops for more provisions, but Guy and Sarah might be back any minute, so it must wait till after lunch. At least, she thought, she could make that delayed phone call to Rona.

'Mum!' Rona greeted her. 'I've been meaning to phone you. How are things?'

'A little hectic, actually,' Avril replied, and told her of Sarah's attack.

'But that's awful!' Rona exclaimed. 'Is she all right?'

'I hope so; they're supposed to be discharging her today. Guy's gone to collect her, but they're not back yet. In the meantime, I've had to get a new lock for the front door. I'll give you a key next time I see you.'

'And ... is Guy staying the weekend, or taking Sarah home with him?'

'They're both staying here.' Avril drew a breath. 'He'll be sleeping in your room, but ... he didn't last night.'

'Mum, I'm so glad,' Rona said warmly.

'Are you? Really?'

'Of course. It's quite serious, then? We wondered, after that weekend—'

'I cut Lindsey off, I know. It was silly, but I was still getting used to the idea myself. And yes, I think it is serious. I'd meant to phone this evening, when you'd both be together, but Max would also be there, and it might have been awkward.'

Rona laughed. 'He's not a prude, you know! He'll be as pleased as I am, and so will Linz.'

'You must all get to know each other, but I don't want to rush things, and at the moment, of course, Guy can only think of Sarah.'

'Do you want me to pass both bits of news to Lindsey? She's going home tomorrow, did you know?'

'No, I didn't. The flat's finished then?'

'Yes; she phoned half an hour ago, to say the bed's been delivered. That was the last out-standing item.'

'I can't wait to see it!'

Rona didn't comment. She doubted that her mother would be included in what Lindsey had referred to as 'the official opening,' since that would also involve inviting Tom and Catherine, rather than the intimate little dinner Rona guessed her twin was planning.

Fortunately, Avril ended the conversation by

exclaiming, 'Here's Guy's car now – I'll have to go. Love to you all, and I'll be in touch later.'

Their return had been delayed because the police were still with Sarah when Guy arrived at the hospital. They'd produced a laptop with a series of staring faces, and asked if she could pick out any of them. She couldn't. The attack had been gone over in detail, the contents of her briefcase noted, and a stop put on her credit cards.

It was Guy who had relayed all this; Sarah herself was still pale and subdued, though the gauze bandage was gone and those on her face were neater.

'They think she got the cuts when she fell,' Guy added. 'There were shards of glass in some of them, and a broken milk bottle was found at the scene. The police think it had been smashed deliberately, to use as a weapon, but thank God that didn't happen.'

'Was there anything confidential on your laptop or mobile?' Avril asked anxiously, as they sat down to their belated lunch.

'The mobile was Pay as You Go,' Sarah replied, 'and my credit needed topping up, so I wish him joy of that. It listed my friends' numbers, but they're not exactly secret. And the laptop should be protected by its password, though there's nothing really sensitive on it either, and, thank God, it's all backed up. All things considered, it could have been a lot worse.'

She retired to bed for an hour after lunch, Avril went out to do her shopping, and Guy dozed over his newspaper. He, too, had advised his office he'd be unavailable today.

After the evening meal, Sarah excused herself. 'A good night's sleep will put me right,' she assured them. Then, in the doorway, she paused, adding with a half-smile, 'And please don't sleep in separate rooms on my account. I'm a big girl now.'

She was gone before either of them could think of a reply.

TEN

Lindsey arrived back that evening with a case of six bottles of wine.

'To thank you for having me,' she said.

'Linz, there was no need for that! Good heavens—'

'It's the least I can do. I've just been to the flat with Nina and Nicole, and it's great! Like a completely new home, modern, but comfortable, and with zingy colours everywhere! I can't wait for you to see it!'

'We'll see it tomorrow, surely, when we help unload your things,' Rona pointed out, but her sister shook her head.

'Actually, no. I'd be glad of your help to load

the car, but I want to unload it slowly myself. Half the fun will be deciding where to put everything, and slotting it in place. Then, once I'm satisfied with it, I'll fix that dinner with you and Dominic.'

'Mum's hoping to see it soon, too,' Rona said. 'She phoned at lunchtime. Sarah was mugged last night on the way back from school, and Mum had to go with her to the hospital.'

Max and Lindsey expressed concern. 'Was she seriously hurt?' 'Is she OK?'

'Guy had gone to collect her and bring her home. She was unconscious for a while, which was why the hospital kept her in, but I think she's more or less all right.'

Rona paused, glancing at her sister. 'She also apologized for cutting you short when you rang, but as we thought, things have moved on between her and Guy. I asked if it was serious, and she thinks it is.'

'Well, that's great news!' Max said with satisfaction.

Lindsey was nodding. 'I thought as much. She was trying to play it down, but I could see she was really interested. Let's just hope nothing goes wrong.'

So the next morning Max and Rona helped carry the boxes and cases down to Lindsey's car and pile them in the boot.

'Let us know how you get on,' Rona said, as Lindsey gave her a hug.

'Of course! And thank you both so much, for

putting up with me for two weeks!'

'Putting you up, not putting up with you,' Max corrected. 'It's been a pleasure.' And, in truth, it had gone much better than he'd feared. There'd been no flare-up of tension between them.

'I'll miss her,' Rona said, as they surveyed the empty-looking studio. Lindsey had stripped the bed, taking the sheets down to the washing machine, and Max now dismantled it and stood it back in its corner, while Rona unplugged the lamp, ready for its return to the study.

'Wasted space, really,' she remarked, looking about her.

'What do you suggest we do? Take in a lodger?'

'No, it's great, really, to have somewhere to stack what we're not using. No doubt in a week or two it'll look as though we never cleared it.'

The post had arrived by the time they reached the hall, bringing a letter postmarked Buckford, which Rona guessed was from the Pynes. She opened it apprehensively.

'Oh, thank goodness!' she exclaimed. 'They are willing to see me – that's a relief.'

'And who might "they" be?' Max enquired.

'Chloë's parents. They suggest Tuesday afternoon, and will expect me unless they hear to the contrary.'

'Well, for God's sake treat them gently,' Max said. 'They'll no doubt be blaming either Nathan or Elspeth for her death – probably both – and this will bring it all back again.'

Rona nodded. 'I'll ring Naomi, and see if

Tuesday's convenient for going back to the house.'

During the weekend, Clive Gregory called round twice to see Sarah, bearing bunches of flowers. Although, as sports master, he'd not been required to attend the Parents' Evening, he still blamed himself for not escorting her home.

Guy returned to Stokely on Sunday evening, and Avril waited, somewhat anxiously, to see if Sarah's new friendliness continued in her father's absence. After her parting comment on Friday, it had seemed pointless to stick to their separate-room intention. Sarah hadn't mentioned it again, and, after a slightly embarrassed breakfast on Saturday, they'd relaxed. It wasn't, in fact, till Avril brought in her breakfast on Monday – Sarah having insisted, against both Avril and her father's advice – on returning to school – that she indirectly referred to it.

'It was very good of you to dish out the TLC on Friday,' she said, her eyes on her plate, 'especially after I've been such a cow. I really appreciated it.'

Slightly taken aback, Avril murmured, 'I only did what anyone would in the circumstances.'

'Phone an ambulance, yes; I'm not so sure about holding my hand and continuing to talk to me, even when I couldn't respond. I'm ... glad Dad's found someone like you. He deserves to.'

Avril felt a lump in her throat. 'Thank you,' she managed to say.

Sarah looked up with a grin. 'Which is not to

179

say I'll be sweetness and light from now on, so make the most of it!'

Avril laughed, grateful for the change of mood. 'Thanks for the warning!' she said.

When Rona phoned Naomi on Monday morning, it transpired that she was busy the next day.

'No problem, though,' she added. 'Tuesday's Mary Strong's day, so she'll show you round. I'll tell her to expect you about eleven.'

Which, Rona thought with satisfaction, would kill two birds with one stone, since she'd been planning to interview the cleaner.

'Is there anywhere I shouldn't go?' she asked.

'Good Lord, no; it's only a house, after all, and Mary will be there. It's hardly an invasion of privacy,' Naomi added with a touch of sarcasm.

So, having left Gus with Max, Rona set off once more for Buckford, wondering what she'd have learned by the time she returned.

'Hirsute' was the adjective that best described Mary Strong. She was a short, square woman, with straight dark hair, very thick eyebrows and the hint of a moustache. The arms beneath her rolled-up sleeves were muscular and thatched with black hair.

'Mrs H said you were coming,' she greeted Rona, stepping to one side to allow her to enter. 'Wanting to have a look round, she said.'

'I'd also be grateful for a word with you, Mrs Strong,' Rona said tactfully. 'I believe you've worked for Miss Wilding for a long time?'

'Bless you, yes. Like family, she said I was.'

'It must have been a shock, when she went off like that.'

The woman flashed her a calculating glance. 'Yes and no,' she said.

Rona's interest quickened. 'You knew she was going?'

'Let's say I wasn't as surprised as the rest of 'em.'

'How was that?'

'She'd been talking of it for some time – vague, like. Said she'd like to get away, go on one of them Sabbath things.'

'Sab...? Oh, sabbatical, you mean?'

'That's it.'

So, despite the impression Naomi had given, the disappearance wasn't totally unpremeditated. 'Mrs Harris might have told you I'm writing about Miss Wilding, so anything you can tell me about her will be very helpful.' Rona hesitated. 'Did she seem happy to you, before she went?'

'Happier than she had been, and that's a fact. It took her an age to get over Miss Chloë.'

'I'm sure.'

'She started going to London, regular like, and that perked her up. I was coming in three days a week then, and she'd say, "If I'm not here on Monday, Mary, just let yourself in, same as always."'

Rona mulled this over. 'Do you know why she went? To the theatre? Shopping? Exhibitions?'

'She never said and I didn't ask. She told me as much and as little as she wanted me to know.

181

One day she said, "Mary, if I do go away, it'll be on the spur of the moment. The family will make a fuss, but that can't be helped. And I'll come back just as sudden when the mood takes me, so mind you keep the house clean." And I have. Everything is exactly as she left it.'

'She didn't say how long she'd be gone?'

Mary Strong shook her head.

'So you don't think ... something might have happened to her?'

'Course not. If it had, we'd have heard, wouldn't we?'

Not necessarily, Rona thought, but did not say.

'Well – ' the cleaner wiped her hands on her apron – 'where do you want to start?'

They'd been talking in the hall, to the accompaniment of the grandmother clock gently ticking the minutes away at the foot of the stairs. Opposite Rona, at the end of the hall, lay the kitchen she'd passed through on her way to the studio, and on either side of her a single door stood ajar.

'Perhaps in here?' She indicated the one on her right, and Mary Strong pushed it open to reveal a small dining room. There was barely room for the oval table and four chairs – Chippendale, by the look of them – but twin mirrors, hung on opposite walls, gave, by their succession of reflections, an illusion of space. A corner cupboard with a display of Crown Derby completed the furnishings. There was a faint smell of lavender – furniture polish, no doubt.

Charming though it was, the room had an air

of being seldom used, and retained no essence of its owner. As Rona emerged, Mary Strong, who'd waited in the hall, pushed open the door opposite and gestured for her to go in. Here, the effect was of a country cottage – a couple of deep, comfortable armchairs, a small television set, book shelves and occasional tables. Over the fireplace hung an exquisite Dutch Interior, and in the empty grate a fire was ready laid, screened by a vase of dried grasses.

And here Elspeth came into focus. Rona could imagine her relaxing after a strenuous day's painting – curling up in one of the chairs, perhaps with a TV supper, planning her next work – or maybe her 'sabbatical'. And from the window at the far end, the studio, surely never far from Elspeth's thoughts, could be glimpsed, solid and reassuring in its grey stone.

A little reluctantly, since she'd have liked to linger, she rejoined Mary Strong, and the woman led the way upstairs. There were two bedrooms over the downstairs rooms, and a bathroom above the kitchen. The latter must have been installed well after the house was built, but was appropriately equipped with a claw-footed bath, deep, old-fashioned basin, and lavatory with polished wooden seat. Rona didn't bother going inside.

The first door was that of the spare room. It contained a bed covered with a quilt, but the underlying flatness suggested a bare mattress beneath. There was a dressing table with a frill round its base, a built-in wardrobe, painted white, and a single chair. The room was completely devoid of atmosphere, and Rona felt mounting disappointment. Apart from some empathy in the sitting room, this visit was proving a waste of time. It seemed Elspeth's desire for privacy encompassed even her home.

Again, Mary Strong was waiting on the landing, and silently pushed open the last door, that of the main bedroom; and here at last the full force of its owner's personality came alive, as though Elspeth had just left the room.

Rona paused, taking it in. A faint, indefinable scent hung in the air, possibly emanating from one of the glass bottles on the dressing table. A silver-backed mirror lay next to them, alongside a cut-glass tray bearing a discarded cameo brooch, its pin still open. The bed was prettily feminine, a lace spread and frilled pillow, and a silk dressing gown hung behind the door. Why hadn't she taken it with her? Rona puzzled.

On one wall hung a set of four small etchings of old-time Buckford, and on another, a signed Russell Flint print. The bedside table held a pretty lamp, a carafe covered with an upturned glass and a small enamel clock, showing the correct time. The faithful Mary Strong must either wind it or replace batteries as needed.

What had been Elspeth's thoughts, the last time she stood here? Had she taken a swift, final look round, wondering if there was anything else she might need – the little clock, the silk dressing gown?

Rona sighed, accepting that though she might

speculate, she'd never know the answer. She returned to the landing, smiled her thanks at Mary Strong, and followed her down the stairs.

'Mrs H said as you wouldn't bother with the studio,' she said.

'That's right – I spent some time there the other day. Well, that was most interesting. Thanks so much for showing me round, Mrs Strong. I hope I haven't delayed you.'

The woman shrugged. 'I'll have missed my usual bus, that's for sure.'

Rona felt a stab of guilt. 'Oh, I'm sorry. Can I give you a lift somewhere?'

Mary's face brightened. 'Well, that's good of you, miss, if it's no trouble. If you'd like to wait in the sitting room, I'll just rinse through my dusters.'

'Of course.'

Rona, glad of the extra time, walked over for a closer look at the painting. She'd always liked Dutch Interiors and this was a particularly good example. After a moment, she moved on to the bookcase and idly examined its contents. Only a couple of volumes were on art, she noted, the majority, of course, being in the studio. Here, the mix was eclectic – Penguin classics, detective stories and several novels with flashes on their jackets, proclaiming them the winners of literary prizes.

She took one down, and as she riffled through the pages, a scrap of paper fell out and spiralled to the floor. Not wanting to mar the room's tidiness, Rona bent to retrieve it – and started

185

almost guiltily as a voice said from the doorway, 'That's me done for today, so if there's nothing else, we can lock up.'

Slipping it into her pocket, Rona cast a last, valedictory, glance round the hall, and went outside, waiting while the alarm was set and the door securely locked. If there were any secrets here, she concluded ruefully, the house had held on to them.

Half an hour later, having dropped off the grateful Mary Strong at a nearby council estate, Rona drove into town, deciding to lunch at the coffee shop before going to meet the Pynes.

Like the Harrises, they lived in a bungalow, but this one, as Rona could see from its widened doorway, had been adapted for wheelchair access.

Mrs Pyne opened the door – Jackie, as she introduced herself – and shook Rona's hand. She was a small, neat woman, in whose faded hair it was possible to detect a hint of her daughter's rich chestnut.

'Please come in,' she said, leading the way into the front room, where a log fire burned. 'I hope it's not too hot for you, but Reg feels the cold.' And, to her husband, 'Rona Parish, dear.'

Mr Pyne, seated beside the fire in his wheelchair, nodded and smiled. 'Please excuse my not getting up,' he said with wry humour.

Rona went quickly to shake his hand. 'It's so good of you both to see me. I know it can't be easy for you.'

'My dear, by this time we're inured to talking about our daughter.'

'I don't want to intrude,' Rona assured him. 'It's your memories of Elspeth Wilding I'm most interested in.'

'Ah, Elspeth.' Jackie Pyne indicated a chair to Rona, and seated herself on the sofa opposite. 'There's no news of her, I suppose?'

'No. But as I explained in my letter, her family have asked me to write her biography.'

Reg gave her one of his peculiarly sweet smiles. 'Forgive us if we know you better as a writer for *Chiltern Life*,' he said. 'We particularly enjoyed your series on Buckford's eight-hundredth anniversary.'

Rona smiled back. 'I'm glad. I enjoyed doing it.' She paused. 'I believe Chloë met Elspeth at the High School?'

'That's right,' Jackie Pyne confirmed bitterly, 'and from then on, she dominated her life.'

'Now, love,' Reg remonstrated gently, adding to Rona, 'There's no denying Elspeth was the stronger character, but Chloë thought of her as the sister she'd never had, and loved her accordingly.'

'How strong an influence was she on her becoming an artist?'

'Very strong.' Reg again. 'If they'd not met, I doubt if Chloë would have considered it as a career. She'd always enjoyed painting, and been good at it, but she was more academic than Elspeth, and could have made her mark in a variety of fields.'

187

'Instead of which,' Jackie put in, 'she was always in Elspeth's shadow.'

'You must have come to know Elspeth pretty well. What was your impression of her?'

'Ah, now there's a question!' Reg said ruefully. 'She was always a complex girl; she could be charming when she chose, and generous to a fault; but where her art was concerned, she was ruthless. Nothing and no one was allowed to interfere with it.'

'And she was so *possessive!*' Jackie took up the story. 'She wanted Chloë all to herself. Several men fell for her over the years, but none of them came to anything. Quite frankly, we wondered if that was down to Elspeth. It sounds unkind, but she was – and no doubt still is – totally self-centred, and if something didn't fit in with her plans, she'd take the necessary steps to remove it.'

'Nathan Tait was the first to stand up to her,' Reg said quietly. 'And look what happened then.'

There was a taut silence, which Rona dared not break. Then Jackie drew a deep breath.

'I felt really sorry for Nathan,' she said more calmly. 'It was obvious he adored Chloë, and she was so happy and excited at the beginning. Flowers and phone calls and boxes of chocolates – bless her, having been in Elspeth's shadow all those years, she wasn't used to being the centre of attention. I think – I'm sure – they could have been happy together.'

'So, what happened?'

'Elspeth happened,' Jackie said flatly. 'It's my belief she was jealous; after all, no one had ever been wild about *her*. But whatever the reason, Chloë started to cool towards him, make excuses when he phoned.'

'She was living at home?'

'Yes – that was another thing; when they left the RCA, Elspeth bought a house and converted a disused building in the grounds into a state-of-the-art studio. Chloë was involved from the word go, helping her plan the studio and so on, and she assumed they'd be living there together, as they had at uni and the RCA. It seemed ideal – but Elspeth soon disabused her of the idea. Said that now she was starting to paint seriously, she needed her own space, and sharing her studio was out of the question.

'We could tell Chloë was hurt, but there was nothing to be done. She looked half-heartedly at one or two places but none of them were suitable, so we suggested she live at home, and rent a studio in the town. Which was what she did, but she still spent all her spare time with Elspeth.'

Though she knew to the contrary, Rona asked tentatively, 'Did Nathan accept Chloë's change of heart?'

'Far from it,' Reg said grimly. 'He positively bombarded her – wouldn't take no for an answer. In the end, she was in such a state I had to have a word with him, ask him to give her some space.'

'And he agreed?'

'Grudgingly, but by then she'd had this big flare-up with Elspeth, and that got to her as much as the Nathan business. It was as though she'd become so dependent on her, she couldn't function without her. And however often she insisted it was over with Nathan, Elspeth refused to believe her. Punishing her, I suppose.'

He stared into the fire for some time, before saying sombrely, 'But though we knew she was upset, we'd no idea how deep it went. Until it was too late.' He looked at his wife.

'Jackie, love, should we show this young lady the letter?'

Rona looked quickly at Mrs Pyne, seeing the tremor cross her face. 'It's private, Reg,' she protested in a low voice.

'I know,' he persisted gently, 'but it explains better than we can. And it shows how hard Elspeth could be.'

Tears had come into Jackie's eyes, but after a moment she nodded, went over to the bureau and took an envelope out of one of its drawers.

'It's from Chloë,' she said unsteadily. 'As you can see, Elspeth returned it unread – we were the ones who opened it. We found it in her desk after she died.'

She held it out to Rona, who hesitated. 'Are you quite sure you want me to read it?'

The Pynes nodded, and Rona took it from her. Elspeth's address had been heavily scored through and replaced by Chloe's, and both postmarks were dated the week prior to Chloë's death. Apprehensively, she slid out the single sheet and read it quickly, then again more slowly.

Dearest Ellie,

It's so stupid *to let this Nathan business come between us! How can I make you believe he means nothing to me, and never really did? All right, we had a bit of a fling, but that's all it was. It wouldn't even have got off the ground if I'd not had too much champagne that evening! I'm sorry I insisted on you meeting him, but I so wanted you to like each other. Instead, it seemed to drive a wedge between us. I've tried to tell him it's over, but he won't accept that, and keeps phoning and sending flowers. To tell the truth, I'm getting a bit desperate.*

I shan't see him again, I promise. I got Dad to ask him to give me some space – perhaps that will do the trick. So can we now put it all behind us? Our friendship's too important to let it end over something so trivial. I'll phone again tomorrow – please, please speak to me this time!

All my love,
Chloë

A different slant on the affair from the one Nathan had related. Which of them had angled it to suit their purpose?

Rona replaced the sheet in its envelope and returned it to Jackie. 'You think this contributed to her killing herself?' she asked gently.

Reg gave a weary shrug. 'She was certainly torn between them, though it scarcely seemed enough—'

He broke off, brushing a hand across his eyes. '"While the balance of her mind was disturbed,"' he continued after a minute. 'Isn't that what they say? And I believe it was *exactly* that. I honestly don't think she planned it. Granted, she was unhappy, but suppose the train hadn't arrived at that crucial moment, offering a speedy way out? Her depression might have gradually lifted, and she'd have come out the other side. That's the thought that haunts me.'

Jackie Pyne, who'd remained standing, patted her husband's hand. 'I'll make some tea,' she said.

Neither of them spoke while she was out of the room, but it wasn't an awkward silence. Reg Pyne continued to gaze into the fire, Rona to sit quietly, thinking over what she'd learned and what she still needed to know.

Jackie returned, with a tray bearing tea and a plate of biscuits, and Rona ventured her last remaining question.

'Did Elspeth keep in touch after Chloë's death?'

They both shook their heads. 'She wrote, of course,' Jackie said, 'expressing her horror and sadness, and "regret" that "differences" had come between them. And I must say she seemed genuinely upset at the funeral; but after that, nothing. I think it would have been too painful on both sides.

'Nathan wrote us a lovely letter,' she continued, passing Rona her cup of tea. 'But although he attended the funeral, he didn't come back here afterwards, so we didn't have the chance to speak to him.'

'Perhaps that would have been too painful, too.'

'Perhaps.'

Rona hesitated. 'I should tell you that I met him in London, last week.' They both stared at her, and she added apologetically, 'I'd have mentioned it earlier, but when you started to speak about him, I didn't want to interrupt. I'd intended to contact him, but actually it was he who approached me; he had lunch with my husband, Max mentioned I was writing Elspeth's biography, and Nathan suggested we meet.'

'And what did he tell you?'

'Basically, what you have, but also that he'd fallen for Chloë way back, at the Royal College of Art.'

The Pynes both looked surprised. 'We didn't know that.'

'It was worship from afar – they never actually met, and he couldn't believe his luck when he found her again, years later.'

'That makes it all the more poignant, then,' Jackie said sadly.

'Like you, he blamed Elspeth for coming between them.'

'There was no other explanation.'

Rona nodded, but she was thinking of the letter she'd just read, and Chloë's insistence that she'd never really cared for Nathan. Was that just to placate her friend, or was the truth that she'd not been as spineless as they all thought, and finishing with her lover had been her own, unprompted, decision? In which case, Elspeth's refusal to believe her must have been doubly frustrating.

Jackie went to the bureau, lifted down the framed photograph on top of it, and handed it to Rona. It was of Chloë's graduation, similar to the one Nathan had sent her.

Rona studied it for a moment – the brilliant smile, the air of happy confidence. 'She's lovely,' she said, handing it back.

'There are a couple of albums upstairs,' Jackie said with touching eagerness. 'Of Chloë when she was younger, and some of Elspeth, too. Would you like to see them?'

And without waiting for confirmation, she hurried out of the room, returning with two faded photograph albums.

'Come and sit on the sofa,' she invited, 'so we can look at them together. There actually aren't many of Elspeth,' she admitted apologetically. 'She never liked being photographed, even as a child.' Rona remembered the face-pulling in Naomi's album.

Not unnaturally, it was Chloë who dominated her parents' album, though there were regular appearances of younger versions of both Reg and Jackie – on the beach, in a swimming pool, in the back garden.

But though Rona murmured appreciative comments as the pages were turned, it was soon clear that Nathan's 'stunning' swan had been by way of an ugly duckling. In her early teens, Chloë was a tall, gawky girl with an unruly cloud of hair, worn variously long, short, up, down, in a plait over her shoulder, or tied back in a ponytail. In the only close-up, her mouth, wide open in laughter, seemed on the large side, and her teeth uneven. Rona accepted she was being uncharitable; Chloë simply looked what she'd no doubt been, a healthy, happy girl, enjoying life to the full. Too bad that life was destined to be so short.

Of Elspeth, as Jackie had belatedly warned her, there was very little, just a few prophetic snaps of the two girls painting, in a garden and once in a summerhouse. In these she'd been caught unawares, and it was pure chance that the familiar curtain of hair fell across her face as she concentrated on the task in hand. Unlike her friend, Elspeth's hairstyle appeared unchanging throughout childhood and into adulthood.

As they came to an end, Rona glanced again at the framed photograph, still lying on the sofa beside her. Though recognizably the same girl, her gawkiness had given way to confidence, her mouth, though still generous, curved in a smile that lit up her face, and her eyes, barely discernible in the old snaps, were large and dark-lashed. Stunning indeed.

Jackie closed the album and sat for a moment with her hand on the cover, a gentle caress. Somewhat belatedly, Rona indicated the pictures on the walls. 'May I?'

'Of course.'

There were four paintings in all, each signed *C Pyne* in the lower right-hand corner. Three were abstracts, soft colours swirling into each other in intricate patterns, soothing and pleasurable to look at. The fourth was of a beach surrounded by cliffs, the tide breaking on the sand in creamy ridges, gulls white slashes in the blueness of the sky. At the water's edge, three figures had been sketched in, a man, a woman and a child, whose red dress provided a contrasting splash of colour.

'She gave us that for our Silver Wedding,' Reg said. 'It's where we always spent our holidays when she was young.' There were tears in his voice.

'What a lovely idea,' Rona said.

There was little more to say, and she didn't return to her seat. 'Thank you so much for agreeing to see me, and especially for showing me the letter. I do hope it hasn't been too upsetting for you.'

'We're always glad of an excuse to talk about Chloë,' her father said. He clasped Rona's hand between his paper-dry ones. 'Good luck with the book,' he added, 'but I hope you've not forsaken *Chiltern Life* completely.'

She smiled back at him. 'No, I'm only taking a sabbatical,' she assured him, the word striking a chord in her mind.

Jackie saw her to the door. 'We'll be interested to read it in due course,' she said.

'I'll send you a copy,' Rona promised.

Jackie waited until she reached the pavement,

then, with a final wave, closed the door. Rona started the car and drove slowly down the road till she was out of sight of the bungalow, where she stopped and switched off the engine. She wanted to collect her thoughts before embarking on the long drive home.

Her day in Buckford had not, after all, been unproductive. Chloë's tragic letter had been an unlooked-for bonus, not least as added proof of Elspeth's supreme self-centredness. And at her house, the talk with Mary Strong had put a new slant on things, and Rona felt she knew her at least a little better.

But not well enough, she added silently, as she started up the car. With luck, Richard Wilding might fill in a few gaps.

ELEVEN

The next evening, just before Max came home, Rona phoned Richard Wilding.

The voice that answered was brusque. 'Yes?'

'Mr Wilding? This is Rona Parish.' She paused, but he didn't help her. 'Perhaps Mrs Harris mentioned that I'd be contacting you?'

'On this biography? Yes, she did.' Scarcely more forthcoming.

'I wondered when it would be convenient to see you?'

A sigh came over the line. 'Is it really necessary?'

'I think so, yes, if I'm to get your sister in perspective.'

'It would have to be an evening or weekend, obviously.'

'Fine; which would you prefer?'

'Oh God, I don't know! Just a minute, I'll have a word with my wife.'

A hand was put over the mouthpiece and Rona could hear muted voices. Then: 'I could spare you an hour on Friday, around six-thirty.'

Damn; that would interfere with Max being home. 'That'd be fine. Thank you.'

'I presume you have the address?'

'Yes, thanks.'

'Friday it is, then,' he said, and rang off.

'And goodbye to you, too,' Rona muttered, and turned as Max came down the stairs.

'Who was that on the phone?'

'Elspeth's unpleasant brother. He doesn't want to see me at all, but has graciously agreed to "spare me an hour" on Friday evening. I'm sorry, Max; I do try to avoid Fridays.'

He kissed her. 'No matter, let's make an evening of it. I'll come in with you, twiddle my thumbs while you do the interview, then we'll have a decent meal somewhere. How about that?'

'Perfect!' she said gratefully.

Having spent all Wednesday and most of Thursday morning working, Rona reckoned she'd earned a respite, and decided to go out for lunch. She phoned Lindsey's office to suggest meeting, but was informed she was out all day visiting a client.

Resigned to a solitary meal, Rona slipped a paperback in her bag, fastened Gus's lead, and set off for the Gallery Café. As she reached the junction of Fullers Walk and Guild Street, however, she heard her name called, and turned to see Magda hurrying towards her.

'Magda, hello! I've been meaning to phone to congratulate you on the fashion show, but never got round to it. Sorry!'

'Glad you enjoyed it. It generated a lot of orders, I'm glad to say.'

'Worth all the hard work, then. I'm on my way to lunch at the Gallery; any chance of you joining me?'

Magda checked her watch. 'I shouldn't – I was going to grab a sandwich at my desk.'

'But you're tempted?' Rona wheedled.

'OK, you talked me into it. But I must be out within the hour; I've an appointment at two.'

'Let's hope they're not busy, then.' The Gallery wasn't known for its speedy service.

They went together up the wrought iron staircase to the walkway above, which housed a delicatessen, a gift shop and a store selling rare books, as well as the Gallery Café. A couple were vacating a table as they entered, and they moved swiftly to claim it, Gus, as always, retiring under the table.

'So, what have you been doing since we last

met?' Magda asked, once they'd ordered.

'Rushing round the county, interviewing people about Elspeth Wilding.'

'How's it going?'

'All right, I suppose. It always seems slow at this stage, but it's a question of gathering information and trying to steer a course between differing opinions of the person in question.'

She poured them both a glass of water, Magda having declined wine during a working day. 'Her sister said the family was willing to speak to me, but I got a pretty cool reception from their brother. Much against his will, he's deigning to see me tomorrow evening, so Max is coming to London with me, and we're going to eat afterwards. I'll be in need of something to restore me.'

'That should do the trick. By the way, I spoke to our mutual friend the other day.'

Rona raised enquiring eyebrows.

'Crispin Ryder. The crowd he brought to the show have ordered well over a thousand pounds' worth of clothes – I wanted to thank him.'

'That's wonderful, Magda!'

'What's more, they asked to be put on my mailing list, so with luck, they'll become regulars.'

'Even better!'

'Incidentally, you must have made an impression – he commented again on how alike you and Lindsey are, and asked if you were also a solicitor. So I blew your trumpet for you – acclaimed biographer, and so on. He was interested to hear you're doing Elspeth Wilding.'

Rona's heart skipped a beat. 'Does he know her?'

Magda looked surprised. 'I don't think so, or he'd have said, surely? Why?'

Rona was on the point of telling her about the photo, but something held her back. Magda could easily mention it if she spoke to him again, and asking her not to would attach too much importance to it. As Lindsey had said, no doubt it was a coincidence, but just in case it wasn't, she didn't want to alert him. To what, she couldn't have said.

'I just wondered, with his being interested, that's all.'

'He was probably only being polite,' Magda said – and no doubt she was right.

Their pizzas arrived, providing a natural break in the conversation, and when it was resumed, Rona turned instead to Lindsey's redecoration and her stay at number nineteen.

'Lucky her!' Magda commented. 'Nothing I'd like better than to throw everything out and start again!'

'Your house is lovely!' Rona protested.

'But it's been the same for yonks, it could do with a facelift. Did *Double N* turn up trumps?'

'I've not seen it myself, but Lindsey's delighted with it.'

'I might just give them a ring,' Magda said thoughtfully. 'No harm in getting their input, at least.' She put down her knife and fork. 'I won't stay for coffee, if you don't mind.' She took her

201

out her purse, but Rona shook her head.

'Have it on me. I talked you into it, after all.'

'Oh, no, I—'

'An extra pizza isn't going to break me,' Rona said, and Magda smiled.

'All right, then – thanks. And our next lunch is on me. Good luck with the Addams Family tomorrow.'

And she was gone. Rona ordered coffee and belatedly took out her paperback, but her attention was wandering. So Crispin was aware she was writing Elspeth's bio. If he *did* know her, surely, as Magda said, he'd have made some comment, if only about her continuing absence? Which meant, Rona concluded, that she'd read more into that photo than was actually there.

She thought for a moment of the handsome, vibrant man she'd met, and all the stories she'd heard about him; and she remembered Naomi's comment, that it seemed unlikely in the extreme that his path should cross with a publicity-shy woman like Elspeth. In which case, she told herself, she should dismiss him from her speculations once and for all. With a sigh, she returned to her book.

Rona had just reached her study when the phone rang, and she lifted it to find Barnie Trent on the line.

'How's my errant feature writer?' he asked her.

'Just about surviving.'

'Not changing your mind, by any chance?'

Rona laughed. 'No, no. A bit disenchanted at the moment, that's all.'

'I don't think you said who you're doing?'

'Elspeth Wilding, the artist.'

'Ah – good choice. I met her several years back, when she had an exhibition locally and we did a feature on it. A charming woman, I thought.'

Rona bit back her surprise. Here was a new angle! But before she could pursue it, Barnie was continuing.

'When we last spoke, I mentioned Dinah was hoping to invite you for a meal. Sorry to be so long coming back, but she's been a bit under the weather lately.'

'Nothing serious, I hope?'

'No, no. The doctor's given her some vitamin pills and she's got her bounce back. So, when are you free?'

'Well, as you know, Max is limited to Wednesdays and the weekend, and tomorrow we're going to London – though that would be too soon, anyway.'

'And we've a school-friend of Dinah's staying over on Saturday. How about next week?'

'I'd have to check with Max.'

'Look, no offence, but since he's so tied up, why not come by yourself this time? You've done it before, and I can't think, excellent chap though he is, that he's overly interested in shop-talk, which, inevitably, we slide into from time to time.'

It was true that, even apart from the business

angle, Barnie and Dinah were more her friends than Max's. She was sure he'd be agreeable.

'Right, then, thanks.'

'So – Monday? Tuesday? Thursday?'

Rona laughed. 'Well, if you have a weekend guest, Monday's too soon, but either of the others would be fine.'

'Right, I'll get Dinah to phone you with a definite date. In the meantime, don't let the disenchantment get you down.'

'I'll try not to,' she said.

'Barnie thought Elspeth was charming,' Rona told Max, on the train to London the next evening. 'In Barnie-speak, that means she gave a good interview, which is pretty unusual, from all accounts.

'Come to think of it,' she went on thoughtfully, 'the more I hear about her, the more contradictory she seems. One version is that she's uncommunicative and camera-shy, another that she's self-centred, domineering and ruthless, as per Nathan and the Pynes.'

'Both of whom have axes to grind,' Max reminded her.

'True,' Rona acknowledged. 'It will be interesting to hear what Big Brother has to say. I hope they won't object to my recorder.'

The Wildings lived in what proved to be a luxury flat overlooking Regent's Park. The hall porter, having enquired her name, phoned to check she was expected before escorting her to

the lift and pressing the button for the appropriate floor.

Rona sailed up in majestic silence, and, as the
gates opened, found herself face to face with
Richard Wilding. For a split second they observed each other, Rona seeing a tall, hard-eyed man
whose hair was liberally sprinkled with grey.
Then he came forward, extending a hand.

'Miss Parish,' he said formally.

'Mr Wilding. Thank you for agreeing to see
me.'

He escorted her through the open door of the
flat and into a large, airy room overlooking the
dark expanse of the park. It was furnished in
exquisite taste, mainly with antiques, and one of
Elspeth's cloudscapes hung in pride of place,
taking up much of one wall.

'My wife, Marcia.'

The woman who came forward was, at a
guess, in her late forties. Her mid-brown hair
was straight and shining, her face a little pinch-
ed, and she was wearing a designer suit in claret,
with a white silk blouse and high heels that
brought her almost to her husband's height.
There was an air of concealed impatience about
her, and Rona had the distinct impression that
her own arrival was inconveniently delaying the
start of their evening.

'Perhaps you'll join us in a sherry?' Richard
said, going to a table that displayed a range of
cut-glass decanters and glasses.

Although she didn't care for sherry, it seemed
politic to accept, and when it came, it was so

pale as to be almost colourless. The first sip proved, as she'd feared, dry enough to shrivel the inside of her mouth. Suppressing an instinctive shudder, she produced her recorder.

'Would you mind if I used this? It ensures accuracy and makes for a more relaxed interview.'

Not that she'd be relaxing herself, in such an atmosphere. Neither of them objected, for which she was grateful, and she switched it on.

'As you'll appreciate,' she began, 'I've only just started my research, but it would be a great help if you could tell me what you remember of Elspeth's childhood.'

'She was enchanting,' Richard said promptly. 'A determined little thing, full of character from the start.'

'In other words,' Marcia put in dryly, 'she idolized her big brother, and still does.'

Richard shot her a warning look, which Rona intercepted.

'No doubt Naomi gave you a different picture,' he said, ignoring his wife.

'Slightly,' Rona admitted tactfully.

He gave a short laugh. 'They're totally incompatible, those two. To be frank, Naomi's always been jealous of her, not only because she was the baby of the family and spoiled by our parents, but because of her talent, which, as you'll have heard, manifested itself at a very early age. Naomi always resented that; I suppose if there's jealousy in a family, it's more likely to be between siblings of the same sex.'

206

'Yet she chose Elspeth as godmother to her daughter,' Rona protested, obliged to defend Naomi in the face of such criticism.

Richard shrugged dismissively, and she wondered, for the first time, if he had family of his own. Marcia didn't look the maternal type.

'You were the middle one?' she checked.

'That's right, slightly nearer in age to Elspeth.'

'And closer in other ways, too?'

He smiled. 'You could say that.'

'Did your moving to London affect that closeness?'

'Not at all, she often—' He broke off, flashed another look at his wife, and continued 'came to stay.'

Rona paused; it seemed she was on the brink of something important, if she could just uncover it. 'I know this is out of context,' she probed gently, 'but were you surprised when she suddenly left?'

It seemed she'd lit the touchpaper. 'Why does everyone keep harping on that?' Richard demanded forcefully. 'Surely she's entitled to a leave of absence? She needed to stretch herself – artists do – and Buckford had become claustrophobic.'

'But it's eighteen months since she left,' Rona objected, 'and she's not even been in touch.'

'She has with us,' Marcia said unexpectedly.

'Marcia!'

'Oh, for God's sake, Richard, this is ridiculous!'

He slapped his hand on his knee. 'I *knew* this

biography was a mistake! I *told* Naomi—'

'But you didn't tell her *why*, did you? That we've always known roughly where she is?'

Rona held her breath. This, she had certainly *not* expected. They were glaring at each other, and it seemed all she had to do was keep quiet and await the outcome. Thank God for her recorder!

Richard passed a hand over his eyes. 'Now you've done it,' he said dully.

'But surely you agree it's gone on long enough? She's had over a year to "do her own thing", though why she has to be so secretive defeats me. What the hell does it *matter* where she is? If she'd been open about it in the first place, like any normal person, the family wouldn't have panicked and alerted the press. As it is, we have to be thankful we were spared *Crimewatch*!'

'That's hardly fair!' Richard flung back. 'She left a message, for God's sake! She wasn't to know it would be wiped before anyone heard it!'

He glanced in Rona's direction, as if suddenly recalling her presence, finished his sherry in a single gulp and banged the glass on the table. 'Your name should be Pandora,' he said bitterly. 'Well, after all that, there's not much point in putting the lid back on the box. All I can ask is that you keep it to yourself, until either Elspeth comes home or the book's published, which-ever's the sooner.'

Rona moved uncomfortably. 'It'll be difficult when I speak to Naomi—'

'Oh, I realize I can't hold you to it.' He stood up abruptly and went to refill his glass, belatedly turning to ask if anyone else cared for a refill. Rona declined, Marcia held out her glass. Husband and wife weren't meeting each other's eye; it boded ill for the rest of their evening.

Richard reseated himself and leant forward, hands clasped, staring at the floor. 'Elspeth felt stifled,' he began. 'My parents were always phoning, wanting to know when they could see her, what she was doing, how she was. And after Chloë's death, it was ten times worse.' He looked up. 'You know about Chloë?'

Rona nodded.

'That, of course, was the final straw – the row between them, followed by her death. Elspeth was so distraught that we brought her back here after the funeral, and she spent days in her room, refusing to see anyone. I was seriously concerned, but after a week or so she grew calmer and even came out with us occasionally, to the theatre or for a meal, and gradually, very gradually, she regained her balance.'

'More than,' averred Marcia, holding tightly to her glass. 'She developed a taste for the bright lights; said she needed to widen her boundaries, whatever that meant, and although she eventually returned to Buckford, she began coming here regularly, staying for a few days at a time. And every evening it was the same: she'd set off alone for the West End. At least, that's where we assumed she was going; she wasn't specific, just told us she was meeting friends, but she never suggested we join her.'

'It was a belated teenage rebellion,' Richard explained. 'During her adolescence, she was totally focused on art – she'd never had any *fun*. Who were we to deny it to her?'

Rona took a deep breath, trying to assimilate this totally unexpected turn of events.

'So when she left, she went with these friends?'

'Oh no,' Richard said quickly. 'She went away for a clean break, to rediscover herself as a painter. And she *has* been painting; she's quite excited about it.'

'So when's she coming back?'

He shrugged. 'When she's ready, I imagine.'

'I ... don't suppose you can tell me where she is?'

He started to shake his head, but Marcia said promptly, 'Scotland.'

Richard came to his feet, flushing angrily. 'Just be quiet, will you? God knows, you've said more than enough!'

Marcia had also risen, and for a moment they held each other's eye. Then she turned and, stalking to the window, stood staring out into the darkness.

Rona subtly changed tack. 'You say she contacted you; how long was that after she left?'

It took Richard a minute to regain his equilibrium. 'Several weeks,' he said then, trying to moderate his voice. 'Until then, we'd been as worried as everyone else. And the only reason she phoned was because she'd come across an

English paper with an article on her "disappear-ance", and was appalled. Fortunately, this was after Toby owned up, so I was able to explain what had happened.'

'Couldn't you have told your family you'd heard from her?'

'That's what I said!' Marcia declared, without turning.

Again, he ignored her. 'She was convinced that if they knew, they'd bombard her with requests to come home – even fly up to see her – and it was to escape all that that she'd gone in the first place. Once she was satisfied they'd had the message, truncated though it was, she made me swear not to say she'd been in touch. If I hadn't, she'd have severed the connection com-pletely. As it is, it's very erratic – sometimes we hear once a month, sometimes it's longer. She bought a new mobile and won't give us the number, so there's no way we can contact her. Come to that, we've only her word for it she actually *is* in Scotland.'

Rona thought over what he'd said. 'Did you tell her about the biography?' she asked.

He shook his head. 'We've not spoken since I heard about it.'

'But you'll tell her next time?'

'Of course.'

'How do you think she'll react?'

'I doubt she'll be exactly overjoyed.'

'Is there any possibility of my seeing her?'

'That, I very much doubt.'

'Could you perhaps ask her? I wouldn't reveal

where she was.'

'I'll ask, but I don't hold out much hope.'

Rona nodded, appreciating it was as far as he could go. 'To come back to Chloë, then; what did you think of her?'

He looked surprised, and a little relieved, at the change of subject. 'A nice girl, quite talented, but she couldn't hold a candle to Elspeth.'

'How would you describe their friendship?'

'Rock solid, I'd have said. They were virtually inseparable from the word go.'

'Would you say, though, that Elspeth was the more dominant?'

There was a snort from Marcia at the window, and Richard frowned. 'I don't know that I'd use the word "dominant", but she was certainly the stronger character.'

'Were you surprised by their estrangement?'

'Not in the circumstances.' Marcia had turned back to the room, and it was she who answered. 'Someone fell for Chloë, and she was as jealous as hell. Added to which, she risked losing her willing slave.'

'For God's sake!' Richard said tiredly.

'You know that's true; she has to come first with everyone. It's a wonder she accepted me, when I stole her beloved brother.'

'Now you're just being ridiculous.'

Marcia simply shrugged.

Again, Rona changed direction. 'When did you realize she was especially talented?'

'When she started at the High School and

someone took her under their wing. That's when she blossomed.' Richard looked at his watch. 'Miss Parish, I'm sorry, but time's running out. We have to be somewhere at seven thirty.'

'Of course,' Rona said at once. 'I'm grateful to you for fitting me in. Perhaps I could contact you again, if I have more questions?'

He nodded, but she had the feeling she'd used up her quota of his patience. She switched off the recorder, slipped it into her bag, and followed him to the door. Marcia remained standing by the window.

'Goodbye, Mrs Wilding. Thank you.'

She, too, simply nodded, and seconds later Rona was descending in the lift. In the foyer, she took out her mobile and texted Max: *On my way; see you in ten minutes.*

Then, her head buzzing with new information, she pushed her way through the swing doors in search of a taxi.

TWELVE

The news that Elspeth was alive and well and living in Scotland, dominated Rona's thoughts over the weekend.

'How do you think I could persuade her to see me?' she asked Max, over a pub lunch on the Saturday.

'If Richard's your intermediary, I don't rate your chances,' he replied.

'Marcia might put her oar in, if only to annoy him. Or, come to that, they both might, to spite Naomi.'

'Happy families!' Max commented.

'I probably caught them on an off-day.'

Marcia had hinted that Elspeth was jealous of her, Rona reflected, but it seemed to her the boot was on the other foot; everything she'd said about her sister-in-law burned with resentment.

She looked up, to find Max regarding her thoughtfully. 'It strikes me you're not enjoying this biography very much,' he said.

She shrugged helplessly. 'I got off on the wrong foot, that's all. The so-called disappearance distracted me from working chronologically, though I'd sworn not to let it, and then learning first that Elspeth *had* left a message, and second that Richard actually *knows where she is* – well, I'm having to rethink everything. Not,' she added ruefully, 'that I'd made much progress anyway.'

She leaned across, took a chip from his plate, and popped it in her mouth. 'Added to which,' she continued, 'there are other problems: now I'm aware of the position, I can't possibly interview the parents, knowing they're worried to death about her, but not able to reassure them.'

'Richard admitted he couldn't hold you to that.'

'But I can't just come out with it, can I? That their daughter's been in touch with him all along, but made him promise not to tell them? And they're expecting to hear from me any minute; I've been holding them at bay, but I can't for much longer.'

She frowned, toying with the roll on her plate. 'Then there's Chloë, another complication I hadn't foreseen. I still think I'm missing something there, something that has a bearing on Elspeth, though God knows what.'

'If you're looking for a let-out,' Max remarked, slapping her hand as she reached for another chip, 'you have one ready-made.'

She frowned. 'How do you mean?'

'Well, you could argue, justifiably, that you were approached under false pretences. Think about it: *Until the contract was signed* – and that could be significant – you were led to believe that she'd disappeared without warning, and no one knew what had happened to her. A different prospect altogether from the fact that she could turn up any minute and play merry hell.'

Rona put her head in her hands. 'What should I do, Max?'

'What do you want to do?'

She thought for a full minute, before looking up and meeting his eyes. 'OK, so it's a poisoned chalice; but as you know, I don't like giving up. To coin a phrase, I've started, so I'll finish.'

He smiled. 'That's my girl,' he said.

Dinner with Barnie and Dinah on Tuesday was a welcome break, and although they touched briefly on the biography, for the most part it was an Elspeth-free zone, and just what Rona needed. Sitting by the log fire, a drink in her hand, and one of the Trents' Siamese cats draped over her shoulder, she could feel herself start to relax, a sensation she always experienced in their home.

'So what's the news at *Chiltern Life*?' she asked lazily, lulled by the loud purring in her ear.

'Nothing particularly exciting. Polly's just got engaged, if that qualifies as news.'

Polly was the receptionist, and looked after Gus when Rona visited Barnie, plying him with chocolate biscuits.

'Oh, that's lovely! Who to?'

'Presumably her boyfriend, but no one I know.'

'Do give her my best wishes. Will she stay on, do you think?'

'Oh, I imagine so,' Barnie said comfortably. 'He's a local lad, so they're not moving away. Different matter with Andy, though. He's leaving at the end of the year.'

Rona was surprised. 'He's not old enough to retire, surely?' Andy, a photographer by profession, had accompanied her on several of her assignments.

'No, he's still a few years to go, but he wants to try his hand at more experimental photography. Hopes to produce a book, I believe.'

'Well, good for him. If he has a leaving party, I'd love to be there to wish him well.'

Barnie smiled. 'I'll see you get an invite.'

Dinah bustled back into the room bearing a tray containing their first course. 'I hope you two have finished talking shop,' she said. 'Dinner's almost ready. Ditch Lychee, Rona; he's not supposed to take liberties with guests.'

'I love having him.' Rona laid her cheek against the cat's soft fur.

'Just as well Gus and the three of them have a non-aggression pact,' Barnie commented, 'or we'd literally have the fur flying.'

Gus, on the rug before the fire, opened one eye on hearing his name, then closed it again, and they all laughed. Rona gently set the cat on the floor, where he proceeded to wash himself, and they all moved to the table.

Talk during the meal was of the Trents' family in the States – daughter Melissa, her husband Mitch, and the children Sam and Martha.

'She's expecting again,' Dinah said worriedly.

'I'd hoped they'd stop at two.'

Melissa's last pregnancy had been difficult, necessitating her mother going out to stay for a while.

'They'll be keeping an extra special eye on her, I'm sure,' Rona said. 'When's it due?'

'June, around Martha's second birthday. Mel will have her hands full, with three under five.'

Rona tried briefly to picture herself in that position, and failed. Yet she knew, uncomfortably, that time was moving on, and that both her parents, though they were too tactful to mention it, were hoping for a grandchild. And, she thought wryly, the way Lindsey was going, it would be up to herself to provide one.

The evening passed all too quickly, and it was time to drive back to the various problems that awaited her.

'I think of you as my oasis,' Rona said, as she kissed them goodbye. 'You restore my soul!'

Dinah patted her arm affectionately. 'Then don't wait for an invitation. You know you're always welcome, so if you feel stressed out, give us a ring.'

'I might well do that,' Rona said.

Rona decided to spend the next day going through the brochures and tour details Gwen had supplied. After that, she hoped to have a clearer idea of whom to contact in the art world for a professional assessment of Elspeth's work – her dealer, for example, and the owner of the gallery where many of her paintings were displayed. It was time, she told herself firmly, to stop procrastinating and start working more methodically on her research.

Down in the kitchen, she filled Gus's bowl, changed his water and switched on the radio, only half-listening to the news headlines as she slid two slices of bread into the toaster. Then a change in the announcer's tone alerted her, and she instinctively paused, marmalade jar in hand.

'The body of a woman was discovered last night at the Buckford house of the artist Elspeth Wilding, and police are treating the death as suspicious. Ms Wilding, who is widely regarded as a major British artist, disappeared from her home eighteen months ago.'

Another change of tone. 'Today's weather forecast is for...'

Rona stood motionless, staring at the radio. Had Elspeth returned unexpectedly, and somehow had an accident? Or, more likely, was the victim Naomi? Oh God, what had happened? Had she had a fall? Somehow electrocuted herself? But the word *suspicious* echoed in her mind. God, not again! Please, not again!

She snatched up the phone, jamming her finger on the button for Farthings.

'Max Allerdyce.'

'Oh Max!' Her voice was shaking. 'Have you heard the news?'

'What news?'

'On the radio. It said a woman's body's been found in Elspeth's house and the police are treating it as suspicious!'

There was a pause. Then he said flatly, 'Good God.'

'What can I do?' Rona demanded frantically.

'Hold on a minute. What do you mean, do?'

'Well, I have to do *something*! I have to know definitely who it is, and how she died!'

'Honey,' he said gently, 'there's nothing you *can* do. Just think for a minute. The family will already be besieged with reporters and cameramen and God knows what. You'd never get through, but even if you did, what would you say? "I'm ringing to find out who's dead?"'

Rona drew a tremulous breath. 'Yes,' she said numbly. 'I see.'

'You'll hear in due course – everyone will. Just keep listening to the bulletins. But promise me one thing, Rona: you will not, repeat not, under any circumstances, drive up to Buckford.'

'All right. I promise.'

'I'll be home this evening, and we can talk about it then. Possibly—' He broke off.

'Possibly what?'

'I was just wondering if Gwen Saunders might know something.'

'Oh Max, you're brilliant! I'll give her a ring! Why didn't I think of that? I was planning to go through the papers she gave me.'

'Well, just remember that whatever's happened doesn't directly involve you. All right?'

'All right,' she echoed obediently, but she was not convinced. Reluctantly, she broke the connection. Then, no longer hungry, she removed the slices of toast from the machine and, opening the patio door, threw them out for the birds.

Gwen Saunders was not answering calls. Though Rona tried repeatedly, and increasingly frantically, to phone her, she was invariably met with the bland voice of the answer phone. Nor did she fare better with her friend Tess Chadwick, crime reporter for the *Stokely Gazette*. Tess's mobile was diverted to voice mail, and all Rona could do was leave a message asking Tess to phone her.

When, frustrated, she eventually replaced the phone, it immediately rang, and she lifted it to hear her father's voice.

'Just checking it wasn't you up in that house!' he said, and though he spoke jokingly, Rona caught the anxious undertone.

'I don't know *who* it was, Pops, and it's driving me mad.'

'You have been to the house, though, haven't you?'

'Yes, three times in all.'

'Then thank God this didn't happen while you were there. Poor soul, whoever it is.'

Avril and Lindsey, both of whom had also been trying to reach her, phoned soon after, but Rona wasn't able to tell them any more than they'd heard on the news.

'Why is it that everything you work on sooner or later involves murder?' Avril demanded irritably.

'I wish I knew, Mum,' Rona replied.

221

Lindsey, however, on a more positive note, suggested they meet for lunch, an arrangement Rona was only too glad to accept.

Meanwhile, her planned routine for the day had gone by the board. Though she forced herself to sit at her desk with the brochures spread before her, she found herself reading the same sentences over and over while she waited for the next hourly update. But the only new fact that emerged during the morning was that the attack was believed to have occurred during a burglary.

But what about the alarm system? Rona thought – and immediately answered herself. When someone was in the house, it was switched off. Had the burglar known that? And since Elspeth had been absent for eighteen months, why had he chosen this particular time to break in?

Before leaving to meet Lindsey, she switched on Channel 4 midday news, waiting impatiently as world events were reported, before, to her horror, finding herself gazing at Elspeth's house, a yellow police tape stretched across the gateway and men in white coats going up and down the path. It was several seconds before she could take in what the reporter was saying.

'— a broken pane in the back door, and though it's not yet been established if anything is missing, there are indications of a hurried search, possibly interrupted by the victim.'

But that's not right, Rona thought; the victim, whoever she was, must have already been in the house, or the alarm would have been on. Unless, on this one, fatal occasion, someone had forgotten to reset it.

Numbly, she switched off the set and went to meet her sister.

'We're not going to talk about it,' Lindsey said firmly, as they sat down. 'If I know you, you've been worrying yourself to death all morning and getting precisely nowhere. So, the subject of Elspeth, her house and everything else relating to her is categorically banned for the duration of the meal. And to make doubly sure, please switch off your mobile. OK?'

Rona smiled weakly and complied.

'So once we've ordered, I'm going to give you a room-by-room description of the flat. It really is something, Ro. The girls have done a fantastic job.'

Lindsey was as good as her word, and Rona, still on edge, was grateful for the respite. They were at the Bacchus, and the rather dim atmosphere, the muted conversation from neighbouring booths, and, not least, the red wine in her glass, gradually combined to steady her.

'So,' Lindsey said, as she ended her virtual tour of the flat, 'the question is, when are you coming to see it for yourself?'

'When we're asked!' Rona replied, with the ghost of a smile.

'How about Saturday, then? Are you free?'

'Yes, I ... think so.'

'Excellent. I know for a fact Dominic's not going abroad for a couple of weeks, so at long last we can have that meeting we've been talking about.' She paused, adding uncertainly, 'I do hope Max likes him.'

Rona laid an impulsive hand on hers. 'I'm sure he will.'

'Are you? They're not at all alike, you know.'

'Don't forget I've met Dominic, albeit very briefly, and I'm quite sure they'll get on fine.'

Lindsey smiled. 'Good! Then all I have to do is plan a menu I can wow you all with!'

When Lindsey returned to her office, Rona found, to her surprise, that rather than being anxious to hurry home for the latest news, she was now reluctant to do so, and opted to defer hearing any developments by taking Gus for an extended walk round the park. By the time they'd completed the circuit and he'd had his free run on the upper slopes, the afternoon had grown chill, and there was a hint of mist in the distance, reminding Rona they were halfway through November. Soon, they'd have to start thinking about Christmas.

When she could delay her return no longer and a blueness was beginning to seep into the atmosphere, she called the dog, refastened his lead and set off for home. It was nearly four thirty. What had been reported in her absence? Had the name of the victim been released? She gave a little shudder, thankful that Max would be back in an hour or two.

She was hanging her jacket in the hall when the phone started to ring. Tess? Gwen?

She caught it up, and a strained voice said, 'Rona? Is that you?'

'*Naomi*!' Rona felt her eyes fill with tears of relief.

'Obviously you've heard the news?'

'I ... thought it might have been you,' Rona said.

'Oh, my dear, how thoughtless of me! I should have got on to you sooner. No, it was Mary Strong, poor woman.'

'*Mary?*' For some reason, Rona had never considered her. Yet why not? Yesterday was Tuesday, after all – Mary's day for the cottage. On Tuesday last week... 'What happened, do you know?'

'Not really. It was the annual dinner at Bill's men's club, and he went there straight from work, so it wasn't till he got home about ten that anyone realized she was missing.'

So while she'd been happily relaxing with Barnie and Dinah, Mary had been lying in the empty house, dying or already dead.

Blocking the thought, Rona said quickly, 'And it happened in the morning, while she was there working?'

'It must have done; they won't know the exact time till the post mortem, but between nine and twelve.'

'Surely it's unusual for burglary to take place in daylight?'

'Yes; but I suppose whoever it was knew the house was empty. Or should have been.'

'You mean they knew it was Elspeth's house?'

'The police seem to think so, but then that's no secret; half of Buckford knows it.' Naomi paused. 'She was lying at the bottom of the stairs, with her head bashed in.'

'And it was her husband who found her?' Rona asked, horrified.

'Bill *and* Lionel, actually. He phoned us in quite a state, saying she wasn't home and hadn't left a note or anything to say where she was. He wondered if she'd been taken ill at the cottage, and asked if he could borrow a key. Of course, Leonard went with him, thank God. The poor man collapsed when he saw her.'

Rona swallowed. 'And there's no clue as to who it could have been?'

'No. The police think he must have broken in while Mary was dusting upstairs. She'd have heard the glass smash, and come down to investigate.' Naomi's voice wavered. 'And if that *was* the case, he didn't panic and run off after killing her, as you'd expect; he searched the bureau in the sitting room, then went upstairs, no doubt stepping over her, and riffled his way through Elspeth's drawers. They were all lying on the carpet, their contents scattered around them. God knows what he was after, but as far as I could tell, nothing was taken.'

Rona pictured the pleasant room she'd stood in only the week before, feeling the essence of its owner. Now, it was marred for her for ever.

'I've not seen Mary myself for some time,' Naomi was saying. 'I suppose she didn't say anything that could throw any light on this?

About seeing anyone hanging around, or anything?'

Rona shook her head, realized Naomi couldn't see her, and said, 'No, nothing. She didn't seem the fanciful type, though. I doubt if it would have entered her head that anything like this could happen. After all, you say she's been going in once a week for the last eighteen months.'

'Exactly,' Naomi said expressionlessly. 'I can't help wondering, why now?'

Bracing herself, Rona put into words the thought that had been haunting her all day. 'I hope to God it was nothing to do with the biography.'

'Oh, I didn't mean that! And I don't see how it could have been; it's not as though it's been announced publicly. Very few people know about it – only family, really.'

There was some small comfort in that. 'Perhaps it'll bring Elspeth home?' Rona mused. Then bit her lip, adding hastily, 'Since it's been on the national news, I mean.'

'If she's still alive herself,' Naomi said. 'After all this time, I'm beginning to wonder.'

Rona closed her eyes on a wave of almost unbearable frustration. Should she say something? At least it would be easier than telling Elspeth's parents. But perhaps this latest development would encourage Richard to make a clean breast of it; she should at least give him the chance to do so.

Almost as though reading her thoughts, Naomi

said, 'I must go; I promised to visit my parents; obviously, this has shaken them pretty badly. But if you remember anything Mary said, however vague or seemingly unimportant, do please let either me or the police know about it.'

'I will,' Rona promised, and, as Naomi rang off, put down the phone. No messages waiting for her, she noted. Then, with a start, remembered she'd not switched on her mobile after lunch.

She retrieved it from her bag and did so, and immediately the red light lit up. Two missed calls, one from Tess and one from Gwen Saunders, both, no doubt, returning the calls she'd made earlier. She tried Gwen first.

'Ms Saunders? It's Rona Parish. I'm sorry I missed your call.'

'I can imagine why you were phoning, Ms Parish.' The usually efficient voice sounded strained. 'This has been a great shock to us all.'

'I'm sure. I've just been speaking to Mrs Harris.'

'Then you'll know we haven't much information as yet.'

A sudden thought struck Rona. 'Did the intruder, whoever he was, break into the studio as well?'

'No; the thinking seems to be that either he was anxious to get away, or, alternatively, he didn't know it existed. Obviously he went round the back, since he broke into the kitchen, but he mightn't even have registered the studio. At a casual glance, it just looks like an outbuilding.'

'I suppose we can be thankful for that.'

'It didn't help Mary Strong, though.'

'No.'

'I believe you met her last week?'

'Yes, I did. She was ... very helpful.' Rona took a deep breath. 'Ms Saunders, can I ask you something?'

'Of course.' The voice sounded cautious.

'Have you been in touch with Miss Wilding since she left?'

There was a long silence. Then: 'Why are you asking me that?'

'Because I rather think you might have been. I ... shan't repeat anything you tell me, you have my word.'

A pause, while Rona held her breath. 'Then the answer is yes, there has been occasional contact between us.'

Bingo! 'Do you know where she is?'

'No. And that's the truth.'

'Then how do you contact her?'

'It's she who contacts me, by telephone. But there have been a couple of times when she wanted something forwarding, and then I sent them to a post box in London.'

'London?' That wasn't what Rona had expected.

'You sound surprised.'

She backtracked, anxious not to betray Richard. 'Not really. Has she given any hint as to when she's coming back?'

'Nothing definite, but I've a feeling it won't be long now. Actually—' The woman broke off.

'Yes?'

'She ... telephoned me this morning. About Mrs Strong. She was very upset, as you might imagine, and wondered if I had any further details. Sadly, I didn't.'

So Elspeth had been in contact this very day! Rona felt a wave of excitement.

'She's still very anxious to keep it from the family,' Gwen Saunders continued. 'I do have your word?'

'Yes, of course, but thank you for confiding in me.'

'To be honest, it's been rather a burden, this knowledge, when Mrs Harris and the others are so concerned about her. But she was adamant I shouldn't tell them.'

Rona said carefully, 'Do you know if she's been in touch with anyone else?'

'Her dealer, I believe, from time to time. About the new collection she's building up.'

So Elspeth's 'disappearance' hadn't been as total as she'd supposed. It seemed the blackout had been restricted to her parents and sister. Rona wasn't sure if that said more about them or about Elspeth herself.

She ended the conversation with Gwen, and phoned Tess.

'This is your friendly neighbourhood reporter,' said Tess's cheerful voice. 'Hi, Rona. Don't tell me you're involved in this Buckford murder?'

'Hello, Tess. No, not really, though I did meet the victim last week.'

Tess gave a low whistle. 'You really are the kiss of death, aren't you?'

'Don't say that!' Rona said sharply.

'Sorree! Joke!'

'Well, it wasn't funny.'

'No, it probably wasn't, in the circumstances. So how come you met her?'

'I'm writing a bio of Elspeth Wilding.'

'Ah, the reclusive artist. Have you met her, too?'

'No. Look, Tess, I was just wondering if you know any more than has been reported in the media?'

'I *am* the media!' Tess pointed out.

'Yes, but you know what I mean.'

'All I can tell you is that the murder weapon is thought to have been a hammer, but whether he'd intended it as such, or brought it to smash the window and the padlock on the gate, is open to debate. It doesn't make much difference to the victim, but my guess is he'd thought the house would be empty and was taken by surprise.

'This woman was the cleaner, right?' Tess added, when Rona remained silent.

'Right. She ... showed me over the house, so I could get the atmosphere.'

'Bet it's changed a bit!'

Suddenly, Tess's breeziness was too much. Rona said quickly, 'It's good of you to have phoned back, Tess, and thanks for the information. I owe you.' And she rang off before her friend could reply.

The kiss of death. For a long minute Rona stood motionless in the hall, until a wet nose nudged at her hand and she looked down at Gus's ingratiatingly wriggling body and waving plume of a tail.

'Oh, Gus!' she said unsteadily, and, bending down, put her arms round the animal and gave him a hug. Then, sniffing, she straightened, feeling in her jacket pocket for a tissue.

As she pulled it out, a piece of paper fell to the floor, and its spiralling descent stirred a memory: it was the scrap that had fallen from the book in Elspeth's sitting room, and which, having stuffed in her pocket, she had totally forgotten. She picked it up for a second time, and smoothed it out to reveal a scrawled string of figures – a mobile number, by the look of it. Absentmindedly, still thinking of the call to Tess, Rona tapped it out.

The ringing continued for several seconds. Then there was a click and a voice said, 'You have reached Crispin Ryder's phone. I'm not available at the moment, but if you leave your name and number, I'll get back to you. Please speak after the tone.'

Rona froze, dumbfounded. A bleep sounded in her ear, then, when she didn't speak, the voice said briskly, 'Thank you for calling,' and the line went dead.

THIRTEEN

'OK, so your hunch was correct,' Max said, 'but I can't for the life of me see why you attach so much importance to it. They're both "celebrities" – it's not surprising they should know each other.'

'Naomi didn't think they did.'

'But as you said, Naomi seems to know remarkably little about her sister. And anyway, the mere fact that she has his number doesn't mean they're bosom buddies. If they met at that do, he could easily have said something like, "If I can be of any help, give me a call", and either jotted down his number or spelt it out for her.'

'Oh, all right, have it your way,' Rona said crossly. 'I just think it's significant, that's all.'

'Significant in what way?'

She shrugged. 'I'm not sure. Just significant.'

Max laughed. 'Feminine intuition? Well, you might be right, but I doubt if it's going to get you far.'

The mist hinted at in the afternoon had thickened, and the lights from the kitchen that usually illuminated the patio and nearer part of the garden were extinguished in an impenetrable, bluish wall that mirrored the interior. Rona, gazing out at it, shivered.

'Lindsey's invited us to dinner on Saturday,' she said. 'To see the flat and meet Dominic.'

'In that order?'

'Tied equal, I think. She was raving about the new decor over lunch.'

'Well, it will be interesting on both counts.'

'She's very anxious that you should like him.'

'Not something I can guarantee in advance. Anyway, what does it matter what I think?'

'God knows,' Rona said shortly, and, with a glance at her averted face, Max let the subject drop.

By the following day, the murder had already lost its place in the headlines. Not wanting to keep bothering either Naomi or Gwen, Rona resigned herself to waiting for bulletins, and, since her deviation to the more recent past had done little good, resolved to return to Elspeth's girlhood.

Although Catherine had given her the address of the ex-head of St Stephen's, she'd suggested Rona's most lucrative source was likely to be the art mistress at Buckford High, and accordingly she phoned the school on the Thursday morning.

'This is an unusual request,' she began tentatively to the girl on the switchboard, 'but I'm trying to trace the person who was head of art in about 1975.'

'Goodness!' the girl said. 'I've no idea, but if you'll hold on, I'll make enquiries.'

A wait of several minutes ensued, while Rona crossed her fingers that the woman was still alive.

'Hello?' A different voice. 'Can I help you?'

'I hope so. My name is Rona Parish and I'm writing a biography of Elspeth Wilding. I would very much like to speak to whoever it was who encouraged her when she first arrived at the school.'

The voice became animated. 'Miss Parish? How very interesting! May I say how much I enjoyed your previous biographies? And how exciting that you're now working on Elspeth! We're all very proud of her.'

'I believe her talent was recognized almost as soon as she joined the school?'

'Yes, we like to claim a little credit there. It would be Miss Pemberton you're looking for; she taught Elspeth throughout her time here.'

'Does she still live in the area?' Rona asked hopefully.

'Indeed yes; in fact, she retired only a couple of years ago. I'm sure she'd be delighted to meet you, but I hope you'll understand if I have a word with her first?'

'Of course.'

'My name is Elizabeth Temple, by the way, and I'm the present head of art. If you could tell me how to contact you...?'

Rona supplied her number, and with mutual expressions of goodwill, the call ended. Now, Rona thought, she'd have to curb her impatience till someone came back to her.

She did not have long to wait. Within half an hour, Miss Pemberton herself was on the line.

'You'd like to discuss Elspeth's early progress, I believe?' she said, in a clear, clipped voice.

'I should indeed, if you could spare the time.'

'Of course; I'm always pleased to speak about my star pupil. Do you live in Buckford, Miss Parish?'

'No, Marsborough, but that's no problem.'

'Then suppose you come up tomorrow morning, and I could give you coffee?'

Rona accepted with gratitude, and made a note of the address. After all the delays and frustrations, it seemed she might actually be making some progress.

Moira Pemberton was younger than Rona had expected – probably in her mid-sixties – and lived with her aged mother in a little house in Greenwood Lane. The old lady was ensconced in the front room, and Rona was shown to a sitting room at the back of the house.

'We converted the front room to a bedsit ten years ago,' Miss Pemberton said briskly, 'when Mother's arthritis made it difficult for her to get upstairs. She's just celebrated her ninetieth birthday, but apart from lack of mobility, you'd never know it. She's as bright as a button, and interested in everything that goes on.'

Rona guessed that if Miss Pemberton lived as long, she too would remain in full possession of her faculties. A tall, thin woman, her silver hair was drawn into a French pleat, her make-up almost undetectable, and she was wearing a grey skirt and twinset with a string of pearls. Not at all Rona's somewhat fanciful idea of an art teacher: though she'd never admit it to Max, she'd envisaged beads and shawls.

A tray bearing cups and saucers and a silver coffee pot was awaiting them, and her hostess lost no time in pouring what proved to be a very good cup of coffee. Shortbread fingers were offered, accompanied by an attractive paper napkin in the shape of a butterfly, and per-mission was given for the recorder.

'I saw at once that Elspeth was gifted,' Miss Pemberton said matter-of-factly, seating herself with her own cup and saucer, 'but she was a difficult child, and at first resisted all attempts to help her. At the tender age of eleven, she knew exactly what she wished to paint, and proceeded to do so, irrespective of what was set in class. But Miss Parish – the flair she showed! One might almost say, even at that early age, the genius! She had a God-given eye for colour and shape, and could make any sheet of paper come alive. I confess I was very excited by her, and pleaded on her behalf that she be allowed free rein. Time enough for the necessary discipline later.

'Once she realized I was, as she considered it, "on her side", she immediately relaxed, and her work blossomed with incredible speed. She painted with the assurance of someone twice her age, seldom needing to redo or retouch any of her work.'

'You say she was difficult; was that only in relation to her art?'

'No,' Miss Pemberton said frankly, 'I fear my colleagues had quite a lot of trouble with her in the early days. She could be totally uncooperative when she chose, as I'd already discovered, but gradually, as she found fulfilment in her art, she became more amenable in other areas.'

'Was she popular, would you say?'

Moira Pemberton considered, nibbling delicately on a piece of shortbread. 'She was *different*. That can often lead to bullying, but thankfully, in Elspeth's case, it didn't. A few girls, I believe, made tentative offers of friendship, but her take-it-or-leave it attitude was scarcely encouraging. Her only real friend was a girl called Chloë Pyne, and I worried about that.'

Rona leant forward interestedly. 'Why?'

'Because Chloë was a very different type, quiet and studious, but content to take a back seat, if you know what I mean. Her work was competent enough, though in a different class from Elspeth's, but as that first term progressed, she seemed to fall under her spell, and started neglecting her other studies in favour of art. My colleagues hinted I was to blame, but I knew it was Elspeth's influence. She could be very forceful.'

Moira Pemberton rose and refilled Rona's cup. 'Chloë, on the other hand, *was* popular, but as they moved up through the school, her friends

238

fell away. I did wonder if that, too, could be laid at Elspeth's door, but naturally I'd no proof, and even if I had, there was nothing I could have done about it.'

She paused, staring into her coffee cup. 'Years later, Chloë tragically took her own life, and once again there were those who blamed Elspeth.'

'Did you *like* Elspeth, Miss Pemberton?'

The woman seemed taken aback. 'What a curious question! Yes, of course I did – and do. Dominant though she appeared, in a sense she was vulnerable too. Also, don't forget, I saw the best side of her.'

She smiled complacently. 'She's been very generous in publicly acknowledging her debt to me, and I've been her guest at several Private Views.'

'You're still in touch?' Rona asked quickly.

'Not, alas, since Chloë died. I heard she took it very badly.'

'And then she seemed to ... disappear,' Rona said artlessly. 'I believe that caused some concern?'

'A lot of nonsense was talked, yes,' Moira Pemberton confirmed. 'Wholly irresponsible, if you ask me. She simply needed to be alone, and who can blame her?'

'Where do you think she is?'

'Somewhere quiet, where she can get on with her work without distractions. That was always what she wanted. She'll come back when she's ready.' Moira Pemberton sobered suddenly. 'A

239

terrible thing, that woman being killed in her home.'

'Yes, indeed.'

'It's enough to put her work back several months.'

No doubt, Rona thought acidly, Mary Strong would have put her murder on hold if she'd realized it would distract her employer.

Possibly divining the direction of her thought, Miss Pemberton flushed. 'That sounds appallingly insensitive, but I only meant that on occasion the muse needs careful nursing, and any upset can interrupt the flow. The woman was her cleaner, I believe?'

'Yes, and had been for many years.'

Miss Pemberton shook her head sadly. 'All the worse,' she said, leaving Rona unclear whether she meant for Mary or Elspeth.

'Did you remain in touch when Elspeth was at university and the RCA?'

'Yes, indeed. She used to come and see me in the vacations, and bring samples of her work.' She nodded at the wall behind Rona. 'That's one of them.'

Rona turned, seeing, to her surprise, a portrait of a small black spaniel.

'Toto, my dog at that time. He's been dead many years.'

'I didn't know she painted animals.'

'She can turn her hand to anything, but as you must know, clouds have always been a passion. She'd lie on the grass out there –' she nodded through the window at the back garden, now dank and November-grey – 'staring up at the sky and watching clouds race across it. "Aren't they wonderful, Pemby?" she'd say. "Never two the same!"'

There was a pause, while Rona braced herself for a question she knew would cause annoyance. 'Wasn't there some sort of scandal concerning one of the masters?'

Miss Pemberton frowned. 'Wherever did you hear that? I'd hoped it was well and truly buried in the past.'

'But it was while Elspeth was at school?'

'I believe so, yes. But what of it? Regrettably, human nature being what it is, these things happen from time to time.'

'I just wondered if it had any affect on her.'

'It affected the whole school,' Miss Pemberton said sharply, 'filling some of the girls' heads with pseudo-romantic nonsense. Elspeth, I'm sure, was above that sort of thing.'

Ah, but she wasn't, Rona thought. And maybe the affect on her was the deepest and longest lasting of all. Though she knew it was unwelcome, she probed a little further.

'What actually happened?'

Miss Pemberton sighed. 'I sometimes wonder if it's wise to have men teaching impressionable girls – especially young and handsome ones.' An unwilling smile tugged at her mouth. 'I may say that some of the staff weren't above making eyes at him, either; he was a personable young man. Colin Palmer; I've not thought of that name in years.'

'And the girl?'

'That's what made it worse, actually. It would have been bad enough if it had been one of the flibberty-gibbets who giggled every time they saw a man. But it was the head girl, Marianne Davis, who had a place at Oxford waiting for her.'

'Do you know what happened to them?'

'Unsurprisingly, there was a clampdown, but I heard later that she was expecting a child, so I doubt she ever got to Oxford.' Miss Pemberton squared her shoulders. 'All in all, it was a nine days' wonder,' she said dismissively. 'I'm surprised you're interested in it.'

'I'd heard the episode referred to, and thought I should check.' Rona leant forward and switched off the recorder. 'Thank you so much, Miss Pemberton. You've been extremely helpful. I won't take up any more of your time.'

Miss Pemberton rose with her. 'I'm glad to have been of help,' she said.

As before, Rona had her lunch at the coffee house, thinking over the interview. There'd been nothing really new, but at least it could be ticked off her list. Which, she thought reluctantly, left Elspeth's parents. They were a glaring omission among her interviewees, and she was tempted yet again to put off seeing them. But as she'd told Max, she couldn't delay indefinitely, and on the practical side, she could make a detour to Chilswood on the way home.

Before her resolve weakened, she took out her

mobile, looked up the number Gwen Saunders had given her, and tapped it out.

'Hello, yes?' It was a woman's voice, breathless and excited.

'Mrs Wilding? This is Rona Parish. I—'

'Oh, Rona! I hope I may call you that? Have you heard? Has Naomi been in touch?'

Rona frowned, puzzled. 'I'm sorry, I don't—'

'Then you haven't! Such wonderful news, I can scarcely believe it! We've had a letter from Elspeth!'

Rona gasped, her planned speech flying out of her head. It didn't matter; Mrs Wilding was continuing unabated. 'It came this morning, out of the blue! She says she's well, and hopes to be home in the spring! Isn't it the most incredible news?'

'Yes,' Rona stammered, 'it certainly is. You must be so ... relieved.'

'Oh, I can't tell you! But since you didn't know, you must be phoning about something else?'

'Yes, I...' With an effort, Rona pulled herself together. 'I'm in Buckford at the moment, and was wondering if I could call on you on my way home? But please do say if—'

'That would be perfect! We've been wondering when we'd hear from you, and now we can show you Elspeth's letter. What time should we expect you?'

Rona twisted her wrist to check her watch. 'In about an hour?'

'We'll look forward to it.'

She switched off the phone and closed her hand round it, her thoughts whirling, until a discreet cough caused her to look up, to find the waitress at her side.

'I said, would you like anything else?'

'Oh, sorry; no thanks. Could I just have the bill, please?'

Has Naomi phoned? Mrs Wilding had asked. And it *was* surprising she'd not heard from her – until she remembered Naomi hadn't her mobile number. Quickly, she dialled home, to find a message waiting.

'Rona – it's Naomi. You'll never believe this, but we've heard from Elspeth! The parents have, too – it was Mary's death that did the trick. You thought it might, didn't you? Please call me as soon as you get this message.'

The bill was placed on the table in front of her, and Rona took out her purse. On reflection, she decided to postpone returning Naomi's call until she'd spoken to her parents. By then, there might be other things to ask her.

It was starting to rain as Rona drew up outside the Wildings' house, and the wind was getting stronger. She turned up her coat collar and hurried up the path, but before she could press the bell, the door opened and Hazel Wilding stood beaming at her. She was a small, round woman with a halo of frizzy hair and a pair of spectacles hanging on a chain round her neck.

She reached for Rona's hand and drew her into the warm hall. 'Come in, come in, Rona! How nice to meet you – I'm Hazel! What a horrible day it's turning into!' She raised her voice. 'Richard! Rona's here!'

For a disoriented minute, Rona expected the Richard Wilding she'd met to materialize, but it was his father who came down the stairs and firmly shook her hand. He was as tall as his son and with the same penetrating eyes, but such hair as he had was sparse and totally white.

'Come into the sitting room,' Hazel said, bustling ahead of Rona into a room where a fire burned cheerfully in the grate. Seeing her glance appreciatively at it, she added, 'When we moved to somewhere smaller, our first requirement was a chimney. For all your central heating, you can't beat an old-fashioned fire.'

She waved Rona towards the sofa facing it, and took an envelope from behind the clock.

'Before we start answering your questions,' she said, 'you might like to read this.'

Rona took it, noticing it had been posted in London the previous day. The letter inside was headed with the same date, but no address was given, and the writing, in thick black ink, was in italic script – a work of art in itself, though not easy to read.

Dear Mother and Father,

I'm sorry not to have been in touch before, but I hope you'll understand that I needed to cut myself off from everything 'safe' and familiar, in order to reinvigorate my work. I also hope the message I left for Naomi to pass on convinced you all that there was no need to worry about me.

Now, however, poor Mary's death impels me to write. What a totally horrendous thing to have happened! I'm still reeling from the shock of it. Who could have done such a thing, and for God's sake, why? I can only pray it wasn't in any way down to my absence. Please pass my sincere condolences to Bill. He must be devastated.

One of my aims in coming away was to paint enough pictures for a small exhibition on my return, and hopefully relaunch my career. I have now almost completed this, and all being well, intend to return home in the spring. So please be patient just a little longer.

Forgive me for any heartache I might have caused you, and I hope when you see my latest work, you'll feel it was worthwhile.

Fond love to you both,
Elspeth

Rona would have liked to read it again more slowly, but Mrs Wilding, who'd been watching her expectantly, was holding out her hand for its return, and she reluctantly relinquished it.

'We could have done with something of the sort a good few months ago,' Richard Wilding said dryly. 'It would have saved a lot of worry, and as Naomi no doubt told you, Rona – I may call you Rona, since you're younger than my daughters? – we didn't get nearly as much of her message as Elspeth had intended, and even that

246

only weeks later. Not that she could have known, of course.'

But she did, Rona thought; though Elspeth couldn't admit it, she'd read of her 'disappearance' and phoned her brother for an explanation. If only, at that stage, she'd allowed him to reassure her parents.

'It's certainly good news that she'll be home soon,' she said diplomatically, 'and also, of course, that she's painting again. I believe she'd been rather in the doldrums before she left?'

'That followed on from Chloë's death,' Hazel said, her eyes filling with ready tears. 'She wasn't thinking straight for a long time after that. You know about Chloë?'

'Yes, a very sad business.'

'Such a *waste*! She was a lovely girl, and round here so often, she was almost like a daughter to us.' She dabbed at her eyes. 'But I mustn't be maudlin. When I heard you'd be contacting us, I sorted out some of Elspeth's things I thought you'd like to see.'

She produced a large folder and seated herself next to Rona on the sofa. 'I kept all the children's drawings when they were little, never dreaming that Elspeth's would be of any more interest than the others'. Now, I'm told, American universities would pay good money for them. Not that they're for sale, mind.'

Rona turned over the large sheets of paper, trying to see them through Max's eyes. To her, the earlier ones looked much like the offerings of children everywhere – bright colours spilling over the lines, round suns and square houses and stick ladies with triangular skirts.

But then, gradually, they became more subtle as an awareness developed – surely precociously – of perspective, line and colour. At the top of each sheet, someone – no doubt her mother – had noted the age at which the picture had been drawn, and by nine or ten the technique was noticeably more assured – horses jumping over fences, their bodies twisting in the air; the musculature in a man's leg as he leapt to catch a ball – the kind of detail, no doubt, that had so excited Miss Pemberton.

'It's amazing how quickly she developed,' Rona said, since some comment seemed called for. 'I believe her grandfather was an artist?'

'Well, he taught art, but he modestly described himself as a weekend painter. I suppose she might have inherited some of his genes.'

Hazel glanced down at some papers in her hand. 'These are her school reports; you won't want to read them now, but you're welcome to take them with you, provided, of course, you return them.' She smiled tremulously. 'Last week, I wouldn't have let them out of the house, but now I've heard from her and know she's well, I can afford to relax a little.'

'I'd love to borrow them, thank you,' Rona said, slipping them into her briefcase, 'and I promise to let you have them back within a week or two.'

For the next hour or so, her recorder primed, she listened to the retelling of Elspeth's childhood – her frustrations, her first day at school, the fateful gift of a paint box, and the transformation it wrought in her. Most of it, Rona had already heard from Naomi, less charitably slanted, but there were new stories too that helped to put flesh on the bones of what was essentially still an elusive figure. And, in the course of the telling, Chloë's name came up again and again.

'It was tragic,' Hazel ended, 'that after all those years together, they were estranged at the time of her death.'

'Why was that?' Rona asked gently, curious to know the interpretation Elspeth's parents put on it. It was surprisingly candid.

'Jealousy, pure and simple,' Richard said uncompromisingly. 'This chap fell for Chloë, and Elspeth couldn't take it.'

'Richard—'

'You know it's true, my dear. She made such a fuss, for God's sake, that Chloë broke off the relationship, but even that wasn't enough. God alone knows if it was Elspeth or What's-his-name who proved the last straw, but between them they pushed her too far.'

'Elspeth fell apart,' Hazel said in a low voice, twisting a handkerchief between her fingers. 'We couldn't reach her. Even at the funeral, though she was standing beside us, she held herself apart, and the anguish on her face broke my heart. I wanted desperately to hold her, comfort her – you do, when your child's hurt, no matter how old she is – but it was our son she turned to. He took her back to London and helped her through the first few weeks. I dread to think what might have happened if he hadn't.'

Richard Wilding cleared his throat. 'I think that's enough soul-searching, my dear. Rona already knows the facts, after all.'

'But I have a feeling she thinks badly of Elspeth for not telling us where she is, and I want to explain that's my fault rather than hers. Because if I'd known, I'd have gone to her – I wouldn't have been able to stop myself – and she didn't want that. She needed to be alone, away from all of us, while she rebuilt her life. Hard though it's been, it was the right thing to do.'

By the time Rona left the Wildings, it was dark and the rain had set in. Max would be home before her, and she texted, rather than phoning, to let him know where she was. Conversation at this point would have dissipated the impressions and nuances of the last couple of hours, and she needed the solitude of the drive home to assimilate them. Time enough to discuss it all with him over supper.

This book she was embarking on had all the trademarks of a tragedy, she reflected uneasily, her eyes on the swathes of light cast by her headlamps. A tragedy for Elspeth, for Hazel, above all for Chloë. If, as was hoped, Elspeth returned home in the spring, it might at least be resolved for her and her mother, but Chloë was beyond anyone's help. How must it feel to be so distraught, so desperately unhappy, that the only way to end it was by killing oneself? And what a burden of guilt, either justified or not, it bestowed on those left behind.

FOURTEEN

'So in the spring you'll be able to interview Elspeth herself,' Max commented, checking the steak under the grill. 'That's quite a turn-up, isn't it?'

'But it's four or five months away,' Rona objected, 'which means I'll have to mark time, in case she contradicts whatever I've written. I need to see her *now*, Max!'

'Then track her down. She has to be *some-where*.'

'Marcia said she's in Scotland, but the letter had a London postmark, and Gwen Saunders sent papers to a post box there. It doesn't make sense.'

'Why does Marcia think Scotland?'

'Because that's what Elspeth told them, though Richard did say they'd only her word for it.'

She sighed, watching him drain vegetables over the sink. 'The trouble is, very few people have spoken to her, and they're all self-contained units. So Richard wouldn't know what she told Gwen or her dealer, and vice versa.'

'Will she have written to Richard, do you think?'

'Probably, to avert family suspicion, though I bet she was on the phone as soon as she heard about Mary.'

'Then he'll have seen the postmark, which will no doubt have confused him.'

'Join the club.'

Max deftly arranged meat and vegetables on the plates, added red wine sauce, and brought them to the table.

'You'll just have to exercise your detective faculties!' he said.

Lindsey's flat had indeed undergone a sea change, its whole character enriched and up-dated.

'Come early,' she'd said, 'so I can give you a conducted tour. I don't want to make too much of it in front of Dominic.'

So they'd arrived at seven with a bottle of champagne, which she put in the fridge while she showed them round. Hall, stairs and landing they'd seen on arrival, transformed from un-inspired magnolia to a rich terracotta contrasting strikingly with the stark white woodwork and knobbed oatmeal of the original carpet.

Their first port of call was her bedroom, another metamorphosis. The furniture was in limed oak, a shelved arch over the bed, with wardrobes on either side, taking up considerably less space than the previous, free-standing units and making the room seem larger. The walls were a soft primrose, with a stencilled pattern in royal blue and gold running round the top, colours picked up by the curtains and duvet.

'It's fantastic, Linz!' Rona exclaimed. 'Makes me think it's more than time we did something with *our* bedroom.'

'I was afraid of that!' murmured Max.

The guest room had been given similar treatment, also with fitted furniture, but with a reversal of colours, blue walls and yellow curtains. However, it was the sitting room of which Lindsey was most proud, and again the effect was striking.

Chairs and sofas were upholstered in café au lait tweed, embellished with duck-egg blue scatter cushions, the walls painted the same duck-egg, and the curtains, hanging richly from floor to ceiling, were in swirls of both colours against a cream background. Lindsey's familiar bureau stood in place, but the dining table in the window was new, again in light-coloured wood.

'Linz, it's perfect!' Rona enthused.

'It's not quite finished, of course, but I want to live in it a while before I buy pictures and ornaments, and in any case I'm going to keep things minimal. It was too cluttered before.'

They were interrupted by a ring at the doorbell, and Lindsey left them to admit Dominic. As he came into the room, Rona was relieved to find her initial liking for him reinforced. With his height, the breadth of his shoulders and his easy manner, he had an air of authority that she suspected was unconscious, certainly in these social conditions. Both sisters held their breath as he shook hands with Max, but to their relief, there was immediate affinity between the two men.

'What a charming room, Lindsey!' Dominic said, looking about him.

'I can't claim much credit, but I am delighted with it. Max, please will you come and open the champagne?'

Left to themselves, Rona and Dominic exchanged a smile. 'Lindsey tells me you've returned to biography. I'm glad; you have a talent for it.'

'Thank you. I'm finding it quite hard, after being able to dash off articles in a matter of days for the last couple of years.'

'Yes, it must require a different mindset.'

Lindsey and Max returned with the opened bottle, and at her request, Max poured it into the flutes.

'To the rebirth of 6a Fairhaven!' he toasted. 'Good luck to all who live in her!'

'I trust you're not going to break the bottle over the bureau?' Rona commented, as they raised their glasses.

'I think we can dispense with that. Congratulations, though, Lindsey; it was a brave decision to scrap everything and start again, and it's worked brilliantly.'

'And thank you both, for housing me while it was going on.'

'At least it made us sort out the studio!'

The evening had started well, and it continued

so. Lindsey, with her usual flair, produced a delicious meal, and it was a pleasure to eat off the new Curzon porcelain. Rona had spent a traumatic few weeks earlier in the year, researching the firm's hundred and fifty-year history; weeks that had encompassed a murder and considerable emotional turmoil. Resolutely, she put it out of her mind.

'I spoke to Mum this morning,' Lindsey remarked, while the men were talking. 'She's coming for coffee tomorrow.'

'She'll love the flat. How's Sarah, did she say? Any repercussions from the mugging?'

'No, she went back to school on the Monday, and seems fine.'

'And Guy?'

Lindsey smiled. 'I saved that topic for tomorrow, when she can't claim there's someone at the door!'

'Good thinking!'

Max glanced across at them. 'Dominic's been telling me about all the places he visits on business,' he said, opening up the conversation. 'I'm wondering if I'm in the wrong profession!'

Dominic shook his head. 'All I normally see are hotels and airport lounges, though I admit I enjoy travelling. Making up for a deprived childhood, perhaps – my mother wouldn't fly, so when we were young, foreign holidays were out.' He smiled reminiscently. 'Not that we *felt* deprived; some relatives had a holiday home at the seaside, and every year we used to trundle off there. We had a great time, rock-climbing and sailing.'

'Not Crispin's parents, by any chance?' Lindsey asked.

'Yes, as it happens; they had this house at a little place called Craiglea, up the coast from Helensburgh, and when they weren't there themselves, were quite happy for the rest of us to make use of it.'

'In Scotland?' Rona asked sharply. 'The Ryders had a house in Scotland?'

'That's right. They were into sailing, and kept a boat up there.'

She felt a stab of excitement. 'Have they still got it? The house, I mean?'

He seemed surprised by her interest, as did Lindsey, though Max was looking resigned.

'As far as I know. I've not been up for years, but I believe it's proved useful to Crispin on more than one occasion.'

'As a love nest?' Lindsey asked, round-eyed, but Dominic only laughed.

Rona met Max's eyes with an almost imperceptible shake of her head; the last thing she wanted was for him to make some reference to Elspeth Wilding. She said quickly, 'We always went to the same place too, didn't we, Linz? I think it's good for children – gives a sense of continuity. When Pops asked if we'd like to go to Spain or France, we always said, "As long as we can go to the cottage as well!"'

The talk continued on a holiday theme until, some time after eleven, Max glanced at his watch. 'Time we were on our way,' he remarked. 'Gus will be crossing his legs.'

They all rose and moved towards the door.

'Don't let us break up the party,' Rona protested, but Dominic shook his head.

'My car will be here any minute.'

'I was wondering if he'd stay the night,' Rona commented, when, having said their goodbyes, they set off for home.

'Perhaps the car was a discreet fabrication.'

But as they turned on to the main road, a sleek-looking Daimler was approaching, and Max, checking the rear-view mirror, confirmed it had turned into the cul-de-sac. 'We didn't leave them long to say goodnight,' he remarked.

'What did you think of him?'

'Very pleasant chap. At a guess, pretty ruthless on the business front, but excellent company socially. Lindsey could do worse than end up with him.'

'It was a good evening,' Rona agreed, 'not least because I now have a very good idea where Elspeth is hiding.'

Crispin Ryder stood at the window of his docklands flat, whisky glass in hand, staring out at the dark water. Pointless to go to bed: sleep was impossible while his mind obsessively circled the problems that were mounting by the day, to the stage where he was no longer confident he could contain them.

How the hell did he get into this? he asked himself, on a wave of impatience. It had started as a joke, a bit of harmless fun – but that was before Grayson became involved. And to complicate things still further, Elspeth was getting restless. She'd been talking of returning home, even before the murder of her housekeeper, or whoever she was.

Crispin sighed, refilled his glass, and returned to his post at the window. She'd been hysterical on the phone, he recalled, blaming herself for the woman's death, and insisting she owed it to the family to go back at once. He'd had to drop everything and fly up to calm her.

And it had taken all his skills to persuade her to stay. Eventually, though, she'd agreed that, for the moment, letters to the family would suffice, and he'd duly posted them on his return to London the next evening. If it hadn't been for tonight's formal dinner, he'd have stayed for the weekend as he usually did – and on reflection, it might have been better if he had. For Grayson had, of course, been at the dinner, foiling Crispin's attempts to avoid him, and enquiring silkily if all was going according to plan.

And as if all that wasn't enough, there was that girl and her bloody biography. It had come as a severe shock when Magda Ridgeway mentioned it. Talk about bad timing! The last thing they wanted just now was someone prying into Elspeth's life and work. Surprisingly, though, Elspeth herself hadn't been too concerned. 'She won't fare any better than the last one,' she'd said, bypassing his attempt to make it one more reason for her to stay in Scotland.

He sipped his whisky, allowing his thoughts to

drift back to their first meeting, nearly two years ago, at the opening of the Newbolt Gallery in St James's. Someone had pointed her out to him, an inconspicuous little thing, he'd thought, hiding behind that curtain of hair. Their paths hadn't crossed during the evening, but outside, in the dark and the rain, they had hailed the same taxi, and, learning the direction she was going in, he'd suggested they share it. Little had he known the consequences that would have, some of them immediate.

In the taxi, they'd embarked on a discussion of the paintings on view, a discussion that was still in full flow when they drew up at her hotel, and she'd impulsively suggested he go in with her to continue it in the bar. So he'd paid off the taxi and followed her, and at some point she'd stopped talking about the general and started on the particular – her dissatisfaction both with her life and her work, her growing conviction that she needed to widen her horizons before she could become a great painter.

As one drink followed another, adding to the champagne consumed at the gallery, Elspeth's inhibitions had noticeably lessened, until he'd felt able to ask how, exactly, she wanted her horizons to expand. And she had looked him straight in the eye and replied, 'I'd like you to make love to me. Would you mind?'

It wasn't until they were in bed that he'd realized she was a virgin – a totally new experience for him – but what she lacked in experience, she more than made up for in the passion he aroused.

After that, she started coming to London every ten days or so, staying with her brother in Regent's Park. And every evening they'd have a meal, then return to the flat and make love.

She'd made it clear from the first she wasn't interested in marriage, and the knowledge that he had other women stimulated rather than concerned her. As she told him frankly, she'd reached her mid-forties without experiencing sex, and intended to make up for lost time.

It had proved an ideal arrangement for both of them, largely because love didn't enter into it, though as time went on they became genuinely fond of each other. And the bonus, as if to prove her theory, was that Elspeth started painting again.

If only it could have continued like that, Crispin thought now, staring out at the sleeping Thames. If he hadn't seen that television programme, if he hadn't mentioned it to Grayson, if, if ... But he had, and now things were fast becoming dicey, and he was running out of options. Grayson, he knew, wouldn't give an inch until the deal was completed, but things had changed and the danger of exposure grew ever greater.

Which, Crispin thought disgustedly, turning from the window at last, brought him full circle, and no nearer solving any of it. He might just as well go to bed.

Catherine said, 'You haven't forgotten it's your

birthday on Wednesday?'

Tom smiled. 'No, but I rather hoped you had.'

'Not a chance! How would you like to spend it?'

'Quietly, with you.'

'You old stick-in-the-mud!' she said fondly.

'Preferable to all the hullabaloo last year – retirement parties left, right and centre, leaving Avril, finding this flat, and to crown it all, the explosive Christmas lunch at the Clarendon, with Rona at the centre of it. It's a wonder I survived it all. Come to that, *your* birthday was drama enough, with Jenny going into labour in the middle of lunch. Let's opt for a quiet day for mine.'

Catherine smiled. 'You might have a point. You don't want me to contact the girls, then?'

He shook his head. 'They'll pop round with presents at some stage, bless them, and we can have a glass of wine, but they both lead busy lives, and birthdays midweek are inconvenient at best.'

'How about the weekend?'

'No, Catherine, seriously. I don't want a fuss. A meal out, perhaps, just the two of us. Treat ourselves to Serendipity. That would be great.'

'It's not that you don't feel up to it?' she asked anxiously. 'You haven't had any more chest pains?'

He reached out a hand, and she took it. 'No, I haven't. It's just that I've got to the age when a birthday isn't necessarily something to cele-brate.'

'Surely there's all the more reason to!' she said.

Lindsey stretched luxuriously, glancing out of the window at the wintry sun.

'There's something gloriously decadent about making love in the afternoon,' she said lazily. 'You could have stayed last night, you know.'

'Far be it from me to embarrass your relatives.'

'They were probably expecting it.'

'Well, I couldn't take it for granted on my first visit, added to which, your mother was due for coffee this morning.'

'Not till eleven! Plenty of time to make your getaway!'

'Was she impressed with the décor?'

'Very. Come to think of it, you could have met her, too, if you'd stayed, but perhaps you'd had enough of my family for one weekend.' She paused. 'You did like them, didn't you, Rona and Max?'

'Very much. I hope it was mutual.'

'I'll phone Ro tomorrow and find out.'

He laughed. 'And report back?'

'It depends what she says!'

'She seemed very interested in our Scottish holidays,' Dominic said reflectively. 'Has she some connection up there?'

'Not that I know of. I'll ask her about that, too.'

'Not on my account, please. It's none of my business.'

'But it is mine.'

'How do you make that out?'

'She's my twin,' Lindsey said illogically.

She slipped off the bed and padded over to the window. Across the road the park rolled away down the hill, and beyond it, the roofs and steeples of Marsborough glinted in the November sunshine. The trees were bare now, their naked branches stencilled against a pale sky, and in the park below, children were flying kites, bright splashes of colour in a monochrome landscape.

Dominic came up behind her, slipping his arms round her and resting his chin on the top of her head. 'Not a bad outlook, is it?' he said complacently.

'It's wonderful, especially from this height. With the house being at the top of the hill, and you at the top of the house, you get a double bonus.'

'Talking of bonuses,' Dominic said softly in her ear, 'how about coming back to bed?'

It was a family rule that work was banned at weekends, but when Max left for the studio the next morning, Rona went straight to the study and switched on the computer. Ever since the dinner party, she had been wondering about the house in ... Craiglea, wasn't it? She'd only half-listened when Dominic spoke of it, the Ryders not having been mentioned at that point, and after questioning him once, she'd not dared ask him to repeat it. Perhaps the phone book would help?

She googled Telephone Directory, Residential Numbers, the BT Phone Book, then typed Ryder under Surname, and Craiglea under Location, and held her breath. And behold a box appeared, giving the name GL Ryder, and not only the number, but – unlooked-for bonus – the address: 57 The Esplanade, Craiglea, Dunbartonshire.

For some minutes she sat staring at it before, with a dry mouth, lifting the phone and tapping it out, holding her breath as she listened to the ringing all those miles away. But the minutes stretched out – two, three – and she released her breath as her spurt of hope withered and died.

Was Elspeth listening to that same ringing? If so, it was clear she was not going to answer it. Nor did a machine cut in; presumably, if the Ryders were seldom there, there was little point in having one. Disappointed and frustrated, Rona ended the call.

'Hi there! Just phoning to thank you for a lovely meal on Saturday.'

'Ro! I was on the point of calling you. Glad you enjoyed it.'

'Sorry we left you with all that washing-up!'

'The dishwasher turned up trumps, and I left the rest till morning.'

'Wise decision. Incidentally, we passed the limousine, just along the road.'

'Dominic being discreet! What did you both think of him?'

'Very impressed. Max says you shouldn't let

him slip through your fingers.'

'Does he, indeed? Well, you'll be pleased to know he liked you, too. He did wonder, though, why you were so interested in the Ryders' holiday retreat, and I must say, so did I.'

Rona hesitated. Anything she said to Lindsey might well get back to Dominic, particularly if they'd already discussed her interest.

'No reason, really,' she prevaricated, 'except that I'd have expected their holiday home to be somewhere exotic, like Barbados or the Canary Isles. Scotland seemed a bit tame.'

'That's all it was?'

'What else?'

'I don't know, but you sounded ... startled, rather than just curious.'

'Imagination, dear sister.'

'If you say so. What are you doing about Pops's birthday?'

'I spoke to Catherine earlier. They're going out for dinner à deux – he doesn't want a fuss – so I said I'd drop in for a drink before lunch.'

'That sounds a good idea; I might well join you.'

'The more the merrier. See you there.'

'I'll pick you up if you like, around twelve? Save you getting out the car.'

'Thanks, sis, I'll be ready.'

Max phoned half an hour later.

'Did you find the number?'

'What number?' Rona asked innocently.

'Come on, I know you too well for that! The

Scottish one, of course.'

'I did, yes, for all the good it did me.'

'No reply? Well, that's hardly surprising. She's probably not there at all.'

'Or she's just not answering,' Rona said stubbornly.

'Be realistic, love; Scotland's a big place, and you're not even sure Elspeth's there, since all communications came from London.'

'I just think Crispin's involved somehow.'

'Because she had his mobile number? Again, a very tenuous link.'

'And because he was in that photo.'

'As were a crowd of other people.'

'Oh, all right – stop being so pragmatic! The point is, I need to speak to her, and now I know she's been in touch, it's galling that I still don't know where she is.'

'Well, it looks as though you'll just have to go on being galled!' he said.

That evening when Sarah arrived home, Avril heard voices in the hall, followed by a tap on the sitting room door.

'Come in,' she called, and Sarah opened it to usher in Clive.

'Good evening, Mrs Parish,' he said.

'Hello, Clive.' Avril waited expectantly, surprised by his presence. It was soon explained.

Sarah's face was flushed. 'We've got possession of the flat!' she said. 'It's great – everything we were looking for; on the other side of Belmont, but still only ten minutes' walk from school.'

'Well done,' Avril said lamely, wondering what was expected of her.

'I did warn you, didn't I? That I'd be moving out when the sale went through?'

'You did, yes.' She felt her heart sink. Though it hadn't been plain sailing with Sarah, they'd become used to each other – and after all, it was through her that she'd met Guy. Now, she'd have to go through the whole process again – the advertising, the worrying about choosing someone compatible.

'So if it's OK, I'll leave at the end of term, in three weeks.'

'Yes, of course.' She really should show more enthusiasm in the face of the girl's delight. 'How exciting for you,' she added.

Clive said, 'We're hoping to get settled in over the Christmas holidays.'

Avril turned to Sarah. 'So you won't be home for Christmas?' Her heart contracted on Guy's behalf.

'Not all of it, but I'll be moving my stuff out at some stage, now we've got somewhere permanent.' She hesitated, glanced at Clive, and burst out, 'And I've got to tell someone! We've just got engaged!'

That did bring Avril to her feet. 'Oh, my dear, that's lovely!' Impulsively, she hurried to kiss Sarah's cheek and shake Clive's hand. 'I'm so glad for you!'

'It only happened this evening, so you're the first to know. Don't say anything to Dad, will you, till I've had a chance to?'

'Of course not.'

'You must come and see the flat when we're settled in.'

'I'd love to.'

'Well, that's really all I wanted to say, so – goodnight, Avril.'

The door closed behind them, and, a few minutes later she heard the front door, as Clive took his leave. It was the first time Sarah had used her name, Avril reflected; a sign, perhaps, of the coming change in their relationship, from PG and landlady to ... what? Superstitiously, Avril shied away from an alternative.

Guy phoned at lunch time the next day, on her return from the library.

'I believe you heard the news before I did?' he began.

'Yes – sorry about that! Are you pleased?'

'I suppose so, apart from the usual fatherly reservations when a daughter leaves him for another man. I like Clive, though; I think they'll be good for each other. And actually, it's helped me make up my mind on something I've been considering for some time. Sarah tells me she'll be moving all her things out, which means this won't be her home any longer, and God knows I've been rattling around here ever since she moved to Belmont.'

'You'll be looking for something smaller, then?'

'Not only that; more of my work is now over

your side of the county, and it would save a lot of travelling if I moved closer to Marsborough.' A smile came into his voice. 'There'd be other advantages, too.'

'Sounds a sensible idea,' Avril said guardedly.

'I might call on your services to help me look for somewhere. As it happens, I'll be over your way tomorrow; we could discuss it over lunch?'

Tomorrow. Tom's birthday. Well, she'd posted his card. Nothing else was expected – or desired – of her.

'That would be lovely,' she said.

'Same time, same place?'

'I'll be there.'

Avril was thoughtful as she put down the phone.

FIFTEEN

Rona tried the Craiglea number repeatedly over the next twenty-four hours, but with continued lack of success. In the meantime, though she tried to concentrate on Elspeth's childhood, she was continually distracted.

First came the news that a man who'd been 'helping the police with their enquiries' on Mary Strong's murder had been released without charge. One week on, and seemingly back to square one. Rona's thoughts strayed to the solid, loyal woman who had shown her over the house. Thank God neither of them had known what was coming.

Then, among Gwen Saunders' notes, she came across a list of private collectors specializing in Elspeth's work, and her mind veered off again. She must contact them at some stage – and, for the first time, wondered how the public would react to Elspeth's reappearance. Would there be a media fanfare, or would she slip back more or less unnoticed?

Oh God, why had she agreed to this biography? Impatiently, she pushed herself away from her desk. What was the point in forcing herself to concentrate, when Lindsey would be here in an hour to take her to Pops? Suppressing a sense of guilt, she switched off the computer and went to make a cup of coffee.

Catherine was at Tom's, as they'd expected, and a selection of minute sausage rolls, vol-au-vents and savouries was set out on the coffee table.

'You really shouldn't have!' Lindsey protested.

'Courtesy of M and S, I'm afraid,' Catherine apologized. 'It's only a snack, but we couldn't have you missing out on your lunch hour.'

Cards and presents were exchanged, drinks poured and the food passed round.

'So, how's the redecoration going?' Tom asked Lindsey.

'All finished, Pops, and now open for viewing. When can you both come round?'

'We'd love to see it, of course, but more importantly, are you pleased with the result?'

'Very. Can't think why I didn't do it years ago. I'll call you tomorrow, and we can fix a time.'

'Fine.' Tom turned to Rona. 'And what of the biography? Coming along all right?'

She wrinkled her nose. 'So-so. The big news is that the family's now heard from Elspeth, and she'll be home in the spring.'

Lindsey stared at her. 'You never told me that!' she accused.

'There hasn't really been the opportunity,' Rona fenced.

'So where is she?'

'That, she didn't say, though I've a pretty good idea.'

'Ro, will you stop being so infuriating!'

'Sorry, but it's only a guess at the moment.'

Lindsey would have argued, but Tom cut in peaceably, 'So you won't be involved in a murder case after all! I must say, that's a relief!'

'Did you look up Miss Burbage?' Catherine enquired.

'Not yet,' Rona admitted, 'but I took your advice and got on to Buckford High. The former art mistress was very helpful.'

Catherine nodded. 'I thought that would be your best bet,' she said.

Lindsey was still sulky when she drove Rona home.

'I can't see why you're being so all-fired secretive,' she complained. 'You could at least tell *me* where Elspeth is.'

'Honestly, Linz, I could be quite wrong, and you know I have to be discreet when working on a bio.'

'I bet Max knows,' Lindsey muttered darkly.

At the Jolly Wagoner, Avril and Guy were enjoying steak and kidney pie.

'Sarah says they're moving in during the holidays,' Avril began diffidently. 'Does that mean she won't be with you?'

Guy made a rueful face. 'Shades of things to come. They're sharing Christmas between relatives, and I've been allotted Boxing Day.'

'Oh, Guy!' Avril put down her fork and looked at him. 'What will you do?'

'Survive, I don't doubt.'

'Come to that, I'm not sure what I'm doing, either. Max and the girls always came to us, but last Christmas Tom and I had just separated, and Max organized a civilized lunch at the Clarendon to break the mould. He's not likely to do it again, though. Tom might well be with Catherine and her family, and for that matter, Lindsey might be with Dominic. For good or ill, time moves on and I suppose we have to move with it.'

'Then make your own arrangements,' Guy said quietly, 'with me.'

She looked at him quickly.

'Only if you want to, of course, but it would pre-empt any awkwardness. And it would only be for Christmas Day.'

'On the other hand,' Avril mused, 'if Rona and Max invite me there, you could come, too.'

He said quickly, 'Oh, I wouldn't want —'

'They were saying they'd like to meet you; this would be the ideal opportunity.'

'Things are in a state of flux, aren't they?' Guy said. 'You and I, Tom and Catherine, Sarah and Clive, even, from what you say, Lindsey and Dominic. By *next* year, it should all have settled down. Your divorce will have come through, for one thing, which should simplify things considerably.' He looked up, suddenly serious. 'You *are* going to marry me, aren't you, Avril?'

'You haven't asked me yet,' she reminded him.

'I'm asking now.' He took her hand. 'Not very romantically, perhaps, over steak and kidney, but very, very, sincerely. Please, darling Avril, will you marry me?'

'Yes,' she said, on a caught breath. 'Oh, yes!'

He turned her hand in his, and kissed the palm. 'That's settled, then.' He grinned suddenly. 'Must be something in the air – first Sarah and Clive, now us!'

'In which case,' Avril said, surprised at the steadiness of her voice, 'there's no question but that we'll spend Christmas together, wherever it is. Also – ' she flushed – 'it seems silly my looking for a new lodger, and you looking for somewhere to live.'

'Daughter moves out, and father moves in? The perfect solution! You're a genius, Mrs Parish! But while that's fine for now, once we're

273

married, we should look for somewhere new to both of us. Agreed?'

'Agreed,' Avril said on a wave of happiness.

Back in the study, Rona dispiritedly switched the computer on again, but instead of returning to her notes, she went on line and googled Craiglea.

Immediately the screen opened on the town's website, listing hotels, sailing club, golf club, and a host of other attractions. A small map in the left hand corner showed a neat little town stretching out along the water. Cautiously, Rona clicked again, enlarging the map to show street names. And there, picked out in orange and running the length of the coast, was The Esplanade.

57, The Esplanade. She felt a rising tide of excitement. Eyes still on the screen, she reached for the phone and tried the number yet again. And still the ringing tone rang out unanswered.

Right, she thought; it seems Mahomet will have to go to the mountain.

'You're *what*?' Max demanded, turning to stare at her.

'Only for a couple of days, to have a look round.'

'Rona, for God's sake! Talk about wild goose chases!'

'If nothing else, it would satisfy me it *was* a wild goose chase.' She paused. 'I suppose there's no chance of your coming with me?'

'Absolutely none. Look, love, you can't just go barging in. If she *is* there – which I strongly doubt – she certainly won't want you turning up on her doorstep. She's entitled to her privacy, and she's shown often enough that she values it.'

'I'm not going to *molest* her, Max,' Rona said sharply, 'and if you think I'm wasting my time, at least it's *my* time. Anyway, it'll be good to get a bit of sea air.'

'Not, surely, at this time of the year. You'll freeze your socks off!'

'Again, they're my socks.'

'Added to which, the hotels are probably all closed for the season.'

'They're not, actually. I've booked a room.'

He sighed. 'There's no talking you out of it, then?'

'Sorry, no; I'm going up tomorrow, for two nights. It'll mean missing our Friday evening, but I'll be back on Saturday. And Max...'

'What?'

'If Lindsey phones – or anyone else, for that matter – don't say where I've gone.'

'Fair enough. You'll phone when you get there?'

'Of course.'

'Then I suppose all I can say is take care, and happy hunting.'

The flight was quick and uneventful, and the hired car she'd booked on line awaited her. According to Multimap, Craiglea was an hour's

275

drive from Glasgow airport, and as an added precaution Rona had brought Max's sat-nav, which she stuck on the windscreen.

With its help, she manoeuvred herself out of the airport, and within minutes found herself on the rain-and-wind-swept M8. She was on her way.

The hotel she'd booked into was on the Esplanade, though how near the Ryder house remained to be seen. She was shown to her room overlooking the front, but what must be a pleasant view in summer was now obscured by a curtain of rain as it continued to lash the windows. Had Elspeth really buried herself here for the past eighteen months?

By the time she'd unpacked her few belongings and made herself a cup of tea, the rain had stopped and a watery sun appeared, so, since she'd no time to waste, Rona changed into appropriate clothing and set out on a voyage of discovery.

The wind caught her breath as she stepped through the swing doors and turned right, in the direction of number fifty-seven. The pavements were wet and shining, and a few hardy souls were about, padded against the vagaries of the weather.

Interspersed with the hotels and boarding houses along the front was a selection of shops – jewellers, gift shops, the Edinburgh Wool shop. Presumably the more plebeian stores and supermarkets were further inland.

The wind in her face was bracing, and Rona fell into an easy stride, keeping track of the numbers as she went. After a while the shops petered out, giving way to residential houses, solid and sturdy in grey stone. Several had vacancy signs in their windows and B&B notices at their gates.

Her footsteps slowed as she approached her goal, while she tried to take in as much as possible without staring at the house too obviously. There was little to distinguish it from its neighbours; no signs or notices here, just a gate, a neat front garden, and a path leading to the door. The windows to either side were screened with net curtains, and Rona wondered, with a tightening of the throat, if Elspeth was inside, watching her.

She continued walking until she came to a street leading inland, and turned into it. Here, the houses were mainly bungalows, hunkering down, Rona thought, against whatever the winter storms might throw at them. At the next corner she again turned right, and, as she'd supposed, found herself in the main shopping street, boasting familiar names like Morrisons and Boots, as well as small, independent establishments – a butcher, a fishmonger and a fruit shop among others.

Most had Christmas decorations in the windows – artificial trees, swags of holly, coloured baubles. It was already getting dark – earlier than at home – and coloured lights strung across the road blinked suddenly into life, turning the puddles on the pavement into rainbows of gold and green, red and blue.

The festive atmosphere reminded Rona that although she and Max intended to invite the family for Christmas lunch, she'd not actually issued invitations – an omission she must rectify on her return home. Perhaps, tomorrow, she'd also take a closer look at the gift shops; one had a display of Rennie Mackintosh-style jewellery and clocks.

At the next crossroads she turned back in the direction of the front, and now she could see lights shining across the water. She'd forgotten it wasn't the open sea that bordered Craiglea, but the Gare Loch, a fairly narrow strip of water that, lower down, opened into the Firth of Clyde.

With the onset of darkness the air had grown colder, and Rona was glad the hotel was only a hundred yards or so down the road. Its warm air enveloped her as she pushed her way inside and took the lift to her room. She stood for several minutes looking at the improved view from her window, the rippling dark water and the lights reflected in it. Then she drew the heavy curtains, sat down on the bed, and phoned Max.

'What's it like?' he asked.

'I was a bit disenchanted when I arrived,' she admitted, 'but that was down to the rain. I've had a walk now, and the town has quite a lot going for it. There are municipal gardens some-where, though I haven't come across them yet, and what's known as a maritime museum. Not that I'll have much time to explore, since Elspeth's my main objective.'

'And how do you propose to achieve that?'

'I thought I'd write a note, explaining who I am and giving my mobile number, and drop it through her letterbox.'

'You mean the Ryders' letterbox,' Max corrected. 'Remember, you've really no reason to believe Elspeth's there, as I tried to point out before you took off.'

'Oh ye of little faith!' she mocked. 'Anyway, not much to report as yet, but it's early days. I'm now going to change and go down for dinner. I only had a sandwich at the airport and I'm absolutely starving!'

He laughed. 'Well, Gus and I are missing you. Take care, sleep well, and I'll speak to you tomorrow. Bye, darling.'

Rona was surprised to see how full the dining room was, though whether the diners were residents or people coming in from the town, she couldn't tell. The menu offered pretty standard fare: a roast, 'catch of the day' – since they were on the coast – pork chop with apple sauce and red cabbage, and a vegetarian option. She ordered cockaleekie soup, followed by the chop and a glass of Merlot.

Then she sat back and looked round the room, surreptitiously inspecting each table in case Elspeth should be among the guests. But unless she'd dyed her hair grey, black or red, there appeared to be no sign of her, and, abandoning her search for the evening, Rona propped up the paperback she'd brought and settled down to enjoy her meal.

Later, back in her room, she took a sheet of the hotel notepaper from its leather folder and, after some thought, composed a brief note to Elspeth, requesting an interview. Knowing her opposition to personal publicity, she wasn't hopeful, but having come this far, she had to justify the trip.

She watched the ten o'clock news as she prepared for bed, read for a few minutes until her eyes felt heavy, then put out the light and fell into a deep and dreamless sleep.

The increasing coldness of the previous evening had brought a thin coating of frost, which, with clear skies and sunshine, promised a more pleasant day. Rona ate the full cooked breakfast before setting off, with more optimism than was justified, to retrace her steps, the sealed envelope in her bag.

More people were about this morning, and she crossed the road to walk along the railings that bordered the beach, breathing in the strong, salty air. Down on the sand, dogs were dashing in and out of the waves, shaking themselves over anyone within radius. Rona felt a pang for Gus; he wasn't used to sand and water, and would have enjoyed the experience.

When she came level to the last of the shops, she crossed back to the landward side, and, her heartbeat accelerating, took the envelope from her bag.

Fifty-seven The Esplanade: the address that had leapt at her out of her computer, and was now literally within reach. Before her courage failed her, Rona opened the gate and walked briskly up the path. But as she leaned forward to post the note, the door opened suddenly, and she found herself face to face with a woman in coat and scarf, who seemed as startled as she was.

Elspeth? Surely it must be, though she looked completely different. Gone was the trademark fall of hair, and with it, Rona's chief means of identification. The figure in front of her could be anyone, with her close crop and small, unfamiliar features.

Rona said hesitantly, 'Elspeth Wilding?' And, as the woman's eyes widened, knew she had struck home.

'Who are you?' she demanded, her fingers gripping the door.

Rona swallowed. 'My name's Rona Parish. I'm writing—'

'Ah!' Elspeth broke in. 'Then I know all too well what you're writing. What I *don't* know is what you're doing here?'

'I was hoping to speak to you,' Rona said lamely.

'Who gave you this address?'

'No one. I just ... worked it out.'

Elspeth frowned. 'I can't imagine how.'

'If you could spare me just a few minutes?' Rona pleaded. 'You've occupied my mind for the last I don't know how long, and it would be so good actually to speak to you.'

'You appreciate I didn't give permission for this biography?'

'Yes, but I do hope you'll agree to it. I've interviewed quite a few people, but it's not the same as—'

'*Who* have you interviewed?' Elspeth interrupted again.

'Your sister, your brother, your parents, Miss Saunders, Mary Strong—'

'Mary? You spoke to Mary? When?'

'The week before she was killed. I'm so sorry—'

'How did she seem? I still can't believe ... oh, look...' Elspeth let go of the door and stood to one side. 'Since you're here, you might as well come in. You can tell me how they all are.'

'Thank you.' Rona slipped the unneeded envelope back in her bag and followed her into the hall. It was immediately apparent that the room on the right had been requisitioned as a studio; through its open door, Rona caught sight of an easel holding a painting, several more stacked against the wall, and a sheet spread over the carpet for protection. But Elspeth, having shrugged off her coat, had passed it and was walking down the hall to the kitchen.

'I'll make coffee,' she said, 'and the first thing is to put you straight about my so-called disappearance. Believe me, I never intended all that hoo-ha. I was horrified when I realized what the family was going through, especially since, as I thought, I'd told them I was going.'

Rona seated herself at the wooden table. 'They never got the message.'

'So I gather.' Elspeth spooned instant coffee into two mugs and added boiling water. 'I immediately phoned my brother – I think he told you – but by then my nephew had come forward and the worst of the panic was over.'

'But you didn't tell them where you were,' Rona said.

Elspeth shot her a quick look, put the mugs on the table, and took some milk out of the fridge. 'I was getting stale, Rona. I needed a complete break, to find my way again. You blame me for concealing my whereabouts, but although I love my family, I didn't want them phoning every few days to see how I was, or even – horror of horrors! – coming up here to check on me. And they would have done, believe me.'

'You missed your goddaughter's party,' Rona pointed out. 'That's why they were sure something had happened to you.'

Elspeth seated herself, wrapping her hands round her mug. 'That, I *was* guilty of, but I told them in the message I couldn't make it, and where I'd left Gill's present. Actually, I hadn't intended leaving till the following week, but a chance came up to go a few days early, and, selfishly, I took it.'

She looked up, meeting Rona's eyes. 'There *were* mitigating circumstances, you know. I'd had a pretty hellish year, and lost all confidence in my painting.'

Rona thought of the canvases in the Buckford

studio, and Max's belief that she'd turned the corner, but it seemed wiser not to argue the point.

'I needed a fresh look, and, to achieve it, a totally new environment. Scotland was the perfect solution. No one bothers me here – I doubt if they know who I am, though I've never made a secret of it – and the scenery really is breathtaking. I'd not intended to stay away so long, but as my talent came back, I decided to paint enough canvases for a solo exhibition, to relaunch my career; and the obvious course was to stay here till I'd completed them. Which I've now almost done.'

She took a sip of coffee. 'Tell me about Mary. How did you come to meet her?'

'Miss Saunders had shown me your studio, but I wanted to get the feel of the house. It's something I like to do when I'm writing biographies; you can tell a lot about someone from their home. So Naomi arranged for me to go back when Mrs Strong was there, and she showed me round.'

'What did she say about me?' Elspeth's voice was low.

'That she wasn't worried, because you'd said you might take a sabbatical, and that you'd told her to keep the house clean, which she was doing.'

Elspeth's eyes filled with tears. 'And they haven't caught anyone?'

Rona shook her head. 'They were questioning a man, but he's been released without charge.'

'I have this terrible fear that her death might be connected with me, though I can't think how. And coming after...'

'Chloë's?' Rona supplied quietly.

Elspeth's head jerked up. 'God, you've not been wasting your time, have you?'

'I'm sorry, I just—'

'Well, I can't fool myself there. Chloë's death was *definitely* my fault. That's something I have to live with.'

She stood up abruptly, took a box of tissues off the counter, and blew her nose. Then she took a deep breath and changed the subject.

'You still haven't said how you tracked me down. Someone *must* have told you.'

'No, honestly, no one did.'

Elspeth regarded her quizzically. 'I gather you have a reputation as a detective, but isn't this rather stretching it?'

Rona sighed. Obviously, Elspeth wasn't going to be fobbed off, but she was reluctant to mention the paper with Crispin's number. It might sound too like snooping.

'It was sheer chance,' she said. 'I saw a picture of you at the opening of a new gallery, and Crispin Ryder was standing behind you.'

Elspeth drew in her breath sharply. 'Now that *is* ironic; I'd no idea he was there, because at that stage I didn't even know him. We actually met later that evening, when we were leaving the gallery. But it still doesn't explain what led you here.'

'Another fluke. Someone mentioned the

Ryders had a holiday home here, and Marcia had said you were in Scotland. It was a long shot, but it ... paid off.'

'Bloody Marcia!' Elspeth said viciously. 'What else did she say?'

'She let slip that you'd been in regular contact with them. Richard wasn't best pleased.'

'I don't know why he puts up with her. So, what are you going to do, now you've found me? Give me away?'

Rona held her challenging gaze. 'It'll be hard to keep it from the family.'

'Well,' Elspeth said on a sigh, 'I shan't be here much longer, so what the hell? Tell them I'm renting a friend's house in Scotland, though I'd rather Crispin's name was kept out of it.'

'Then how do I explain tracing you?'

'God knows! I'm not even sure you've told *me* the full story!'

Then, when it was clear from Rona's expression that she wasn't going to elaborate, she added, 'Say I contacted you, if you like. That I'd heard about the biography and wanted to set things straight.'

'And how shall I say you heard of it? I suppose the truth is that Richard told you?'

'Yes, and at this stage, you might as well tell them so; the rest of the family won't be pleased I've been in touch with him, but you can say I swore him to secrecy.' Elspeth sat back and folded her arms. 'So, is there anything else?'

'Well, as I said, I'd be very grateful if you'd give me an interview.'

'What do you call this?'

'About your work, I mean, and your childhood. How your talent developed, and what direction you want to go in now. For instance, what have you been painting up here?'

'Landscapes and seascapes, for the most part. This place is an artist's paradise.'

'No more clouds, then?'

Elspeth smiled wryly. 'Isn't there a song, *I've looked at clouds from both sides now*? I've certainly done that, and then some! Which isn't to say I mightn't revert to them in the future. In the meantime, I've been doing something completely different. I even managed to persuade a local fisherman to sit for me. But all in all, I'm glad I've nearly finished. I'm ready to go home.'

She took the empty mugs and put them in the sink. 'So how are they all? The parents, Naomi and Lionel?'

'Very well. Delighted to have your letter, and looking forward to seeing you again.' Rona paused. 'I know you were going out, so I won't hold you up any longer, but my flight isn't till tomorrow afternoon. Could I possibly come back in the morning, or even this afternoon, with my recorder?'

'Can't it wait till I get home?'

'I'd prefer not to, so I'd have something to be working on.'

'Well, I suppose it's too late now to shut the stable door.'

'That's great! Thank you! Then when—?'

They were interrupted by the ringing of a

mobile. Elspeth frowned and hurried out to the hall, where she'd left her bag when Rona arrived.

'Hello? Yes? What—?' She tensed, and her voice sharpened. 'What's happened?'

Rona stood up, unsure what to do. Should she just leave? But they'd not fixed the appointment.

She moved uncertainly forward, and, as Elspeth remained intent on the phone, gestured towards the improvised studio, miming, 'May I?'

Elspeth made a distracted gesture and hurried back into the kitchen, shutting the door behind her. After a moment's hesitation, Rona went into the front room and stood looking about her. Surprisingly, despite the net curtains, it was bright and airy, an uncurtained side window providing extra light.

First, she examined the canvas on the easel. It showed mountains and valleys, streams and gorse-covered hillsides. While a traditional enough scene, it had been imbued with Elspeth's particular magic, so that the strong colours sang and burned almost three-dimensionally, seeming to leap off the canvas. She didn't need Max to recognize an outstanding work of art.

She turned and surveyed those lined up against the wall, and it was abundantly clear Elspeth had found her new metier. There was a portrait of a small girl examining a shell, the total concentration of childhood lovingly conveyed; another, of the fisherman she had mentioned –

rough jersey, craggy face and blue, far-seeing eyes. One painting depicted a heron, feathers ruffled in the wind, alone on an expanse of sand, and among the rest, rough seas, topped with creaming surf, boiled and rolled under a lowering sky; lochs lay dreaming under summer suns, surrounding mountains mirrored in their depths; a herd of deer stood poised for flight, their alarm tangible. Traditional, nineteenth century scenes, most of them, but treated in a totally new way, alive with twenty-first century urgency. Scotland had indeed proved Elspeth's salvation.

An irritating buzz distracted her, and she turned to see a bluebottle climbing up the side window to within an inch of its opening, only to give up and start again at the bottom. Hoping to get rid of it, she knelt on a chair and tried several times to shoo it out, but on each attempt it managed to evade her.

About to abandon it, a flash of white caught her eye in the gap between chair and wall, and she glanced down to see a sheet of paper half-hidden under the chair. Thinking it would facilitate her attempts, she reached to retrieve it, and, as she bent closer, saw it was a pencilled drawing.

Elspeth must have mislaid it. Rona stood up, about to move the chair and rescue it, but Elspeth's voice stopped her in her tracks.

'Rona? Where are you?' There was an odd note in her voice, almost of hysteria.

'Here.'

As she reached the hall, Elspeth seized her arm and propelled her to the front door, her face white and strained.

'I'm afraid you'll have to go,' she said jerkily. 'I can't speak to you any more.'

Rona turned to stare at her. 'But I thought you said—'

'I've changed my mind. I'm sorry, but it's out of the question. Goodbye.'

And Rona found herself out on the path, gazing at the closed door.

SIXTEEN

'Without any explanation?' Max demanded incredulously, on the phone that evening.

'None whatsoever. Something in that phone call really spooked her, and as far as I know, the only person who has her number is Crispin. Richard certainly hasn't.'

'I wonder what rattled his cage?'

'I don't know, but I wish he'd waited one more day. She'd just agreed to an interview.'

'Have you tried to contact her again?'

'Not yet; I decided to wait till she'd calmed down, so I spent part of the time writing up our meeting while it was fresh in my mind. After that, I thought I should see something of the countryside while I'm here, so I took the car and pottered along the highways and byways. Elspeth's paintings had whetted my appetite.'

'Tell me about them.'

'They're fantastic, Max. Mostly landscapes and seascapes but a couple of portraits and an amazing picture of a heron – you could almost feel the feathers. I know they stand motionless for a long time, but even so, she must have sketched it first, surely?'

'Birds are certainly a new subject for her. I must say, I envy you that private view. So, will you try again?'

'I'll go back in the morning, but I can't say I'm hopeful.'

'Well, at least your hunch proved right about her being there. Pity, as you say, the phone call scuppered it.' He paused. 'What time do you get in tomorrow?'

'Three forty-five at Luton.'

'Want me to meet you?'

'No point, my car's at the airport. I only have hand luggage, so all being well I'll be home by four thirty.'

'Like to go out for a meal?'

'That would be great.'

'OK. See you soon, and good luck for tomorrow.'

As Rona had feared, there was no response to her knock the next morning. The net curtains still screened the windows, the door remained firmly shut. And this time, she knew, Elspeth might well be watching her dejected retreat down the path.

After an early lunch in the hotel bar, she checked out and drove to the airport. Not a wasted journey, by any means, but falling short of what it might have been. All she could do now was await Elspeth's return to Buckford, and hope to see her then.

'What's she like?' Max asked curiously, as they sat over dinner at Dino's.

'Not at all what I expected. Very small, for one thing – about five foot, I'd say – and she's had her hair cut really short. It suits her, but it's certainly not the image everyone has of her.'

'Apart from her appearance, though, people had widely differing opinions. How did she fit with those?'

'I wasn't with her long enough to judge.'

Max topped up her glass. 'Do you think she has a thing going with Crispin Ryder? She doesn't sound his type.'

Rona shrugged. 'They could just be friends. I wonder if he visits her up there? According to the press, he's still hitting the London scene pretty regularly.'

'But you think it was him on the phone?'

'I could be wrong, but Richard said she's changed her mobile, and as far as I know, no one else has the number.'

'Are you going to tell the family you found her?'

Rona considered, sipping her wine. 'I have her permission, but I think I'll wait till the opportunity arises. It's not as if they're still worried about her, after all. But enough of all that: what did you get up to while I was away?'

'Apart from the all-night orgies, you mean?'

'Apart from those.'

'Not a lot. I took Gus for a long walk this morning up in the woods, and had a pub lunch on the way back. They've got all the Christmas decorations up.'

'That reminds me, we really must speak to everyone about Christmas lunch. I'd meant to look in the Craiglea gift shops, too, but I was so thrown by Elspeth's volte-face, it went right out of my mind. I think I might take a day off on Monday, and make a start on Christmas shopping before the shops get too manic.'

'Rather you than me,' Max said.

The following morning, Rona phoned round the family with her invitation, with mixed results. Lindsey accepted with thanks; Dominic hadn't mentioned Christmas, but she was sure he'd be 'doing his pater familias thing'. Tom gently broke the news that he'd be spending Christmas Day with Catherine's family in Cricklehurst, but softened the blow by offering to host Boxing Day lunch. And Avril took the wind completely out of her sails by asking if Guy Lacey might be included in the invitation.

'Of *course*, Mum!' Rona assured her, masking her surprise. 'That would be great! What about Sarah?'

'She's just become engaged, and is going to

her fiancé's parents. Guy will see her on Boxing Day.'

Which seemed to be the form for fathers this year.

'We really ought to fly up to Newcastle soon, and see your family,' she said to Max, having relayed all this.

'Oh, I meant to tell you – Cynthia's invited us for New Year. Father will be staying with them over the festive season.'

'When did this come up?'

'She phoned on Friday evening, just after I'd spoken to you. Then all your goings-on put it out of my head.'

'Well, it'll be good to see them all, and it'll save us having to dash up before Christmas. You'd better organize the flights, though; you know how booked up they get.'

Over breakfast on Monday, Max glanced up from his paper. 'Wish I was coming to London with you; I see this is a viewing day for the Spanish paintings auction. If you get tired of shopping, go and have a look at the famous Castillo. It's in Bond Street, so wouldn't be out of your way.'

'I might well do that.'

'What train are you catching?'

'The first after the rush hour. Nine-something. Wish me luck!'

'Oh, I do!' he said.

Rona had a successful morning, managing to

cross several names off her presents list, though she regretted the Rennie Mackintosh clock she'd seen in Craiglea; it would have looked just right on Lindsey's mantelpiece, in place of the one she'd relinquished to Hugh.

She had a salad lunch in Oxford Street, checking her list again, and admitted to herself that she'd run out of steam. She'd made a good start; perhaps she'd leave the rest for another day, and trawl some of the Guild Street shops at home. And since it was still only two o'clock, she'd follow Max's suggestion and go to have a look at the paintings.

Having left her parcels in the auction house cloakroom, she was directed to a sale room on the first floor. It was very crowded, and though the walls were covered in paintings, the largest group was clustered round a picture at the far end. Rona could guess which it was. She elected to work her way down to it, in the hope that by the time she reached it, the crowd might have diminished slightly.

Having bought a catalogue to take home to Max, she flicked quickly through it. Ribera, Murillo, á Greco, Velázquez – all were represented, and she moved slowly down the room, delighting in the still lifes and the rich clothes of saints and noblemen. The treatment of materials was a special interest of Max's – the bloom on velvet, the sheen on satin, the drape of a skirt, and she knew he'd have revelled in this display. Too bad he'd not been able to accompany her.

And so she came at last to the canvas in pride

of place, where a crowd was still gathered, and checked it in the catalogue. The painting itself had been afforded a whole page, printed in colour, and Rona paused for a moment, frowning, before glancing at the information on the opposite side.

Felipe Castillo, she read: *1602–1669. Doña Inez de los Reyes. Oil on canvas 59.5 x 90 CM: 231/2 x 35 IN*. The estimate given was £500,000–£750,000.

She manoeuvred herself into a position where she was able, between heads, to see the picture that had caused such a stir. And a little frisson she couldn't analyse ran down her back as she studied it more closely.

The painting was of a seated woman, half in profile, wearing a richly embroidered gown of red velvet, her head reverently bent towards a missal held in both hands. What was there about it that disturbed her? she wondered, half-listening to the comments from those about her. Why did it—?

'Rona!' exclaimed a voice just behind her. 'We must stop meeting like this!'

Still preoccupied, she turned in bewilderment to see Nathan Tait smiling at her.

'Oh ... Nathan,' she said lamely.

He examined her face, eyes narrowing. 'Are you all right?'

'Yes ... yes, fine. I ... just wasn't expecting to see you, that's all.'

'Not too unpleasant a shock, I hope,' he said, an edge to his voice.

She forced a laugh. 'Of course not.'

He took her arm and drew her out of the mêlée around the painting. 'I admit I had the advantage of you: I *was* half-expecting to see Max here, with or without you.'

'He'd have loved to come, but he couldn't manage today. I've combined my visit with Christmas shopping.'

'No wonder you're a bit fraught. My studio's just round the corner; come back for a cup of coffee, and you can tell me how you're getting on with the biography.'

'Oh, thanks, but I'd better not. I ... should be getting home.'

'Nonsense! It's barely three o'clock, and you look in need of a rest. Do you good to draw breath before being plunged back into the crowds.'

'Really, Nathan, it's good of you, but—'

'No buts.' He hadn't relinquished her arm, and now his grip tightened as he started leading her back up the room.

'Nathan, really—'

He ignored her, guiding her on to the staircase as they descended against the flow of the crowd. 'Don't worry, the studio's only two minutes away.'

'I must at least collect my parcels,' she protested, as they reached the foyer, and he waited while she redeemed her cloakroom ticket. Blast the man! Rona thought; he'd obviously taken offence at her lack of enthusiasm on seeing him. Heaven preserve her from the artistic temperament! But if the only way of soothing ruffled feathers was a cup of coffee – which, actually, she felt in need of – then so be it. Although she'd have liked longer to study the painting she'd come specifically to see. Again, that odd little niggle of unease.

Nathan took possession of her parcels, and they emerged on to Bond Street.

'Just along here,' he said encouragingly, turning back towards Oxford Street. Then, 'You got that photo of Chloë?'

'Yes, it was good of you to send it. I did thank you, didn't I? By email?'

He made a dismissive gesture. 'She *was* beautiful, wasn't she? I wasn't exaggerating?'

'She was lovely, yes. You ... must still miss her.'

'Oh, I do. Every day. This way.' They turned into a little side street, and, halfway along it, stopped in front of a narrow door. Nathan took out a key and unlocked it, ushering her ahead of him into a small hallway containing only a lift and a flight of stairs.

'The studio's on the second floor,' he told her. 'Normally I use the stairs, but since you're tired, we'll take the lift.'

They rode up in silence, rising above one hallway, visible through the open grill, and clanking to a halt on the next one. A corridor led towards the back of the building, and Nathan unlocked the third door along. The room they entered was, Rona saw, a typical artist's studio – paints, trolleys, stacked canvases, easels. There was also a chaise longue draped in velvet – presumably for the use of models – and, behind it, a counter containing an electric kettle, a microwave, mugs and a jar of instant coffee, reminding her of Elspeth.

Nathan waved her towards the chaise, and, as she somewhat reluctantly seated herself, commented, 'You really didn't want to come here, did you?'

She looked up apologetically. 'It wasn't that, it's just that I like to catch a train well before the rush hour, added to which, as you said, I am a little tired. Christmas shopping's an exhausting pastime.'

'All the more reason to relax for a while. You've an hour before you need worry about the rush hour.' He moved behind her to the counter. 'Coffee OK?'

'Lovely, thanks.'

There was a click, and music filled the room, from a CD player, Rona guessed. She forced herself to relax, letting the soothing strains wash over her as her thoughts drifted back to the painting. Why should she—?

'There you go.' Nathan pulled over a small, paint-stained table and plonked down a mug. 'Milk? Sugar?'

'Neither, thanks. I'm in need of undiluted caffeine!'

He half-smiled and perched on a stool opposite her, his own mug in his hands. The coffee was steaming, but Rona lifted hers at once and took a sip. The sooner she drank it, the sooner she could leave.

'So, how's the biography progressing?'

'Well, the thing you soon learn is that you can't hurry them. It's some time since I did one, and I confess I'm finding it rather frustrating.'

'Especially with the subject being, as it were, out of the picture.' He smiled thinly at his own joke.

'Yes.' She'd no intention of telling him about Scotland. 'But there are plenty of people who *are* around, and I'm working my way through them. Including,' she added incautiously, 'Chloë's parents.' Immediately, she could have bitten her tongue out. She really must concentrate on what she was saying. Forget the picture, she could think about that in peace, once she was on the train.

Naturally, Nathan pounced. 'You've seen the Pynes?'

Rona nodded and took a hasty gulp of coffee, burning her mouth, but giving herself time to dissemble. 'They've known Elspeth since she was a child. I wanted their opinion of her.'

'And what was it?'

'Much the same as yours,' she said, hoping to recover lost ground. 'That she manipulated Chloë.'

'What did they say about me?' he asked softly.

Rona brushed her hair off her face, feeling suddenly uncomfortably hot. 'That you'd...'

'That I'd what?'

She took a long drink of coffee. Not much left now, and then she could go. Think! Think! He

300

must be right – she was more tired than she'd realized. '...been devastated by her death, and attended her funeral.'

'That's not what you were going to say, is it?'

Rona looked at him, blinking to clear his image, which was unaccountably blurring round the edges. He leaned forward suddenly, his eyes intent on hers.

'Let's stop playing games,' he said. 'You know, don't you?'

'Know – what?'

'That I killed her.'

She gasped involuntarily. *What* had he said?

'By ... making her choose between you and Elspeth?' Her voice sounded slurred.

'No, by pushing her under the train.'

Oh God! Oh my *God*! And like a distant echo came Lindsey's comment on hearing of Chloë's death: *Murdered, no doubt?*

'I was hardly going to let her dump me in favour of that ... that *lesbian*, now was I?' Nathan demanded viciously. 'What would people *think*? And I wanted Wilding to suffer as much as I was doing. Which,' he ended with satisfaction, 'she most certainly did.'

Rona tried with increasing desperation to marshal her thoughts. He couldn't possibly mean it literally – could he?

'All went according to plan,' he was continuing. 'No one doubted for a minute that it was suicide. But then you had to come along and stir things up again. So I made it my business to meet you, and after doing so, concluded,

301

wrongly, that I could still contain it. Which, God help me, I went on believing, until Max mentioned that Elspeth had some of Chloë's letters.'

Max? Rona's brain struggled to make sense of that.

'And that, I might tell you, rang alarm bells big time. Because if, trying to placate Elspeth, she pretended she'd no feelings for me and I was pestering her, it was just possible doubts could arise. Elspeth herself didn't worry me; if she'd known anything she'd have accused me long since, and in any case, she's probably dead herself by now. But you were a different matter; you dig out facts for a living, and sooner or later you were bound to read the letters and make the fatal connection. You might even have already done so – witness your behaviour today – but unless you could produce them, you'd have no proof. Clearly, I'd no choice but to remove them a.s.a.p.'

Rona stared at him, her mind spinning out of control.

'So,' he continued, 'the next day I went to Elspeth's house to get them. Her *empty* house. Simple enough, you'd think. But that bloody woman was there, wasn't she, and had to stick her nose in. And after all that, I couldn't even *find* the bloody things. The only possible conclusion was that you had them.'

He smiled, and a chill ran down Rona's spine. 'I couldn't believe my luck when I saw you just now, the more so since it was clear at once that you suspected me.'

She shook her head violently, trying to stand, but her limbs felt leaden and refused to respond.

'I'm sorry about this, Rona, though more for Max's sake than yours. We go back a long way. However, self-preservation is the order of the day, and it's clear drastic action's required yet again. I must say, it's becoming quite a habit.'

He watched impassively as she tried again to rise. 'No point in struggling,' he told her. 'I emptied tranquillizer capsules into your coffee. You'll be out of it soon.'

Rona's mouth felt dry and oddly fluffy. 'The letters,' she tried to say. 'There was nothing—'

'Too late, I fear; even in your present state, you must realize you know too much. So,' he placed his mug on the table and stood up, 'you were anxious to leave, weren't you? Let me help you on your way.'

Powerless to resist him – to do *anything* – Rona was pulled to her feet and her arms – seeming not to belong to her – pushed into the sleeves of the jacket she'd removed on arrival. All she wanted was to lie down and sleep, but though she tried to tell him so, he didn't seem to understand.

His voice echoed in her head. 'Here's your bag, and we mustn't forget your parcels, though you'll have to carry them; I'll need my hands free to support you.'

She'd no idea what he was talking about, and was beyond caring. With his arm round her waist all but carrying her, they left the studio, descended in the lift, and went out into the

303

winter street. Briefly, its cold air revived her a little and her eyes fluttered open as she tottered along, one foot dragging after the other. She was aware of people about her – why weren't they helping her? – and the nearby roar of traffic.

'A liquid lunch, I'm afraid!' Nathan's disembodied voice apologized, as they lurched into someone.

More crowds. Louder traffic noise, and the draught of its passing on her face. She stumbled as Nathan changed his hold, easing her in front of him, but the pressure of his body and the closeness of people on either side kept her upright. She swayed dizzily, the edge of the kerb beneath her feet. Then, suddenly, pandemonium.

She felt a sharp jab in the small of her back, and, simultaneously, a violent tug on her arm pulling her sideways, so that she fell heavily against the people beside her. Screams, an ear-piercing screech of tyres and brakes, shouting, and, finally, oblivion.

It was some time before she came fully round, to find herself lying on a narrow bed in a cubicle. At her involuntary movement, a nurse appeared, smiling down at her.

'Where...?' Her mouth and throat were bone-dry, and the attempt to speak made her cough. Gratefully, she drank the full glass of water handed to her.

'You're in a Medicentre, in Oxford Street,' the nurse told her. 'You were involved in an incident, but don't worry, you're not hurt.'

Rona stared at her. 'Oxford Street?' she croaked.

'You don't remember? Never mind; some ... people are waiting to speak to you, but I'll tell them you're not ready yet. Just lie and rest for a while. Your friend is on his way.'

'My ... friend?' A blurred picture of Nathan formed in her mind, bringing a wave of panic, and she struggled to sit up.

The nurse put a restraining hand on her shoulder. 'Mr Allerdyce; he's listed as an emergency contact in your pocket diary.'

'Max!' Rona relaxed. 'He's my husband,' she said.

'Oh, I'm sorry. With the name being different...'

Rona nodded. Too much effort to explain. 'He ... laughs at me ... for ... filling that in ... every year.'

'He won't again,' the nurse said darkly. But Rona's thoughts had moved on. She had to know...

'I ... was with someone,' she began cautiously.

There was a subtle change in the woman's manner. 'No more questions, now, till you're feeling stronger. Settle down and go back to sleep till your husband arrives.'

And she did. The next thing she knew, Max, white-faced and anxious, was bending over her.

'God, Rona, are you all right?' he demanded, stooping to kiss her.

'I think so. But Nathan—'

'Nathan? Nathan Tait? What's this got to do with him?'

He waited for her to answer, and when she didn't, repeated, 'Where does Nathan come into it? All I know is you were involved in some kind of "incident", and the police are waiting to speak to you.'

It was coming back now, the nightmare studio and Nathan's eyes intent on her.

'He told me he killed Chloë and Mary Strong,' she said flatly, 'and I think he tried to kill me.'

'*What*? Darling, that can't be right! He's our *friend*!' Max was staring at her, convinced she was still confused, but when she nodded confirmation, he said heavily, 'We'd better get the police in.'

So Rona went through the story – meeting Nathan at the viewing, his insisting they go to his studio for coffee, the tranquillizers dissolved in it, and his bizarre confession. Whether or not his story could be verified, she neither knew nor, at that stage, cared. All she could think was that she must let Elspeth know Chloë hadn't killed herself.

'Do you think they believed me?' Rona asked Max in the car on the way home.

'God knows; I had difficulty believing it myself. You're still a bit woozy, and it *was* a tall story. But I've now learned a bit more; when I went for the car, a reporter was hanging around, wanting to know how you were. He told me he'd been speaking to an eye witness, who

306

swore the man you were with – Nathan, presumably – tried to push you under a bus. I still can't get my head round that.'

The jab in the back. The sideways jerk.

He glanced at her, but she made no response.

'He – the reporter – kept saying "allegedly" – covering his back, I suppose – but the man he spoke to noticed you both particularly, you, because you looked ill and Nathan, because he seemed so tense. There was a crowd of people waiting to cross, but he pushed his way to the kerb, where he manoeuvred you in front of him. The witness thought this odd, as you seemed pretty unsteady; then, as the bus approached, he swears he saw Nathan brace himself and give you a shove.'

Max drew a deep breath. 'The terrifying thing is, if he hadn't happened to be watching, it would have been written off as an accident, and you'd ... almost certainly have been killed. As it was, he instinctively grabbed you and pulled you clear, and with you suddenly removed, Nathan stumbled forward himself.'

Rona gazed at him, horror-struck. 'Under the bus?'

Max nodded.

'Is he ... dead?'

'I don't know; apparently he was rushed to hospital.'

It was too much to take in, and, after struggling with it for a while, Rona gave up and thankfully sank back into sleep, only regaining consciousness long enough to stumble upstairs and into bed, where she slept solidly for ten hours, till the last of the barbiturates were out of her system.

SEVENTEEN

'Any news of Nathan?' Rona asked Max anxiously, when he brought her breakfast in bed the next morning.

'The paper's not come yet.'

'He said you told him about Chloë's letters. Is that true?'

Max frowned. 'Not that I— oh, hang on; I might have said something. He phoned me at Farthings one day when I'd just mixed some paint, and frankly my only concern was to get him off the line as quickly as possible.'

'But what did you say?'

'He asked about the bio, and if you'd come across anything to do with Chloë, and I said I thought there were some letters. That's all. Why?'

'That's why he went to Elspeth's,' Rona said flatly, 'to get them.'

Max stared at her. 'Oh my God.'

She reached quickly for his hand. 'You weren't to know. There's absolutely no way you can blame yourself. Max,' she went on quickly, to distract him, 'before all this happened, there

308

was something else bothering me, about the Castillo. I was trying to work it out when Nathan suddenly appeared, and he assumed my uneasiness was down to him.'

'What about the Castillo?'

'It was very odd. I ... kind of *recognized* it.'

'Well, that's hardly surprising; it's been in the papers and on television.'

She was shaking her head. 'No, I mean I'd seen it *personally*, but it ... wasn't in colour.'

Max shrugged. 'Perhaps you're thinking of some of his other work? He did a lot of court portraits.'

She buttered her toast, unconvinced. 'If only I could *remember*!' she said helplessly, brushing a fly away from the marmalade.

Max swotted at it. 'I thought these things were supposed to die out in winter,' he said.

Rona straightened suddenly, eyes widening. A fly on the windowpane. A sheet of paper on the floor beneath.

'God, Max! Oh my God! I know where I saw it! In Elspeth's studio, in Craiglea!'

He smiled, shaking his head. 'Darling, that's simply not possible.'

'It was the fly that reminded me,' she insisted. 'I was trying to guide one out of the window, leaning over the back of the chair, and this sheet of paper was on the floor behind it. It was a pencil sketch. I only had a brief glimpse, but I *swear* it was the same as the Castillo – the bent head, the missal in her hands.'

'A coincidence, that's all. There might be

some vague similarity, which your memory exaggerated. I've done the same myself.'

Down in the hall, Gus gave a sudden bark.

'Sounds as though the paper's arrived,' Max said. 'If my reporter pal did his stuff, there might be news of Nathan. Incidentally,' he added, nodding towards some carrier bags propped against the wall, 'not content with saving your life, your Good Samaritan even rescued your parcels and put them in the ambulance with you. We must find some way of thanking him.'

Rona ate her toast thoughtfully, her mind still on the sketch. She *wasn't* imagining the resemblance, she was sure. Damn it, except for its size and the fact that it wasn't in colour, it was *identical* to the Castillo portrait.

Max came slowly into the room, the newspaper in his hands, and something in his expression started her heart thumping.

'Max, what—'

'You're not going to believe this,' he said heavily. 'How's this for a headline? *Art world rocked by doubts thrown on masterpiece.*'

Rona gazed at him wordlessly, coffee cup in hand.

'*In a dramatic move last night,*' he continued, '*Meredith's Auction House withdrew the much-acclaimed portrait of Doña Inez de los Reyes from its forthcoming auction after doubts concerning its authenticity were expressed by an eminent art specialist.*'

He lowered the paper and they met each other's eyes.

310

Carefully, Rona put down her cup. 'She wouldn't!' she whispered.

'She just might,' Max replied.

'But ... *why*?'

'To prove she could, that she could be accepted as an Old Master. It's possible that what you saw was a preparatory sketch.'

'I was going to hand it back to her,' Rona said aridly. 'I wonder what she'd have done, if I had.'

Max ran a hand through his hair. 'We mustn't jump to conclusions, though. For one thing, this expert could be proved wrong. For another, it might have nothing whatever to do with Elspeth. It was just seeing the headlines immediately after you...' He broke off, then added, 'But if we *are* right, we can guess what that phone call was about – someone warning her the murmurs had started. No wonder she wanted you out.'

He sat down on the bed and took her hand. 'Remember my advice, when the Harvey biography fell through? Only to write about people who've been safely dead and buried for a hundred years? Pity you didn't take it.'

She could only agree.

That week seemed totally surreal. Rona felt on the brink of an avalanche, not daring to move in case it precipitated disaster. Her main dread was that Naomi would contact her, and, if so, what she could say to her. But there was no word, nor, logically, any reason for one, since Naomi had no way of connecting the art scandal with

311

her sister.

Were she and Max right in their deductions? Rona prayed not, but, as the story continued to dominate the press, the pencil sketch haunted her. Yet, even if it were what she suspected, there was no way she could betray Elspeth. Particularly since, thankfully, no one had paid out any money for the painting.

Max agreed. 'It's still possible you were mistaken,' he reminded her, 'which could lead to a court case and God knows what else. Let the experts hammer it out. If it does prove a fake, more likely than not they'll never know who did it, and, as you say, at least it was caught in time.'

But suppose somehow they *did* find out, Rona worried, and it *was* Elspeth? How would that affect the biography?

Thursday brought news with an even more personal impact, reporting that 'Well known artist Nathan Tait, who was involved in an incident in Oxford Street on Monday', had died in hospital without regaining consciousness. Police had been waiting to question him. A summary of Nathan's career followed.

So much for Rona's hope he might corroborate her story. Now the burden of proof rested solely on her, and she'd not much hope of a positive outcome. The police might find dregs of the tranquillizers in her mug at his studio; but that would prove only that he'd drugged her, which they already accepted. There was nothing to back up the motive behind it.

She would have to accept there was no way of

reversing the verdict on Chloë's death; she'd already sent a hurried note to Elspeth, repeating what Nathan had told her, and hoped it would prove some crumb of comfort in the maelstrom in which Elspeth now found herself. But the Pynes also had a right to the truth, and she resolved to see them at the earliest opportunity.

The same went for Bill Strong. His was a much more recent grief, but knowing who had killed his wife, and why, would at least answer questions and hopefully help the healing process.

The third and final bombshell of that momentous week came with the six o'clock news on the Friday, as Rona and Max sat in the kitchen with pre-dinner drinks.

'The body of a woman recovered this morning off the west coast of Scotland has been identified as that of the renowned artist Elspeth Wilding, who dropped out of circulation in May last year. An overturned rowing boat was found nearby. Miss Wilding's career began...'

It was totally and incontrovertibly the last straw, and Rona, increasingly traumatized by the week's events, finally burst into tears.

The following Wednesday's post brought a letter forwarded by her publishers, Jonas Jennings. The original postmark, she saw incredulously, was Craiglea, Dunbartonshire, and the date 3rd December, the day before Elspeth's body was found. Rona's legs gave way, and she sat down

313

suddenly on the stairs. It took an effort of will to slit open the envelope and withdraw its contents.

Dear Rona, she read, *By the time you read this, you will no doubt have learned both of my death and the truth about the 'Castillo' painting, and drawn your own conclusions. I have written to the appropriate authorities, but feel I owe you a personal explanation of how this all came about, not to mention an apology for bundling you out of the house so unceremoniously last week.*

It all started so innocently. As I think I mentioned, I'd been worrying for some time about my lost talent, and my need to get away by myself for a while, to develop a new style. I was discussing this with Crispin one evening, and he offered me the use of the family's holiday home in Craiglea. He went on to suggest I try copying a famous painting, to get me back in the swing of it. Willing to try anything by that stage, I agreed.

He brought me up here, and together we bought the necessary equipment and chose which painting to copy. We settled on a small Monet, and it was his idea that I adapt the existing painting, bringing some of the background figures to the fore, and eliminating others. The result, which I admit to being delighted with, was that my painting was unmistakably in Monet's style, without being a replica of an already-known work.

The next time he visited me, Crispin, too, was

314

delighted with it, and took it back to London. Two weeks later, he phoned me, very pleased with himself. He'd sold it, as a genuine Monet, for an exceedingly large sum to the friend of a friend and, despite my protestations, insisted on splitting the proceeds with me.

I was horrified, but, I'm ashamed to say, at the same time highly flattered that my work could be taken for that of as great an artist as Monet, and decided to try my hand with a picture based on the court portraits by Castillo. I could tell you I wasn't intending to pass it off as genuine, but that protestation rings a little hollow, after accepting payment for the fake Monet.

You'll appreciate that this malpractice would never have been possible at home, where dear Gwen paid regular visits. It almost seemed fate had a hand in the timing, but whatever combination of circumstances was to blame, it explains my prolonged absence – I'd intended to be away only a month or two – and, of course, keeping my whereabouts secret.

However, having finished the portrait, my conscience finally got the better of me, and I refused to let Crispin take it to London. By this time, too, I was beginning to paint on my own account. The 'exercise' of copying great artists had worked so well that, to Crispin's annoyance, I did only the two fakes before abandoning the practice to concentrate on my own work, which you saw when you were up here.

What I didn't realize was that, without my knowledge, he'd removed the 'Castillo' and, *probably drunk with the success of his last gamble, overreached himself – and me – by submitting it, with the help of some shady colleagues, for inclusion in the forthcoming auction of Spanish paintings. He'd seen a television programme on the so-called art fraudster John Myatt, and realized that, if the artwork was good enough, it was possible to fool the experts.*

Since it all fell apart, he's been on the phone constantly, begging me not to confess, but my fear is that some other artist might come under suspicion. I reminded him that John Myatt was given a relatively short prison sentence, so he was likely to get off lightly – a fact I admit to resenting, since the whole fiasco had been his idea, and had ended for me in total disaster. He's sailed close to the wind for years and had a good run for his money; I reckon a short, sharp shock might jolt him into a more respectable lifestyle!

For my part, I have to accept that my career is over and, even more sadly, my reputation irreparably damaged. Which is why I've decided to take the steps I have; it will be painful for the family, and that, I truly regret. At least we've been apart for a while, which might help to ease the blow.

So to you, Rona. I'm sorry our acquaintance was so short; I think I'd have enjoyed working with you. You are, of course, free to make use of this letter as you choose, but you mustn't feel under an obligation, one way or the other. By the time your book comes out – if, indeed, you

*decide to proceed with it – the main facts will in
any case be common knowledge. The above
might at least offer an insight as to how it came
about.*

*It only remains to wish you the best of luck in
everything you undertake.*

Yours,
Elspeth

Rona sat on the stair for a long time after she'd
finished reading, going over what she'd learned.
There'd been no mention of her note about
Nathan's confession; that it hadn't arrived in
time was an additional sadness. Her overriding
emotion, though, was deep anger towards Crispin Ryder; his amoral behaviour had contami-
nated a great artist, who, in the normal scheme
of things, should have had many productive
years ahead of her. What a waste! What an
appalling waste!

But what of Naomi? And Richard? And their
parents? She'd already written letters of condol-
ence, but how would the scandal affect them?
Would they want her to continue with the book?
And if so, how could she request their memories
of Elspeth, when their grief and shame would
far outlast the writing of it?

Thankfully, it would be up to her publishers to
reach a decision, but whatever it might be, on a
personal level, Rona herself would never, now,
be able to create the word-portrait of Elspeth
she'd been hoping for.

Gus, surprised by her continued immobility,

nudged her hand, and she leaned forward to hug him, aware that the central heating had gone off and she was cold. She was also very much in need of company. She and Max would discuss the letter this evening, but he was busy now, and for the moment she wanted her sister. She went to the phone.

'Linz, it's me. Any chance of slipping out for a coffee? ... Bless you! Ten minutes at the Gallery? Perfect.'

So once again her professional life was on hold. Well, she thought philosophically, she'd weathered that crisis before and would again. Barnie, bless him, would have something to occupy her in the meantime, but, for the moment, she'd take a leaf from Scarlett O'Hara, and think about it tomorrow.

Reaching for Gus's lead, she went to meet her sister.

I9780727879417
MYSTERY FRA
Fraser, Anthea.
Unfinished portrait /

PROSPECT FREE LIBRARY

915 Trenton Falls Rd.
Prospect, New York 13435
(315) 896-2736

MEMBER
MID-YORK LIBRARY SYSTEM
Utica, N.Y. 13502

150100